WINGS
OF
HEALING

GUARDIANS OF THE NORTH

By Honor Bound
Heart of Valor
Bright Sword of Justice
Between Earth and Sky
Wings of Healing

ALAN MORRIS

GUARDIANS OF THE NORTH

WINGS OF HEALING

BETHANY HOUSE PUBLISHERS
MINNEAPOLIS, MINNESOTA 55438

Published by Bethany House Publishers
A Ministry of Bethany Fellowship International
11400 Hampshire Avenue South
Minneapolis, Minnesota 55438
www.bethanyhouse.com

Printed in the United States of America by
Bethany Press International, Minneapolis, Minnesota 55438

ISBN 1-55661-696-1

This book could not have been written
without the help and encouragement of my father.

Thanks for keepin' the faith in me, Pop.

ALAN MORRIS is a full-time writer who has also coauthored a series of books with his father, best-selling author Gilbert Morris. Learning the craft of writing from his father, Alan has launched his first solo series, GUARDIANS OF THE NORTH. He makes his home in Florida.

CONTENTS

PROLOGUE

March 27, 1877
Fort Macleod community

D*r.* James Burke rose as he usually did, made coffee, then sat on the front porch of his house rolling cigarettes and leisurely smoking for an hour. He mentally went over all he had to do for the day: the Williams woman should be giving birth this day—he didn't know how he knew, he just did, and was rarely wrong about these sorts of things; the Knox boy needed a follow-up on an infected throat; and Big Jack Benson needed some help castrating some colts. And those were just the things he knew about. As always, other situations would surely arise as the day aged.

Coughing heavily, Dr. Burke was about to rise, get his bag, and start his day when he was surprised to see a covered wagon headed directly toward his house. *Strange,* he thought. *I'm pretty far out of the way here. Someone must have given them directions to me, or else they're lost.*

He greeted the excited young man who jumped from the wagon and began to babble about his wife being severely ill. After he calmed the man down, he then saw to the woman. Donovan, their name was, the young husband told him. Dr.

Burke coughed and nodded. He could tell at once that Mrs. Donovan was pretty bad off. Though her skin was pale, she was burning up from a very high fever. Burke could hear her labored wheezing from the fluid in her lungs even before he climbed in the back of the wagon: pneumonia, he was sure of it.

"How long she been like this?" Dr. Burke asked Donovan as he took the woman's feeble pulse.

"About a week now. She got sick right after we left Dufferin. We're going to the mountains to live."

Burke cocked an eye at the thin young man. He couldn't have been more than twenty, with an oversized nose and a shock of brown hair falling down into his frightened eyes. He surely didn't look like the type to tame the mighty Rockies. It was probably his wife's idea.

The woman stirred at that moment and began babbling to someone named Missy, as if she were right there by her side.

"She's been doing that the last couple of days. Just talks to her best friend back in Dufferin. What do you think, Doc? Will she be all right?"

Dr. Burke wanted badly to lie to the lad, but it never did any good to do that. Instead, he dodged the question. "The high fever's real bad, son. I can see you've been forcing water down her, and that's good for preventing dehydration, but she's got a lot of fluid in her lungs. That ain't good."

Donovan swallowed with a click. "Will she. . . ?"

"I'd be praying for a miracle, was I you. I'm sorry, Mr. Donovan."

The poor man took the dire news fairly well. Dr. Burke could not turn them away, so he allowed them to stay at his place while he went on his visits. When he returned late that night, Dora Donovan was dead.

Though he didn't know it, Dr. James Burke suffered from lung cancer that would normally have claimed his life in two years at the most. Instead, he contracted Mrs. Donovan's early flu-like symptoms of chills, heavy sinus drainage, fever, and uncommonly inflamed throat. The fluid ran to his cancerous lungs as if summoned.

Four days later, Dr. Burke was dead.

PART ONE

SHADOWS

When the sun sets, shadows,
that showed at noon
But small, appear most long
and terrible.

Nathaniel Lee
Oedipus

CHAPTER ONE

A New Dress

Reena O'Donnell breezed into the unfamiliar Pelham General Store, then promptly drew back in shock.

"Hep you, ma'am?" the man just inside the door asked.

The gift of speech completely deserted Reena for the moment. She looked around the interior of the store quickly, searching for someone else—*anyone* else—to help her. There was no one. The urge was strong to step back outside and look at the sign over the door to make sure she hadn't wandered into the wrong store.

"Ma'am?" the person in front of her asked again, then grinned. He was a shambling hulk of a man, and his grin revealed the complete absence of any teeth. His gnarled, unkempt beard was spotted with what appeared to be tobacco juice and some sort of red crumbs that were most certainly the remains of cinnamon candy.

Reena realized that she was staring at him with open astonishment and fumbled for something to say. "I . . . um . . ."

The man's friendly, open expression quickly faded away and turned to one of suspicion. "You an Indian? You speak English?"

"An Indian. . . ? Oh, the dress!" Reena wore a simple buck-skin dress decorated with colorful beads, cowrie shells, and thimbles. She laughed, but it lasted just a bit too long and sounded hollow even to her. However, it gave her a few moments to gather her thoughts. He was the most disgusting-looking man she'd ever laid eyes on.

"Yep," he drawled, the friendly look returning, "I kinda figured you fer an Indian while I watched you come down the street. But seein' them beautiful blue eyes you got, I knowed I was wrong. That don't happen much."

As he talked, Reena heard the sloshing of liquid in his mouth and knew with horror what was coming next. She wanted to bolt out the door right then and never come back, but her feet seemed frozen in place.

The man snorted, hawked deeply, then turned and spat into a spittoon behind him.

Reena closed her eyes and somehow kept herself from turning and walking away. But this store was her last hope in town. . . .

"You all right, lady? You look a little green."

"I'm . . . I'm fine. I just . . . need to look at your dresses. If you have any."

"Sure, we got plenty of dresses. Come thisaway. My name's Pelham, by the way, just like on the sign outside, but most folks call me Hog."

I can't imagine why, Reena thought wryly. As she followed him to the back of the store, she found herself overwhelmed by his unpleasant odor. Mr. Hog Pelham had obviously been indulging himself in the whiskey and pickled onions, among other things she didn't even want to contemplate. As he proudly prattled on about his new store, Reena turned her attention to the mounds of merchandise in disarray.

Every available inch had been utilized. A great variety of farming implements and other hardware lined the walls on nails and hooks. Kitchen supplies, such as butter churns and brooms, occupied one whole corner. Unopened crates and boxes were scattered everywhere on tables, amidst staple grocery items, saddles, harnesses, men's hats, guns, and Reena even spotted a weather vane rooster. An old yellow dog was curled up on some denim pants on a table, sound asleep.

Reena almost ran into Pelham and realized that he'd stopped and asked her a question. "I'm sorry, what?"

"I said, will these here do ya?" He waved his arm expansively over a table covered with an assortment of dresses. "They ain't in any particular order, as you can see. Hope to have 'em on racks by next week." He looked around the cluttered store sheepishly. "Along with a few other things."

"Is Mrs. H—Pelham around?" She'd almost asked for Mrs. Hog, but that wouldn't do. It was scary to think that Hog had a wife in the first place, she realized.

"Why? You wantin' drawers?"

"Drawers?" Reena asked blankly, and at once she knew it was a mistake coming here.

Pelham leaned toward her, bringing his foul odor perilously close to Reena's nose, and whispered, "Unmentionables."

Reena had to take a step back. "No, no, I was just wondering—"

"'Cause I got 'em, if'n you need 'em. Couldn't help you much pickin' 'em out, though." His mud-colored, bloodshot eyes took on a different light. "That is, unless you'd maybe want a man's opinion, if'n you catch my drift."

The revulsion in Reena was almost too much to bear. She had to get away from this man. She also sensed that another disgusting spittoon episode was just around the corner. "No, thank you, catching your *draft* is enough, Mr. Pelham."

He gave her a blank look. "Huh?"

"If you'll excuse me, I'll just look through your merchandise."

"You betcha," he said, then wandered off to sort through his myriad of crates.

None of the dresses were sorted according to size, so Reena had to look through every one of them. Surprisingly, they were not of poor quality. She even found a couple of good copies of Charles Worth's famous designs. After a quick search, she was disappointed to find that not one was close to her size. She closed her eyes and muttered, "This can't be happening. Why did Dr. Burke have to die?" Then her eyes flew open at the absolute selfishness and callousness of the thought.

Dr. Burke had been D. W. Davis's wife's brother. Davis owned the I. G. Baker Store, where Reena had always bought her clothes, and he always carried her size in a grand assortment of fashions. Pelham's stock was puny in comparison. Davis had closed the Baker store for Dr. Burke's funeral out of respect for his wife, and it wouldn't open again until too late.

Reena quickly felt guilty for her remark, then turned to find Pelham. "Mr. Pelham?" she called.

The proprietor's head popped up over a stack of boxes. "Ma'am?"

He looked uncommonly eager, and Reena wondered if he thought she'd decided to take him up on his "unmentionables" deal.

Suddenly, Reena felt an urgent need inside her to *find a dress*! The Mountie Spring Ball was *tomorrow*! "You don't have any dresses in my size, Mr. Pelham. I was wondering if you had knowledge of any other—"

His eyes lit up. "I *do* have one that ain't out there. Maybe that one'll fit ya."

Reena felt a surge of hope and rushed over to him, stumbling over an open box on the floor. "Where is it? May I see it?"

"Suuuurrrre you can see it. It's just a matter of findin' it," he said as he pulled on his matted beard thoughtfully. "Lessee . . . " he muttered. "Daisy left on Friday, and when I bought it from her I put it . . . where?"

It probably won't fit, so don't get your hopes up. No, don't think that, think positive—it will *fit! It will be just my size!*

Pelham snapped his fingers. "Got it! It's right here behind the counter."

This time, Reena didn't mind the smell in his wake; she just

18

wanted that dress. She followed him close behind, eager, even wanting to give him a little shove to hurry him along. She was almost around the counter with him before she stopped herself and moved back to the customers' side.

Pelham rummaged around underneath the counter, then produced a medium-sized box. Grandly he lifted the lid and withdrew the dress. "How about that? Now, *that's* a dress!"

Reena's heart sank.

It was green. Very green. It was a dazzling shade as bright as high summer grass. Reena reached out to run her fingers lightly over the bodice and was somewhat surprised to feel the heaviness of good satin. Hesitantly she took the dress from Pelham, shook out the folds, and held it out for inspection. She sneezed explosively, for around the bodice were sewn outrageously fluffy and wide black feathers. But the satin material had good body and fell out in thick folds . . . but only to her knees.

"But this . . . this is a saloon girl's dress!"

"Yep, and a mighty pretty one. Daisy was just about your size, so it oughta fit. Daisy had to leave town in a hurry and needed money, so I bought it from her. Here, hold it up to you and give it a try."

Reena sighed, knowing by instinct and sight that it *would* fit her. With a feeling of disbelief that she would even consider trying it on in front of him, she pulled the dress closer around her tall, slim body and looked down.

"Looks perfect, little lady," Pelham said admiringly.

Reena didn't want to look up at him and see the look in his eye. She could imagine only too well what his thoughts were about seeing her in that dress. However, an idea was forming in her mind.

Looking up at Hog Pelham, she ignored the lecherous gleam in his eyes and said, "I'll take it."

————

From the guest room of Megan's house, Reena worked on the dress.

The bodice had a low, graceful cut that showed her throat and shoulders but was not an unacceptable décolleté. She removed the feather mantle and refashioned three of the smallest black feathers with a green glass button to make a spray for her hair. Then she added a two-inch ruffle of ecru lace at the neckline.

The dress had five layers so that the saloon girl wouldn't be encumbered with petticoats! It had an underskirt of green satin, then a petticoat of green net, then another tightly gathered underskirt of the green satin, then a layer of flouncy, gathered black net, and finally the overskirt of heavy green satin. Reena removed all of the layers under the top skirt and fashioned a long straight skirt, fitted and reaching to her ankles, of the green satin. Then she added two scallops for a front slit, providing a teasing glance of her black satin shoes and even a glance of ankles. She shortened the overskirt to her hips in front, with a sweep of material gathered to her knees in back, and added a light underskirt of the green netting to give it body. Taking the leftover satin and black netting, she fashioned a wide belt to encircle her small waist, with a three-layer small gathering in the small of her back that served as a demi-bustle.

Finally, needing to actually see the progress she was making, she decided to slip on the dress and inspect it. The first feeling she had was of sadness for the previous owner. The girl who'd worn this—Daisy—wasn't in the best of professions, so Reena breathed a quick prayer for her. The very fact that Daisy had sold this dress spoke of desperate circumstances. But then again, she might have decided that the saloon life of lecherous men and stale liquor wasn't for her. Maybe she had finally met a nice man who had taken her away from all that. Reena preferred the latter situation for the poor girl.

With a sigh, Reena turned her attention back to the matter at hand. She couldn't exactly show up at the Mounties' ball wearing buckskin. The thought of it made her smile.

Reena's missionary work with the Blackfoot Indians hadn't made an elegant wardrobe the first priority. In fact, it wasn't a priority at all. Since she'd felt God's call to come to the North-West Territories in 1872, her selection in clothes had naturally turned to the simplicity and practicality of the Indian people. If you were cold, you dressed accordingly, and the same for hot summers. The selection from her stylish wardrobe in Chicago for her trip had been deliberately sparse, due to the fact that she knew there would be no opportunities to attend socials and teas in the barren area. Therefore, she'd brought only one suitable dress acceptable for such a situation, and it had quickly faded to ruin. Her purchases at I. G. Baker's store had been few, and her favorite dress had deteriorated to nothing two days before when a young Blackfoot girl had spilled buffalo grease on it while playing "white woman" in it.

Now, looking in the mirror, Reena wished for a pair of satin gloves—green, of course—with eighteen buttons that stretched up over her elbows. She wasn't that fashion conscious by any means, but the gloves would have made a perfect complement for her new creation. Megan had black lace mitts she could borrow. Reena nodded to herself in the mirror. *Not bad. Not bad at all, if I do say so myself.*

"But what will *Hunter* think?" she asked herself in a hushed, bewildered tone. "His opinion is all that matters to me."

She found herself looking at *herself* rather than the dress— the ebony flowing hair, the bright blue eyes that shone almost aqua sometimes, the tan, oval face. Her natural olive skin coloring had absorbed the sun's rays like a sponge, leaving her with a year-around golden tan. It wasn't ladylike, she knew, but she couldn't carry around a parasol all day in her work with the Indians.

The hard work Reena performed every day had toned her arms and shoulders to a sinewy suppleness. Moving her eyes on down, she stopped and felt a ray of hope. Either her hips were expanding on their own, or the dress made it appear so. "That's great news," she said aloud with a twist to her mouth. "Maybe at the age of twenty-five you'll start looking like a real woman instead of a boy. Maybe like Megan. Now *that's* a woman's body." Megan was Reena's sister, and her shapely body was the envy of all women who knew her.

Reena was following the same pattern she always did when inspecting herself. Though she was a beautiful woman, she found herself noticing only her flaws, picking at them like an irritating scab on a wound. It was a habit of introspection she'd always followed, as natural as getting up in the morning.

Shaking off the thoughts about her appearance, Reena examined the dress and how it fit her. "Fits great, actually," she mumbled. "I couldn't *ask* for a better fit." She turned around a few times, craning her neck to see the back, and finally gave a firm nod. "I like the hips. Definitely like the hips."

Reena smiled at her reflection. For a brief instant she entertained the idea that she was indeed an attractive woman with a fantastic smile, and she could see why men noticed her even when there were many other women around. This thought lasted only a fraction of a moment, then flew away without the acknowledgment that it was ever really there.

Taking a deep breath, she said, "Hunter will like it. I like it." Then her eyes twinkled with mischief. "But I know someone who won't."

———

"That's without a doubt the most scandalous dress I've ever laid eyes on!" Megan Vickersham exclaimed.

Reena spun with her arms outstretched, giggling. "If you don't like it, sis, just say so. You're always so dubious."

Megan pointed to the door of the guest room from which Reena had just emerged. "Go take that monstrosity off and put on your real dress. It's almost time to go." Megan, possessor of the enviable figure that looked great in any dress, was the exact opposite of her sister. Four inches shorter than Reena's five foot eight, her hair was a golden brown, and her light skin glowed white when they stood next to each other. Whereas Reena's natural grace showed with her every move, Megan was a bit on the clumsy side. With neither sister knowing it, they both admired traits in the other that they would never possess.

"But, Megan, this *is* my dress," Reena said.

"We don't have time to joke, Reena! Hunter will be here any minute, and you want him to see you in *that*? With your shoes and *ankles* showing? I'd never be caught in something so gaudy!" Megan nervously moved over to the front window and peeked out, as if Hunter would walk in right that moment. She waved a hand at Reena in a shooing gesture. "He's not in sight— now, go!"

"Megan . . ."

Jaye Eliot Vickersham entered the room from the kitchen, absentmindedly munching on a pastry, resplendent in his Mountie full-dress uniform. When he saw Reena he stopped, looked her up and down, swallowed, and said, "Why, hello, Reena. That's a nice dress. I don't think I've ever seen it before."

Reena cast a triumphant smile her sister's way.

Megan looked at her husband in disbelief. "Vic. . . !" Her mouth worked, but nothing came out.

Vic tapped his sharp chin with a finger, considering Reena. "You know, that dress is very . . . er . . ."

"Ghastly!" Megan erupted, finally finding her voice. "Hideous!"

Vic looked at her, his chocolate brown eyes widened in surprise. "Well, darling, those weren't exactly the words I was searching for. I think they was 'different' and 'pleasing.' "

"It's *not* 'pleasing'! It offends the eyes *and* one's morals!" Megan's face turned soft. "Reena, please be a dear and go change into your *real* dress. You've had your little fun, but the hour is growing very late, as they say."

Reena glanced at Vic's angular, kind face. "She won't believe me, Vic. This *is* the dress I'm wearing tonight. Tell her."

Vic turned to his wife. "Darling, this *is* the dress Reena is wearing tonight." Turning back to Reena, he asked, "How was that, my dear?"

"Lovely. You do it much better than I do."

A rapping on the door caused them all to look at it—Reena

23

with anticipation, Vic with pleasure, and Megan with undis-guised horror.

"Ah, that would be Hunter," Vic said jovially and took a step toward the door.

"Jaye Eliot Vickersham, don't you *dare* answer that door!" Megan ordered, pointing a finger at him.

Vic understandably froze in his tracks.

Megan's stabbing finger swung around to Reena. "You. Go change. No more playing around."

Reena laughed and shook her head. "You just don't under-stand, do you?" She went to Megan and placed her hands on her shoulders. As if speaking to a child, Reena stated, "This . . . is . . . my . . . dress . . . for . . . tonight." Then she turned to the door, leaving Megan sputtering about poor Hunter having to be seen with that . . . that . . . *thing* tonight in front of *everybody*, and opened the door.

Hunter Stone's entire face lit up when he saw Reena.

"Hello, Hunter," Reena greeted warmly.

"Reena," he breathed, "you look lovely. Beautiful dress."

Behind her, Reena heard her sister make a strangling sound.

———————

They walked to Fort Macleod together, arm in arm, the best of friends. The Vickershams' house was only a few hundred yards from the fort, so they enjoyed the late afternoon before it turned chilly. They could already see people—both settlers and Indi-ans—filing through the gate into the parade ground.

Reena felt fine, as fine as she had in days. The air was crisp and full of the scent of freshly blooming flowers. Megan was actually laughing at her own behavior now, and Reena's arm was through Hunter's, holding it tight. She looked up at him and admired the clean angle of his jaw, the solid cleft chin, and Roman nose. He must have noticed her inspection because he turned his clear gray eyes to her.

"What are you looking at?"

"You." *Those eyes, Hunter Stone*, Reena thought for perhaps the hundredth time, *are incredible.*

Hunter grinned. "You look happy, Reena."

"I *am* happy," she returned. She was grasping his arm with both hands now, never wishing to let go, wanting to tuck this moment away in her thoughts for later when she was about to go to sleep—the look of approval on his face, the cut of his sturdy figure in the scarlet uniform, the sinewy muscles corded in his arm under her hands, the smell of fresh shaving lotion floating around him in a cloud—all of it she could draw on and treasure later.

Megan was laughing with Vic. "Old habits die hard, I suppose. Used to be, *nothing* mattered to me but clothes."

Reena turned to her and grinned. "I know. If you met someone and they weren't wearing clothes up to your standard, you'd have nothing to do with them."

"Makes you wonder, doesn't it?" Megan asked in a strangely hushed tone.

"About what, my love?" Vic asked.

Megan smiled at her husband's endearing terms that he unfailingly used with her. "About God's love. How could He love someone like I used to be?"

"Mmm. The same goes for all of us, darling."

Vic's wistful comment set them all to thinking about his stunning discovery of the previous year and how it had affected both his and Megan's life.

Quietly, Hunter asked, "All set to go tomorrow?"

"Yes," Vic answered, looking at Megan quickly to see her reaction to the subject. "All packed and ready to go. I should be back in a week or two, hopefully with a towheaded boy in my wake."

Reena glanced over at Megan furtively, searching for signs of anxiety, but her sister kept her eyes trained on their destination without a marked change of attitude. Her eyes met Vic's over Megan's head, and she saw the same sort of bewilderment that was a shadow in his eyes when he talked about the subject.

Vic had come across a murdered woman in the mountains

the previous year. It was a shock when he realized that he knew her, had actually had a relationship with her several years before when he wasn't a Christian, but the real shock had been in the diary he'd found.

The woman had named the baby Jaye. After Jaye Eliot Vickersham—his father.

It had, of course, stunned Megan. She and Vic had only been married for two weeks when he gave her the news. At the time, they had just made it through a different ordeal—very traumatic in itself—and she could only thank the Lord that they were safe and promise Vic that she would do everything in her power to make a home for the boy with them, if that's what he wanted.

Vic wanted it more than anything. The clues to Jaye's whereabouts from the diary had been ambiguous and vague, but he'd started searching for him in October of 1876. The mother, whose name was Fran, had been a wandering spirit with no choice but to leave the boy with a relative. The life Fran had led made Vic glad she'd made that choice. However, the diary gave only a cousin's name—first name only—and the mention that the city was near Maple Creek, two hundred miles to the east of Fort Macleod.

Vic had gone there—apprehensive, nervous, feeling a bit foolish—and after searching and asking questions, he had discovered that Fran's cousin Stella had departed abruptly without telling anyone where she was going. He did get a last name for Stella—Smith—but that was all he discovered about the woman. Dejected, Vic had left his name and address with the local magistrate, asking him to send word *at once* should any further information come to his attention.

All winter the boy had been on Vic's mind. The "what ifs" rang through his head constantly, but there was absolutely nothing he could do short of charging around the whole North-West Territory blind, hoping for a miracle.

Finally, after an agonizing three months, Vic had received a letter from the Maple Creek magistrate stating that one of Stella's friends had heard that Stella—and hopefully, Jaye—had ended up somewhere outside Battleford. The good news was that there was a small Mountie post in Battleford that Vic could use as a home base while he searched; the bad news was that Battleford was a good three hundred miles away to the northeast.

Vic wasn't daunted, though. At least it was a lead, and that was what Vic had been praying for. Now the only mystery nagging at Vic was what kind of life Jaye had endured with this cousin who'd had a boy dumped on her. Was Stella responsible? Did she love the boy as her own? Were they rich, poor, happy, miserable? Vic knew he had plenty of time to ponder these questions on the way to Battleford.

Now that they had almost reached the fort and the sound of merrymaking, Reena said to Vic, "I hope you find him this time."

"We'll all be praying for you, of course," Hunter assured him.

"Thank you," Vic said fervently. "You both know how much that means to me." A thought occurred to him. "I hope the town stays healthy, since there's no civilian doctor here anymore."

"Dr. Burke's death was so sudden," Megan exclaimed. "What did he die of?"

"Influenza, I've heard," Hunter said. "And I've also heard that a few more people have it, and one has pneumonia."

"Oh my," Reena breathed. "Then what will they do? There's no doctor except for the regimental one. What's his name, Hunter?"

"Nevitt. And he's an artist, too, believe it or not."

"So what will the civilians do? Dr. Nevitt doesn't have time to travel all around the country treating everyone."

Hunter shook his head. "I don't know."

When they reached the huge gate, they nodded to a few people who were filing inside. "Looks like a bigger turnout than last year's ball," Megan commented.

Reena stepped through the gate, still clinging tightly to Hunter's arm, and the annual celebration of the North-West

Mounted Police Spring Ball assaulted her senses.

The first thing Reena noticed was the mouth-watering aroma of roasted beef, pork, and pheasant. The spits were set up away from the regimental band and dance area to keep the heat and smoke away from all those who had come to enjoy the festivities of the ball. She saw the huge side of beef turning slowly over a lively fire, with men gathered around gossiping and watching the dancers. It was indeed more crowded inside the fort than she'd ever remembered before.

The band, consisting of eight scarlet-clad men with banjos, violins, and flutes, was seated by the barracks piping out a lively tune. Hunter had told Reena that the men had paid for the instruments themselves and that the instruments had been shipped all the way from Winnipeg by dog team. The dance area was already crowded, and everyone had to shout to be heard over all the noise. There were many Indians present also, even a few from Reena's Blackfoot tribe, to whom she waved.

Strung around the barracks and inner buildings were colorful beads, banners, and mottoes tacked up by the Mounties that morning. Though no one was naïve enough to believe that the winter snows were completely over, April 1 was the day when everyone began to look forward to warmer weather and the renewal of life with the return of greenery.

Beside her, Hunter pointed. "There's Becker and Jenny."

Amid the dancers, Reena saw the two and had to suppress a laugh. Dirk Becker was Hunter's height, six foot three, but carried even more natural solid muscle—a huge young man. Jenny Sweet could only be described as petite, and when they were together the sight was comical. Becker towered over her like a lion in full bloom of youth beside a small gazelle. They were laughing as she watched, and Reena was glad to see that.

"I'm going to say hello," Hunter said, and started to disengage from Reena's grasp.

"No, Hunter. Let them dance. They look so happy right now—just like I'm feeling."

Hunter glanced at her with a strange look of contemplation

on his face, then urged in a quiet, conspiratorial voice, "Come on." He grasped her arm and turned back toward the gate.

"But . . . Hunter, we just got here!"

Hunter paid her no mind. To Vic and Megan he said quickly, "We'll be right back."

Reena followed him out the gate, noticing that Vic and Megan were too surprised to speak. Outside, Hunter turned left away from the town, passing the back of a barracks. "Hunter, what are you—" She was cut off when Hunter quickly opened a door she hadn't seen and pulled her inside. "What are you doing?" she asked breathlessly, beginning to worry about his abrupt behavior.

Stopping and turning, Hunter took her in his arms, a playful grin at his lips. "This is the officers' mess. I knew no one would be here; they're all out there." He jerked his head toward the noise on the parade ground.

"And what could that possibly—"

Hunter cut her off by planting his warm lips firmly against hers. She felt his strong arms around her and for a moment was so stunned at his carefree behavior that she stiffened. Then, never able to resist him, she threw her arms around his neck and returned his kiss with her own fervor. Both of them were smiling through the kiss, and finally Reena had to pull away and laugh with joy. "You horrid man! How could you take advantage of a missionary woman like this?"

"I don't see the missionary woman being very offended. Besides, if the missionary woman had known about this room, *I* might very well be the victim of a forced kiss."

Reena shrugged and felt the light of her love for him burn even brighter. "You're right. Kiss me again."

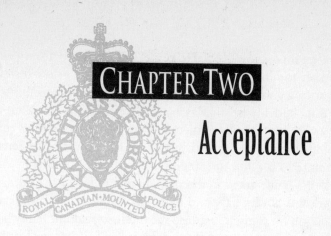

CHAPTER TWO

Acceptance

Dirk Becker had seen Hunter and Reena duck out of the fort and wondered briefly where they were going in such a hurry. He didn't dwell on it, however, because it was almost time for another swing under Jenny's arm, which would require all his concentration in order to keep from sprawling flat. It was no problem, of course, to swing *her* around, since she barely came to his shoulder. But when *he* did it . . .

Here it comes! Dirk thought, and he could see that Jenny was already grinning in anticipation. So were others around him, much to his chagrin. They'd already seen the awkward maneuver performed once, and they were looking forward to witnessing it again. Dirk made a face at Jenny and practically squatted down to make his pass under her arm.

This time he *did* fall—right onto his left side. All the dancers around them laughed uproariously. Jenny covered her mouth with her small hands, giggling helplessly. Her pretty hazel eyes danced. "That was fun, Dirk. Do it again, please?" she asked in a little girl's voice.

Dirk felt a flash of resentment, then laughed himself. What

a sight he must have been! He could feel himself blushing and knew that the long scar that stretched from just below his eye to his strong jawline was standing out bone white against his red face. But suddenly he didn't care and stood up to give a mock bow to his appreciative audience. They all applauded his gallantry in the face of embarrassment. Then he turned to Jenny and pointed a playful, threatening finger at her. "And you . . ."

"Yes?" Jenny asked innocently, unable to hide her grin.

Dirk was always happy to make her laugh, even if it meant humiliation for himself, because she did it so seldom. Jenny had grown up under a callous, abusive man who'd ultimately lost his life in a fiery explosion caused by the very whiskey he peddled illegally. The emotional scars she carried of the mistreatment from her father and his men were deep. The trauma had been so great at times that Jenny had suffered from strange catatonic episodes of which she was neither aware of nor could remember. But to everyone's relief, these occurrences had disappeared less than a year ago.

So when Jenny laughed, Dirk felt overjoyed. Nevertheless, in a stern voice he told her, "It's not polite to laugh at your beau when he falls down while dancing. We men have our pride."

The band abruptly shifted to a slow waltz. Jenny held her arms out in a grand manner and took on a proper English accent, so unlike her back-country drawl. "Ladies are allowed to laugh whenever and wherever they like, thank you very much. Even though you've caused me discomfort by your clumsiness in front of so many peers, I shall allow you to continue dancing with me."

"Your graciousness astounds me, ma'am." Dirk slipped his arm around her tiny waist and took her hand, aware of the ever present jolt whenever he touched her. The waltz was his favorite dance, but Jenny was still learning it and kept her eyes trained somewhere below his chin while she counted steps. Dirk wanted to smile, but he knew how uncomfortable she was about dancing in front of other people.

It had taken much begging and pleading and coaxing on his part to even get her to step out on a dance floor with him, but finally she had—last Christmas Eve at a social given by D. W. Davis. Jenny had constantly kept her eyes roaming from couple to couple, obviously feeling as if everyone was watching her, waiting for her to make a mistake. When she did make a slight misstep, her eyes had rounded, and Dirk could see the sudden urge to bolt from the floor. He'd smiled at her reassuringly and immediately complimented her graceful movement. Despite his assurance, Jenny had the look of a cornered animal, but she hadn't dashed from the dance floor. He had only been able to persuade her to dance one more time that night, but it was a start.

As Jenny stared below his chin now, she said in a tentative voice, "Dirk?"

"Yes?"

"How can you—as a Christian—think that dancing is all right? I mean, I've read about some preachers who say it's a sin. What do you think?"

"You've graduated, my dear."

"What do you mean?"

"Here I was thinking you were counting steps as you stared at my neck so intensely. But you were thinking about springing that question on me, weren't you?"

Jenny looked guilty, then asked, "Do you mind?"

"Of course not! You can ask me anything you want about God or Christianity, you know that. But to answer your question, do you know who the greatest dancer in the Bible was?"

Jenny shook her head.

"King David—my personal favorite in all of the Old Testament. He was paid the highest compliment that has ever been given." Dirk paused, trying to whet her appetite for the Word of God. Jenny wasn't a Christian, and there was nothing he wanted more on this earth than for her to find the peace and comfort of God.

"What was the compliment?" Jenny asked.

"God chose David to lead Israel because David was a man after God's own heart. Isn't that the greatest compliment you've ever heard?"

"Yes," Jenny answered in a quiet, thoughtful voice.

"And no one danced before God more than King David. He danced out of pure joy and worship for his Father. I have no doubt that at times he danced with one of his many wives before the Lord, too."

"He had more than one wife?"

"Many, actually. But don't hold that against him. It was just the custom at the time."

A teasing glint came into Jenny's eyes. "Do you think that would be a blessing? To have so many wives?"

"Me? Absolutely not. The only thing I'm good at juggling is knives, and by the look of my face, I'm not very good at *that*." He saw Jenny run her eyes over the terrible scar on his face, then become thoughtful again. Somehow, even before she asked it, he knew what was coming.

"How come you don't blame God for that? For doing that to you?"

Dirk laughed, and it was a rich, ringing baritone. "Jenny, God didn't do this to me! Why should I blame Him for *my* stupidity?"

"But . . . He allowed it to happen, didn't He? Why didn't He stop it? He could have made that horrible man you were competing with just . . . I don't know, walk away or something."

The waltz ended, and Dirk decided they could use a rest and some punch. Taking her arm, he told her gently, "Jenny, there are consequences to our actions and sins on this earth. God allows them to happen so He can teach us—discipline us and show us the right way to go. And though it may sound strange, He does that because He loves us so much. Do you understand?"

"Well . . . not really."

They reached the refreshment table, and Dirk poured them two glasses of strawberry punch. Two Mounties came up to him

34

and began teasing him about being a danger to the other dancers around him.

Jenny had never received a formal education until she'd come to Fort Macleod after her father's death. Being around Dirk and Megan and Reena, she'd admired their knowledge of books, social customs, and life in general. A yearning had begun to burn within her that she'd never known was there—a hunger for learning that was almost frightening in its intensity. After Megan had taught her to read, Jenny devoured every book she could find, amazed over and over again at the things she'd been missing in her miserable life. Jenny was blessed with a quick intelligence and ability to learn. Were these abilities blessings from God? Jenny had a strong feeling they were, but she wasn't ready to acknowledge it yet.

She'd never even heard of God except in vile conversation from her father and his men. Now, in her new life, she found herself surrounded by caring people who provided something she'd never known—dear people who were truly concerned about her well-being. Sometimes it still took her breath away when she contrasted the love around her to the hatred and abuse she'd known for her first seventeen years.

Watching Dirk—handsome beyond belief, scar or no scar, it didn't matter to Jenny—as he joked with his companions, she continued to wonder what he saw in her. She didn't consider herself beautiful in any sense of the word. She knew she drawled like a mule skinner when she talked. She did not share Dirk's faith, something she knew was very important to him. So why did he insist on courting her? Instead of being overjoyed, as something inside her said she should be, she was troubled. They were so completely *different*, from their upbringings to their beliefs to their very goals in life. Dirk wanted to save the world for God, whereas Jenny just wanted to *survive* after her years of intense suffering. Sometimes a small voice inside told her that her thinking was selfish. But nevertheless, that was how things were right now, and she sometimes found herself actually resenting Dirk and his pious ways.

After all, hadn't she heard somewhere that judging others was a sin? Who was he to tell her that her life was wrong? At the same time, she *knew* she wasn't worthy of his concern. She *knew* God could never love a person like her who'd never given Him a thought in her life. Her way, she'd come to realize, was to forget the past—which was proving to be impossible, since it haunted her every day—and get on with some semblance of a life. Most probably alone. All alone.

Dirk turned to her now, seeming a bit uncomfortable that he was taking so much time talking to his friends. He flashed her his boyish grin, revealing strong white teeth. He was trying to reassure her that he hadn't forgotten about her while his companions rambled on around him, and he was worried that she felt neglected.

Just with that easy smile from him, something gave way inside Jenny, and her dark thoughts completely reversed themselves. He was always so kind and caring and tender with her. She'd never known anyone like him in her life and had certainly never had a true gentleman show feelings for her. She felt a surge of guilt that she could even think his intentions were less than honorable.

Thinking back to his story of David, Jenny couldn't understand this business of dancing before God. Why would that please Him? But she *had* understood about paying for sins on earth, and she'd experienced uncomfortable feelings when he'd said it. It was like something shaking loose inside herself, something that had always been there but had decided to make its presence known for the first time at that exact moment.

And it frightened her more than she could say.

The morning after the ball, with dawn barely touching the horizon, Megan stood in her bedroom, carefully and lovingly polishing the glass figures her father had commissioned to be made for her eighteenth birthday. They were colored a soft robin's-egg blue, each one a little larger than her hands. They were blown sculptures of couples—one pair sitting on a window bench seat with the man reading to the woman, another pair walking hand in hand, and the last pair sitting on a swing, the man turned to his love and staring lovingly into her eyes.

Accompanying the gift, her father had made a rosewood stand with two shelves. He'd attached ribbons to the bottom of the top shelf and down to the swing, thereby suspending it so that it actually swung. Megan had been overjoyed to receive the gift and believed it was the finest thing anyone had ever given her. It meant so much to her because it was the only gift her father had ever given to her personally. Megan, Reena, and their brother, Liam, had always known that the presents they received came from their mother, and their father had probably always been as surprised as his children when they opened them.

But that year had been special—Megan couldn't really remember why, other than it was the magical age of eighteen for her. Still, she couldn't recall Reena receiving a gift so personal from him on her eighteenth birthday.

Megan still remembered the look on her father's face when she'd opened it. Jack O'Donnell was nothing if not confident; his success in the tough banking world of Chicago had brought about a natural ease with himself in a manner that showed clearly to others. But when Megan had looked up at him with joy over her gift, she'd seen a strange look of uncertainty in his eyes she didn't witness again until the death of her mother. Thinking about it since, Megan now understood that her father hadn't a clue as to what an eighteen-year-old girl would consider a good gift. At that moment he'd worn an expression that Megan had always longed to see on his face—one of a loving father concerned about his daughter's feelings. It was a moment she would never forget, and she was sure it was because of that look that she treasured what she held in her hands at this moment.

Her favorite figure was, and had always been, the man sitting so comfortably in the swing. Of course, when she held him in her hands he looked awkward, with one leg turned sideways and his arm in an unnatural position. But when placed in the swing, turned to his love, he seemed to convey his deep *feelings* of love for her, as if he were at that moment bursting to tell her how he felt.

Suddenly, Vic burst into the bedroom, startling Megan. Vic was speaking even as he opened the door. "Darling, I want you to—"

With a gasp of horror Megan felt the figure slip from her hands. Desperately she reached down and caught the man's outstretched arm, as if he were offering her assistance in keeping him from shattering on the wooden floor. Megan closed her eyes briefly in thanks, then looked at her husband. "Vic, are you insane?" Instantly she hated the shriek in her tone, but she couldn't seem to stop herself. "You almost made me break this!"

"I'm sorry, darling, I—"

"Ohhh! What are you doing charging in here like that?"

Vic reached for her, and she actually took a step back, afraid that he would make her drop the figure again. Realizing how slick it felt in her hands from the sweat of her palms, she quickly wiped it with the cloth and carefully replaced it on her dresser. The glass couple swung together briefly before coming to a stop.

"I'm really sorry, Megan."

Feeling foolish now, Megan turned and went into his arms. *His arms are always open for me*, she thought, mentally kicking herself. *Not once since I've known him has he denied me an embrace.* Surprising herself, she sobbed.

"What is it?" Vic asked, holding her closer.

"I'm so unkind sometimes, Vic, and you're always patient with me. I should be the one apologizing to you for being scratchy."

"I know how important those figures are to you—"

Megan pulled back suddenly, her eyes wet. "It's just so *far*, Vic! How many miles?"

He smiled and smoothed a lock of her golden hair back from her face. "Three hundred."

"But . . . that's the end of the *earth*!"

Vic laughed his easy laugh. "Of course not, my dear! Fifty

miles a day—six days. Some time to look around and find the boy, say three days, then six days back. Two weeks and a day. That's not so bad, is it?"

"But all kinds of things can happen! You could break your leg, or your horse could break his leg, or you could meet up with a bear—*anything* could happen!"

Vic shushed her and drew her to him again. "Now, now, none of all that. We both know that the Lord will guide my way and everything will be all right, don't we?"

"Yes," Megan answered, her voice muffled against his shirt. He smelled of woodsmoke from the fire he'd built for her.

"Of course we do."

They stood there for a while, enjoying the embrace they would both sorely miss in the time to come. Finally Megan said, "Vic?"

"Yes?"

"Why *did* you come charging in here like that?"

Giving a little half laugh, Vic said, "I wanted you to come see the sunrise with me once more before I left."

There was a short silence, then Megan burst into a fresh bout of tears.

———

"Mmm," Vic moaned with delight, "I'll sure be missing these apple pancakes, I can assure you."

"And I'll miss your groaning while eating them," Megan smiled. She was wrapping biscuits she'd made that morning for him, along with dried beef, salt pork, a few large potatoes, and cornmeal.

Vic eyed the huge sack while chewing, then said, "Darling, my poor horse will soundly object to the weight of that monstrosity. He has to carry the food for the two of them, you know." Vic was taking two horses—one to ride and another to carry the supplies.

"I don't care about that silly horse. I'd give you *four* sacks if I could, but I know it would be no good in a few days."

39

"Well, there'll be plenty of game along the way. And there's a post on the Red Deer River where I can resupply."

Megan thought again, *Three hundred miles! He'll be so exhausted. . . .* She moved behind him and began massaging his shoulders, imagining how sore they would be—*all* of him would be—for the next two weeks.

A deep, satisfied rumbling sound came from Vic's throat, then he tilted back his head against her. "I'll miss you."

"Oh, Vic, I'll miss you, too."

"You know, if you need anything—*anything*—Hunter is just across the way there."

"I know."

"He's already told me he would stop by every other day or so to check on you."

Impulsively, Megan leaned down and kissed his forehead. "I'll watch for him. Don't worry about me. Just take care of yourself."

Vic took her hand and guided her to the chair beside him. "Listen, dear—I didn't want to tell you this because it might have spoiled your evening last night, but . . . I heard from Dr. Nevitt that four more cases of the flu were discovered yesterday. This is a frightening time for me to be leaving. Please promise me you'll take care of yourself. If you feel the slightest cold coming on, you'll go to Dr. Nevitt—all right?"

"Yes."

"Promise?"

Megan smiled and squeezed his hands. "I'll be fine, Vic. Stop worrying."

"Ha! I will if you will."

They talked for a few more minutes of inconsequential things, but in the back of Megan's mind was the ominous thought of not having him around for two weeks. Actually, she was very afraid of being alone for that long, but she didn't dare tell him. He had enough worries of his own in trying to find his son.

Finally they could put off his departure no longer. Vic gathered his things, saddled and loaded the horses, then led them to the front porch where Megan was standing. The morning was chilly, but not unpleasantly so, and the sun was rising into a cloudless, endless stretch of blue.

Vic tied the horses to a post and took Megan in his arms. Megan told herself she would *not* cry, and to her surprise she succeeded. They stood there, just holding each other, drawing what little comfort they could to last them for the long days ahead.

When Vic pulled away, there was a concerned light in his eyes. "There's one more thing I have to ask you, Megan. Have you thought about the possibility that I'll really find him this time and bring him home?"

Megan tried to give him a reassuring smile, though his very words sent a mild panic through her. It was *all* she'd thought about for the past few days. Megan was a schoolteacher—a good one, she'd found to her surprise—but she'd never in her life been around a toddler. She'd dreamed of being a mother, of course, but that happy event had always been down the road in the future, something to play with in the mind, something to *prepare* for. Now she felt as if motherhood was being forced on her, and it caused a bit of ugly resentment to rise in her.

Nevertheless, she smiled and told him in her calmest tone, "Of course I've thought of it. This little boy will have his father's goodness and sweetness in him, and I'll love him as much as I do you. I'll take him as my own, Vic."

Looking relieved beyond measure, Vic kissed her lovingly. "I know you will. I was just wondering if you were prepared, and I can see that you are. I love you, darling."

Megan watched him mount the horse and fought off a sudden, frightening desire to beg him to stay with her, leave tomorrow or the next day, or the day after that. But with effort she kept the smile on her face as he blew her a kiss and turned away.

Just before rounding the fort and fading from sight, he turned and waved again. Megan waved back.

And then he was gone.

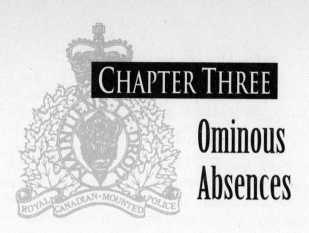

CHAPTER THREE

Ominous Absences

Jenny waited in the schoolhouse for Megan. It was a huge building: so big, in fact, they had squared off one large section and didn't even use it. It was difficult to keep warm on cold days, and much of Jenny's time was spent stoking the several stoves located along the walls with firewood donated from the children's families.

Megan was later than her usual seven forty-five arrival time. Jenny knew what today was—the day Vic left on his journey to find his son—so undoubtedly he and Megan had lingered an extra bit of time saying good-bye. Jenny couldn't imagine what Megan was feeling. Not because Jenny didn't know what it was like to be left alone—her father had done that since she was ten—but how did it feel when it was someone you loved and cared the world about? Vic's trip through hostile country could be dangerous, and Jenny figured he would be gone for two to three weeks. Megan would be feeling very down this morning, so Jenny began preparing some hot tea for her.

Lydia Meecham helped her. Lydia was a precocious seven-year-old who loved playing pretend. Her blue muslin dress trimmed with pink satin ribbon was old, but clean. Her brother, Timmy, sat at his desk drawing, his favorite pastime. The two children were always the first to arrive at school, and Jenny knew it was because Lydia liked her so much. They'd hit it off instantly the very day Jenny had come to Fort Macleod after her father's death.

"Why do you think Miss Megan's late?" Lydia asked her.

Jenny smiled reassuringly down at the blond-haired girl with the deep crimson birthmark on her right temple and explained about Megan having to say good-bye to her husband for a few weeks.

"So she's *already* having a bad day, huh?"

"Yes, Lydia, I suppose you could say that."

"That is unless she's prayed to Jesus, and He's helped her."

Here we go again, Jenny sighed inwardly. *Even the children are after me.* "Yes, that's probably true."

Behind them, Timmy sneezed wetly. "Excuse me," he muttered as he pulled out a man's handkerchief from his back pocket. Jenny could see the initials stitched on it—F. M.—Fitz Meecham, their dead father. He'd been a farmer initially, but something had gone wrong, and he'd turned into a vicious outlaw who'd murdered innocent people and had stolen livestock all over the Territory. Jenny supposed that was another reason she cared for these two more than the others. They had the same wayward and now dead fathers in common.

"Bless you, Timmy," Jenny said and was alarmed when he sneezed again. "Do you feel all right?"

"Not really. Just got a cold, I think."

Lydia said accusingly, "You kept me up all night with your sneezing."

Typical brother-sister concern for each other, Jenny thought with amusement. But something about Timmy's sneezing bothered her, something she'd heard just yesterday.

The door opened, and more children came in, laughing and playing, then Megan entered. She looked tired, and it was only the beginning of the day. Smiling at Jenny and the children,

Megan removed her wrap and woolen cap, all the while greeting each one. They looked up at her with adoring eyes and huge grins.

When Megan got to Jenny, the younger girl offered in a low voice, "Why don't you take the day off, Megan? I can handle the lessons."

"Thanks, Jenny, but I'm going to have plenty of time to sit in that empty house by myself for the next few weeks. I don't want to start today."

"Is Vic. . . ?" The way Jenny asked, it seemed as though they were talking about someone on the verge of dying.

"Yes, he's gone. He left early."

Jenny tried to gauge Megan's emotions, but all she could detect was a sadness which, she supposed, was probably all that was there, except for maybe a fear of loneliness buried deep and ready to surface. Jenny promised herself to spend as many evenings with her as Megan could stand. She wasn't foolish enough to believe that she could replace Vic, but she could be of some company while he was away.

Jenny's attention was diverted when she heard another child sneeze. One of them was talking in a nasal tone, too.

"Goodness, I'm late," Megan muttered as she set about getting the lessons for the day together at her desk. "It's already time to begin." When Megan looked up, Jenny saw her round-eyed, surprised look. "Where *is* everyone?"

Their usual attendance was twenty-two, with children of all ages. Jenny usually took the youngest ones and Megan the older ones, but occasionally they would swap so they could give every child some of their attention. Today, at five minutes past eight, there were only twelve children in the schoolhouse.

Jenny had a very bad feeling, and just when she opened her mouth to mention it to Megan, little Lydia sneezed. "Megan," Jenny said in a tiny voice, staring at Lydia, "something's wrong."

"Of course something's wrong!" Megan replied with a small laugh. "We have a lot of hooky-players today."

"No, Megan . . ."

"What is it?"

"Boys and girls," Jenny called to get their attention, "does anyone here know where the others are? Deke, you live near Sandy King. Where is she today?"

Deke, a burly boy of twelve, shrugged his shoulders. "I don't know, Miss Jenny. I try to stay away from her because she always hits me."

Among the giggles, Mary Anston told him, "That's because she likes you for some reason, frog-face."

Normally this would bring a secret smile to Jenny, but not today. Immediately she put a stop to the howls of glee and said, "Now, I saw many of the children who aren't here at the ball last night. Where are they?"

A small, quiet little girl raised her hand tentatively.

"Yes, Carla?"

"Petey and Danny Prejean are sick. When my pa and me stopped by this morning to pick them up, their mama said they had the chills and a fever."

"Jill Keisler, too," added Mary.

"And the Gilliam twins," another child offered. "They've got the flu."

Jenny had heard enough. She turned to Megan, who looked as alarmed as Jenny felt. "Megan, I think I should go to Dirk and report this."

"I agree. I'll stay with the children."

On the way out the door, Jenny heard another sneeze.

———

With a grunt, Dirk came down on the mare's back as she did her best to dislodge him. She was a stubborn one, for many times the mares were better fighters than some of the stallions. Snorting and whipping her head, she took them into the air again. With a strange little twist, she nearly threw him this time. Dirk felt himself overbalance to the left, then, with a desperate whip of his raised arm, he managed to straighten himself.

"Close now, little girl!" Dirk heard himself shout at her. He'd been on her for almost a full minute now, and he sensed her fatigue and the inevitable breaking of her will. He heard the Mounties who were watching begin to call encouragement to him. They, too, saw that he was close to taming her.

After three more weakening jumps, the mare shook her head vigorously and settled into a trot around the corral. Dirk reached down and patted her sweaty neck, murmuring to her gently as he did all the horses he trained, "You're a good'n, you are." His father had taught him that. In his back-country Mississippi drawl he'd told Dirk, "That gal has been through a pretty humiliatin' experience. You need to let her know she ain't done nothin' wrong. She's done somethin' right." That simple advice to the fourteen-year-old Dirk had stayed with him ever since.

When he brought the mare to a halt by the group of Mountie spectators, he threw the reins to a constable and swung off.

"You broke her real good, Sergeant!" an excited, fresh-faced new recruit called. All eyes turned to him, and he blushed deeply from the silent inspection. "What's the matter? Why's everybody looking at me like that?"

The attention shifted to Dirk as he walked right up to the young man. *He doesn't know better*, he thought, *but he's about to be educated.* Then he heard more words from his father come out of his own mouth to the lad: "She's not 'broke.' There's nothing broke about her. Look at her . . . do you see anything *broke*?"

The young man, obviously frightened of this huge sergeant who was only a few years older than himself, tore his eyes from the imposing figure and dutifully looked the mare over. "No, sir, there's nothing—"

"Broke, that's right. She's *trained*—there's a big difference. She's still got her spirit, and she'll make someone—maybe even you—a fine mount. If she does become yours, you treat her with the same respect she'll give you, or you'll answer to me."

"Yes, sir, but I didn't mean—"

Dirk's scarred face softened. "I know you didn't. Just remember, all right?"

"You bet, sir!"

Everyone at Fort Macleod knew that Dirk Becker was without a doubt the finest horse trainer around. No one questioned his wisdom, or his phrases, for that matter. The word "broke" concerning horses had forever been banished from the fort.

Dirk removed his hat and wiped his sweating brow. Looking at the wild horse corral, he pointed and told a constable, "Bring me that chestnut next. The one with the—"

"Hey, Sarge, isn't that your lady coming this way?" the constable asked, looking over Dirk's shoulder.

Dirk turned, and his face lit up. "So it is. Hanson, you take the chestnut."

"You got it, Sarge."

As Dirk walked to meet Jenny, his good humor at her surprise visit faded away. From the look on her pretty face, he could tell she was deeply troubled about something. She gave him a small smile, but it was forced.

"Hi, Dirk."

"Jenny," he smiled.

"I was watching you. You sure ride well."

"Thank you. What brings you out on such a fine day? Playing hooky?"

A shadow passed over her face. "There's something wrong."

Dirk remembered what day it was, and he glanced over to Vic's house in the distance. "With Megan?"

"No, no. It's the school—or rather, the children. Almost half of them are absent this morning."

"Half?"

"Yes. It sounds like there's something going around, and they're all sick. I'm worried."

Dirk had heard about an unusual number of people falling ill, but he'd simply blamed it on the change of weather. However, he *had* heard the word "flu" a lot lately in conversation.

"I was thinking," Jenny continued, "that you could speak

to Superintendent Irvine about it. Someone needs to go check on these children and find out what's wrong."

"Of course I will. I'll even get Dr. Nevitt to go with me—" He stopped abruptly and looked at her. "No, I won't. Dr. Nevitt just left for Fort Walsh this morning."

They looked at each other with a dawning realization. Quietly, Jenny said, "That means that since Dr. Burke died, there isn't . . ."

Dirk finished her sentence for her, knowing that she didn't even want to speak the words. ". . . a doctor around for many miles." He patted her arm gently, attempting to convey a calmness he didn't feel. "I'll go see Superintendent Irvine right now."

"Dirk?"

"Yes?"

"The children . . ."

"I know. Go back to the school, Jenny, and try not to worry. I'll take care of it, and everything will be all right."

As he strode away, Dirk wondered if he'd just lied to the girl he loved.

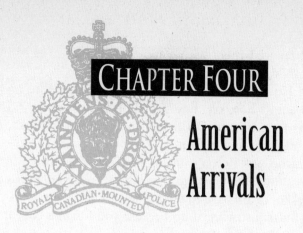

CHAPTER FOUR

American Arrivals

Y ou want *me* to take those lunatics to Warren, sir?" Sergeant Preston Stride asked. He'd served in a British army regiment in England before coming to the Territories, and he was every inch the tough, no-nonsense leader of men who was admired by all the Mounties. Tall and erect, he had close-cropped red hair and serious blue eyes that could turn stormy at a dereliction of duty so small as dirt under the fingernails. Now those eyes stared at Hunter Stone in disbelief.

"Yes, Sergeant. You."

A deep voice behind them said clearly, "*Veni . . . vidi . . . vici.*"

They turned to the wagon and looked at the man who thought he was Julius Caesar. He was standing in the bed of the wagon, as he'd done ever since they'd put him in there, gazing down at them as if from a lofty height, exuding arrogance and spouting Latin phrases. His name was Cabell, but no one could convince him that he was not the Roman statesman and general. He'd made a nuisance of himself in town like his two friends, and all were being taken to the asylum in Warren.

Cabell favored them with a monarch's graciousness and translated, "I came, I saw, I conquered."

Behind Hunter, Stride heard Del Dekko cackle in his high-pitched twang. "Boy, oh, boy . . . ain't *he* something?" Del nudged his friend Faron O'Donnell in the ribs joyfully. "See what you're gonna miss out on?"

Faron, who was Reena's uncle, gave Del a disgusted look and said in a thick Irish brogue, "Ye'll be keepin' yer elbows to yerself, Dekko, or I'll have to crack one of 'em."

"Ah, you're just worked up because you lost the coin toss and will miss out on all the fun."

"*Iacta alea esto*," Cabell announced ominously, his dark gaze sweeping over them with meaning. "The die is cast."

"Bah!" snorted Faron. "Hunter, me lad, can't ye make him shut up? A man can't think clearly when so much gibberish is bein' thrown at 'im!"

Cabell's two companions took no notice of his antics. One sat in the corner behind Cabell, as far from anyone as he could get, swatting at things that only he could see. His eyes were bloodshot, with black circles underneath, as if he hadn't slept in a week. Once in a while he would moan softly. No one knew his name.

The other man was Ebbie Shank, and he seemed to believe he was a menagerie of farm animals. At the moment he was a rooster, strutting around the wagon with his hands cocked beneath his armpits, jerking his head forward with each movement. His eyes were wide and staring. Every so often he would bellow, "Cock-a-doodle-doo!" in a surprisingly good imitation.

Cabell looked down on Hunter and Sergeant Stride with beetled brows and announced, "*Oderint dum metuant*. Let them hate me, just so long as they fear me."

Hunter felt a tingle run along his spine at that one. The man had the richest, most authoritative voice he'd ever heard, and this was the first time he'd spoken directly at someone with a clear meaning. Though obviously mentally disturbed, apparently the man was aware of at least *some* of his surroundings.

"Whoa, don't look like he cares for you boys in red too much!" Del said. "Better watch him—he might call a Roman legion down on you!" With a barking laugh, Del almost dug his elbow into Faron's ribs again, then thought better of it. Faron was glaring at him a little too intently.

Cabell fixed Del with his glare. "*Senectus ipsa morbus est.* Old age itself is a sickness."

Del's eyes rounded as the meaning sunk in. He turned to Faron and asked, "Did that feller just insult me?"

"Aye, that he did. But it isn't as if you don't deserve it, Dekko."

Del looked back at Cabell with newfound respect.

"Sir," Sergeant Stride said to Hunter, "you know I'd never—"

"Cock-a-doodle-doo!"

Stride cast a distasteful glance at Ebbie Shank, then continued. "You know I'd never shirk a task or disobey an order, but . . . why me?"

Hunter hid a smile. Preston Stride had probably faced death more times than any of them with his British battlefield experience, but right now he was pale at the prospect of this unusual assignment. "There's no one else I can spare, Sergeant. It's you."

With a sigh, Stride saluted and said resignedly, "Yes, sir."

Grunting pig noises came from the wagon, and Hunter turned to find Ebbie Shank sniffing Cabell aggressively. Cabell looked down at the man sniffing his shirt and oinking, then said, "*Et tu, Brute?*"

The silent, squatting man behind them swatted at an imaginary fly and poked himself in the eye, crying out.

Hunter didn't envy Stride's forty-mile trip with these lunatics.

Stride called to Del, "Are you ready, Mr. Dekko?"

Del looked at Cabell warily and found he was staring at him again. "Umm . . . you know, Faron, maybe you oughta take this one. I'm feelin' a little—"

"Nossir!" Faron cried, looking happy for the first time. "Just because that Caesar fella has you spooked, you'll be tryin' to back out? Not with this son of Eire!"

"Son of *what*?"

Cabell actually pointed at Del and roared, "*Tamquam sco-pulum, sic fugias inauditum atque insolens verbum!*"

"Oh no!" Del murmured. "What's he throwin' at me now?"

Cabell translated, "Avoid a strange and unfamiliar word as you would a dangerous reef!"

Del, almost shaking with superstitious dread, said to Faron, "Forget I asked about that word, Faron. I'm gonna avoid it, just like that fella said. In fact," he said, rising to get his horse, his eyes still on Cabell, listening carefully for any more Latin thunderbolts, "I'm gonna do exactly as Mr. Caesar says on this trip."

From the wagon, Cabell said sagely, "*Sesquipedalian.* A foot and a half."

"Baaaa! Baaaa!" bleated Ebbie Shank beside him.

After the "lunatic wagon" had gone, Hunter sat down beside Faron in the chair Del had vacated. Removing his hat, Hunter began fanning himself with it, commenting, "You've got a nice spot to watch the world go by, Mr. O'Donnell. Shade . . . nice padded chair . . . log to prop up your feet. It's hot out there in the sun today."

"Aye, lad, probably the hottest day of the year so far. Gonna snow, though."

Hunter wiped the sweat of his brow, smiling. "What makes you say that?"

Faron shrugged. "I just feel it."

Hunter watched him twirl a stick in his fingers, then his gaze inevitably fell on Faron's arm—or what was left of it—and the empty sleeve pinned up at the top of the bicep. "How are you getting along?"

"High, wide, and handsome," Faron answered, then looked down at the sleeve himself. "Somethin' like that makes a man reconsider his priorities in life. Gives him character."

Hunter nodded, then tried to imagine himself with only one arm, as he'd done many times since he'd met Reena's uncle. It was impossible, of course. Yet he admired how determined Faron was to manage for himself. Hunter wondered if he would have had the same courage as this tough old Irishman.

"You know," Faron told him, "I think about that day a lot. The day the bullet shattered me elbow, not the day they took me arm."

"Yes? What about it?"

"I recall prancin' into that clearing, confident as Napoleon, and seein' ol' Crazy Horse and his braves just comin' awake. I didn't think about it at the time, o' course, since the bullets started flyin' thick and heavy, but I'd be willin' to wager that that was the first time ol' Crazy Horse had ever been that startled." Faron cackled and shook his head. "I only saw him for a split second and haven't seen the lad since, but the look of surprise on his face was as out of place as beauty on the queen."

Grinning, Hunter told him, "I'd say that's a fairly good assumption, Mr. O'Donnell. Crazy Horse is quite a legend, from everything I've heard."

"Hunter, me lad," Faron said, leaning forward to rest his one good elbow on his knee, "I think it's time for me to ask ye—why do ye insist on callin' me 'mister' after all these months?"

Hunter met his steady gaze. "Because you're Reena's uncle, and she loves and respects you." He paused and shrugged his broad shoulders. "And so do I."

Faron stared for so long that Hunter began to think he'd said the wrong thing. Then the corners of Faron's mouth turned up, just slightly, and he said, "You know, if I were to leave this world today, I'd have no worries for me favorite niece. Not with you around. That's comfortin' to this ol' heart, son, very comfortin'."

"Thank you, sir. That means more than you know, coming from you."

Faron leaned back and waved his hand. "It's got nothin' to do with me. You've made yourself what ye are, and I'm glad Reena found ye." He breathed deeply of the warm spring air, then let it out slowly. "When I think back to that snivellin' little man—ah, forgive me, it ain't polite to speak o' the dead so. Every time I think about that Louis feller she was goin' to marry before she came out here . . . you never knew him, eh?"

Hunter paused, remembering, then said quietly, "I knew him for a short while."

Faron eyed him. "And it sounds like we're of the same opinion o' the man. Anyways, I knew way back then he couldn't make Reena happy. O' course, *me* knowin' it ain't the same as *Reena* knowin' it, God bless her. Impossible, silly match-up. The best day o' Reena's life was when he broke off the engagement to her. I wonder if she thinks that way now."

Smiling slightly, Hunter said, "We have better things to talk about than Louis."

"Hah! 'Course you do! Slap me down for bein' a silly old man!"

"You're not silly, sir. Your concern for Reena shines through. It's noble and honorable, and that's why I'm going to tell you something I haven't even told my closest friend, Vic." Hunter hesitated, not sure how to say it.

"What is it, lad?"

Hunter heard galloping horses, and his attention was taken by the sound of challenges at the gate. Standing, he looked to the sentries fifty yards away, then saw them swing open the gate for some dusty riders to enter. The sentries pointed the riders directly to Hunter, the only officer in the fort at the moment.

Faron said eagerly, "What were ye goin' to tell me, Hunter?"

"Excuse me, but I need to see about this. Maybe we can talk later." He turned to the riders, and his first impression of the leader was that he had some sort of allergy to the sun. The only skin showing was around the eyes. His lower face was covered with a dusty blue bandanna, and he wore calfskin gloves. They came to a stop in front of Hunter and Faron.

The leader nodded once, then pulled off the bandanna. He was an albino, Hunter saw. The pink, translucent skin even *looked* fragile in the shaded sunlight beneath his wide-brimmed hat. He had a turned-up nose and a wide, broad mouth. Small red eyes were set deep in pink pouches surrounded by crow's-feet. Looking Hunter up and down, then Faron, he exuded an intangible, dangerous quality that Hunter didn't like.

"My name's Jerome Matsen. We rode up from the States because we've got a little business to see to. I hear we can't go about it until we get your permission." His strange eyes swept down Hunter's form quickly, as if needing Hunter's permission about anything was beneath him.

Hunter nodded. "I'm Sub-Inspector Hunter Stone, and this is my scout Faron O'Donnell. What business would you have in our country, Mr. Matsen?" *It's not going to be good, I know that*, he thought.

"Horse thieves," Matsen returned. "Indians. We aim to get 'em back, with or without your help."

Or permission, he wanted to add, Hunter mused. "And how do you know the thieves are here?"

Matsen gave him a condescending look. "Tracked 'em, of course. How else?"

Beside Hunter, Faron raised a finger and pointed. "Ye'll be watchin' yer manners around here, Matsen. This ain't your country."

Matsen grinned, revealing strange, pointy teeth. "Well, from the sound of it, it ain't none of *yours*, either! How 'bout it, boys?" he asked his seven companions. "You ever see a one-armed Irishman?"

The other men laughed gruffly, their horses skittering at the sudden sound.

Hunter took a step forward, and the laughter died out instantly. Through tight lips he said, "I'll escort you to wherever this leads. Then, I'll be happy to escort you back to the border."

"Hey, I feel safer already having one of you big, strong

Mounties protecting us from the forces of nature and the Indians."

"Wait outside the gate. I'll saddle my horse."

"Need any help?" Matsen asked, still showing his small teeth. "Wouldn't want you to get that pretty red uniform all dirty, would we?" Then he jerked his horse's head around and signaled his men to follow, readjusting his bandanna as he rode out of the fort.

Faron said, "I'll just bet that lad's mother is proud of *him*, don't ye think? Hunter, ye aren't thinkin' o' going with that bunch alone, are ye?"

"Hardly. If you would, go find five or six men to saddle up. I've got a bad feeling about this one."

"Aye, I'll be comin' along, too. Maybe I'll find a good excuse to slap that fella who insulted meself and me heritage."

"From his behavior, Mr. O'Donnell, I'd say there could be a good chance for that." On his way to the livery to saddle his horse, Hunter reflected that he'd prefer to be escorting a man who thought he was Julius Caesar rather than someone like Jerome Matsen. The latter duty seemed far more dangerous.

Hunter tried not to think about his distasteful companions as they rode along. Instead, he concentrated on the sights around him.

They were riding through badlands directly toward a large lake to the north. The grasses around them were still brown from the winter's frost and snow, but in only a few weeks he knew the broken prairie would be transformed into a carpet of green. He thought of the brilliant yellow bloom of the prickly pear, along with the lustrous purple and gold of the shooting star, that would soon intermix to provide a colorful display of spring. Melissa blues, the gorgeous butterflies indigenous to the area, would soon swoop and flutter everywhere.

Hunter took a deep breath, imagining the scent hovering over all the pristine wilderness. Then Faron spoke in a low voice beside him, and the pleasant thoughts drifted away like smoke.

"Ye know where we seem to be headin', don't you, lad?"

"Yes, it looks that way."

"And what will ye be doin' about it?"

Hunter gave him a direct look. "Uphold the law to the best of my ability."

Faron considered this, rubbing his beard. "Aye," he said simply, "that ye will."

Hunter felt the chilling of déjà vu with every mile. If they were going where he thought they were headed, a very bad scene from the past could repeat itself today. He turned to look at Matsen and was surprised that the man's pink eyes were already on him. They revealed a strange mixture of wariness and amusement over the bandanna. *Apparently he's amused about everything. He thinks everyone and everything around him are here for his enjoyment.*

The man riding beside Matsen, a man named Dunston, with narrow shoulders and features, was rooting around in an old cotton bag with many holes in it. Cursing softly, he finally produced a near rotten apple and gazed at it with disgust. "Well, I sure ain't that hungry," he commented and threw the apple away. Then he inspected his age-worn bag with the same look of contempt and carelessly tossed it away, too.

After a moment, Hunter held up a hand and ordered, "Hold up."

Everyone looked at him questioningly; even Matsen appeared curious.

Hunter looked at Dunston and said, "Go pick that up."

"What?"

"You heard me."

"You want me to go pick up that apple? That's some prairie dog's dinner, and he'll be glad to find it."

"Not the apple . . . the bag."

No one moved, and all of the Americans regarded him as if he'd just told them to dismount and perform cartwheels. Matsen's tiny eyes narrowed even more until only the pupils showed.

"You're crazy, mister Mountie," Dunston said.

"You can do it of your own free will, or else you won't be joining your friends for the trip back home. You'll be sitting in our jail."

"We're wasting time here," Matsen grunted, jerking the bandanna from his face. "Maybe we'll just go on without you boys and get them horses back ourselves."

"Then maybe I'll just arrest you and save you the trouble." Hunter sensed his fellow Mounties tensing at the mention of possible trouble. Matsen's men, though seemingly calm, were more alert all of a sudden.

Matsen snorted derisively. "You're gonna arrest us because this dummy dropped a bag? I don't think that'll even hold up in *your* court, much less an American one."

"Maybe not," Hunter said evenly, "but it will sure delay your getting those horses back. Inspector Walsh, the acting magistrate, is away for about a week. You'd be our guest until he got back for your trial."

Matsen cursed, then told Dunston, "Get down and pick up that bag."

Dunston hesitated, not fully believing all the fuss over a little sack.

"Now!" Matsen roared, then turned to Hunter with hostile red eyes.

Dunston dutifully retrieved the bag, and Hunter heard him remark in a sullen tone, "These Mounties think they're gods or something."

Hunter couldn't help but feel satisfaction over the incident. He didn't like these men and believed there was more to the story of the horses in question than had been revealed. Hunter had seen men like Matsen before. They danced back and forth over the line of right and wrong—not to mention the physical line of the border between the two countries—so often that they'd become experts at getting what they wanted with a little help from the law itself.

FOUR / AMERICAN ARRIVALS

After Dunston remounted, still grumbling, Hunter's brief pleasure at putting Matsen in his place vanished when he remembered their mission. The pony tracks they were pursuing pointed directly toward Reena's Blackfoot camp.

61

CHAPTER FIVE

On the Threshold

Is God's love the same love you have for Stone Man?"

Reena smiled down into the dark, round eyes of the eight-year-old Blackfoot girl who had used Hunter's Indian name. The children of the village loved to play matchmaker more than anything. At every opportunity they brought up Hunter, like some sort of measuring stick for everything Reena taught them about love.

Another girl caught on to the hinting. "Yes . . . is God's love as great as Stone Man's love for you?"

Reena gave them a playful look of sternness. "I know what you children are doing, you know. And it's not going to work."

Pure innocence met Reena's accusing gaze. "What do you mean?"

"The answer to your question is that there is no way to compare God's love to our love. It's far greater . . . and more complex and forgiving than ours."

"Com . . . plex?"

Reena searched for another word and came up with "intricate," which they still didn't understand, and finally told them,

ALAN MORRIS / WINGS OF HEALING

"It's just . . . *different*." She attempted to explain it more, then had to give examples from the Bible of God's unfailing forgiveness. She loved these times, when the English teaching had passed and the Bible teaching began. The children were a much more attentive audience than the adults of the tribe. Their questions were endless, but they were practical. When they finally grasped something of God's goodness, Reena loved the dawning comprehension on their little faces.

"But," one of the girls asked when Reena paused in her teaching, "would you not forgive Stone Man for anything if he asked you to?"

"Yes, I suppose so." Reena saw where this was going but let it proceed naturally so that all the children could follow along.

"Then why is God's forgiveness greater than ours?"

"I'll tell you why. If Stone Man began courting another lady, I would be very upset and sad, right?"

Heads nodded eagerly.

She smiled at the children's delight in hearing her talk about her feelings for Stone Man, then continued. "I would be angry with him," Reena continued, "probably even for a little while *after* he asked me to forgive him. That's—"

For one little girl, whose name was Sun Flower, the agony of the unknown was just too great. "Would you throw sticks at him?"

"Throw. . . ?" Reena fought down a smile when she realized that the behavior Sun Flower was talking about was perfectly acceptable in their village. "No, I wouldn't throw sticks at him. Or rocks, or anything else. I would be angry and hurt, though, and I would have to build up my trust in Stone Man again. God isn't like that. When we ask Him to forgive us for a sin, He welcomes us back into His arms with joy and without question. Then guess what?"

"What?" they all asked breathlessly.

"Then God even forgets that we hurt Him. It's like we never even did it! Do you see the difference?"

That slow appearance of comprehension that Reena loved so

much spread over their faces as one, then she saw a few nods. *Oh, Lord, I love these children so much. Thank you for sending me to them. Thank you for letting me be the one who helps them understand you more and more every day.*

Suddenly, Reena noticed that the children had become nervous and were looking around. After having lived with them now for a few years, she too had developed an innate alertness to possible danger. It was a way of life for them, for with the constant threat of attack from a warring tribe or strangers, the Indians were keen to sense when something was about to happen.

Reena too felt and witnessed the possible danger in the air. When surprise visitors appeared—red or white—the Blackfoot women and children rushed to hide in the lodges near the small stream that ran by the village.

Reena shooed the children away at once. "Go! Now!" They scurried away, most of them joining hands with their mothers, who were doing the same thing. Reena looked around to see from which direction the visitors were coming and was pleased to see Hunter leading a group of Mounties and other men toward them around a copse of aspens. Her smile faded, however, when she saw that Hunter wore his "lawman" face, as she'd come to call it. He wasn't here for a pleasure visit. Usually he greeted the braves rushing to meet the intruders with grins and a calm assurance in his bearing. Today, Reena could see from a distance of fifty yards that his broad shoulders were braced unnaturally and he was not smiling. Reena half ran to meet him.

Hunter found her in the crowd, and instead of looking relieved or pleased, he seemed to become even more tense. *What's happened?* Reena wondered.

Holding up a hand to stem the flow of questions coming his way from the braves, Hunter told them, "I need to see Plenty Trees . . . go get your chief."

A few caught on to what he was saying and rushed off.

Reena fell in step beside Buck, Hunter's horse. While patting his sweaty neck, she looked up at Hunter. "Hi," she said more merrily than she felt.

"Hello, Reena."

"Lawman attitude today, huh?"

"I'm afraid so," he said stiffly.

"Is it bad?"

Hunter hesitated, and his eyes cut over to the civilian men with him. "Bad enough."

"Hello, darlin'! Don't ye even have a word for yer old one-armed uncle?"

Reena turned. "Uncle Faron! I didn't even see you!"

"Aye, I've grown used to that whenever Hunter's around."

For the first time Reena looked at the men with the Mounties, and she sensed Hunter's problem immediately. They were obviously rough men—Del called such men "prairie trash"—and her first impression was that surely these men were Hunter's prisoners. But their hands weren't tied, and they were armed. One of them wore a bandanna over the lower half of his face. Reena had the sudden crazy thought that the men were here to rob them, but Hunter wouldn't be a part of that. The man with the bandanna was an albino, and though Reena had seen people like that before, an edge of danger glinted in this man's eyes.

"Hunter, what's happening?"

"Let me explain when Plenty Trees gets here."

Reena noticed they were moving away from the village toward the horses corralled in a circular band of lodgepole pine. Her curiosity rose even more. She looked questioningly at her uncle, but he would abide by Hunter's judgment. He attempted to give her a smile of reassurance, but it didn't curb Reena's growing distress.

"That's them," one of the civilians growled behind Reena. "I recognize the brand from here."

"Stinkin' horse thieves," another muttered.

"Shut your mouth!" Hunter ordered at once. "Not another word out of any of you."

Reena gave the cowed rider a brittle glare, but the man didn't notice. The albino did, though, and Reena could tell that he actually smiled beneath the kerchief. Then the words of the man Hunter had put in his place hit her. "Horse thieves?" she murmured, then looked up at Hunter. "Horse thieves? Is he talking about. . . ?"

Plenty Trees arrived and carefully headed off the riders from his precious stock of horses. Reena knew he trusted Hunter and the Mounties unquestionably, but she could tell he didn't like the look of the riders behind them.

Hunter halted the column with a raised hand. "Good day to you, Plenty Trees. I hope you and your people are well."

"Thank you, Stone Man." They exchanged the ritual pleasantries with meaning—two men who respected each other.

"Chief Plenty Trees," Hunter continued, a shadow passing over his handsome face, "I ask permission to examine those ponies behind you. If you allow me to do that, I will explain to you why."

Plenty Trees looked puzzled, but a few braves behind him shifted nervously and began whispering among themselves. The chief said graciously, "Of course, Stone Man. You are welcome here."

Without a word, Hunter moved Buck over to the corral and dismounted. Reena watched as he ducked beneath the rope, speaking in a low, calming tone to the suddenly nervous horses. White men smelled different than Indians, and Reena had seen the reaction before. Hunter moved among them easily, however.

Shifting her attention to the braves, Reena saw their eyes had moved from Hunter to the Americans. Their faces were outraged, some filled with actual hatred. The albino and the rest of the men were staring back with open hostility, but also with the hint of victory. Reena didn't like the ugly atmosphere that had suddenly invaded the beautiful day.

Among the ponies, Hunter slid his gloved hand lightly over the brand on the flank of a pinto. The brand was "LS." Not all of the horses in the corral possessed it, but it didn't matter because Indians didn't brand horses. Hunter hung his head for a moment while shielded from the group beyond. He *hated* what he had to do now.

With a deep sigh he went to Buck and mounted, then moved toward Plenty Trees and the other onlookers who were all watching him intently. His men saw the tense look on his face and glanced nervously at the Indians. Matsen, true to form, also watched Hunter's face and his grin began to spread.

Hunter nodded to Plenty Trees, then turned to the Americans. "Matsen, what's your brand?"

"LS" came the instant answer. "Stands for my boss, Landon Striker, in Montana Territory," Matsen said and began to gloat.

Hunter despised the man more than ever. Regretfully, he told the chief, "Plenty Trees, you are in possession of stolen horses. I call on your honesty and ask if you were aware of this fact."

Plenty Trees looked behind him at the braves, and when he faced Hunter again, he seemed more confused than ever. "I did not know this, Stone Man. How can that be?"

"Ask some of the men behind you, Chief. While you do that, I'm going to be forced to take the horses."

"*All* of them?" the chief asked in absolute astonishment and despair.

Inwardly, Hunter cringed. "Of course not, Plenty Trees. I meant only the horses carrying that man's brand." Horses were the very life of a tribe of Indians. If they had no horses for hunting and fighting, they could not survive. Plenty Trees' reaction had been genuine and understandable. Hunter gave a nod to Sergeant Cook to gather the ponies in question.

Suddenly, one of the braves yelled something in Blackfoot and gestured at the Americans angrily. Matsen kept the bemused smile on his face and didn't say anything. Reena moved to stand beside Plenty Trees. When the brave was finished with his speech, there were a few nods of feathered heads, and Reena said, "Hunter, he says these men stole the ponies from them in the first place. They were taking back what was theirs to begin with."

I knew it, Hunter thought in agitation. *The bad part about this was that the brave was probably telling the truth.*

"That Indian's lying!" Matsen called.

"Shut up!" Hunter roared. The last thing he needed here was violence, and if the Americans didn't keep quiet he would have it. Matsen looked sulky, but he didn't say anything more. Turning back to the Indians, Hunter said in a calmer tone, "I understand what the brave is saying. Please tell him I don't doubt his word, but my job is to confiscate stolen property and have it returned to its proper owner. Those horses—"

The brave spoke angrily again, this time directly to Hunter and in English. "*We* are the proper owners!"

Hunter continued in his calm tone, hating himself for sounding so sensible for what he had to do. "Plenty Trees, we *must* give those horses back. Do you understand?"

"Hunter . . ." Reena began, then couldn't think of a thing to say. He was right, of course, and there was nothing anyone could do about it. She glanced over at the angry brave, momentarily resenting him for bringing this calamity down on all of them. Stealing horses was a way of life for Indians—indeed, had been for a thousand years—and they saw nothing wrong with it. In their eyes, if a brave was stealthy and smart enough to penetrate defenses and make off with a few ponies, he was to be admired, not punished. They simply could not understand that to the white man the offense was punishable by death.

The Mounties had the horses in question tied on a string and brought them over. Plenty Trees watched them ominously, yet he knew that he must comply with the Mounties and their law. Reluctantly he said to Hunter, "You may take the ponies." Fire glowed in his eyes as he swung around to the Americans. "But I want those people off my land."

"You'll have it," Hunter assured him.

Reena moved over to Hunter and looked up at him. Quietly she said, "I know you have to do this. I understand, and I'll do my best to make them understand. But this isn't good for relations. They trust you, and I think some of that trust will be gone after today."

"I know," he nodded, "but, Reena—what can I do? I wish it weren't me who had to do this, but there was no one else—"

"It's all right. It wouldn't matter if it was you or any other man in a scarlet uniform. I just think you need to find a way to make it right with them."

Hunter's eyes softened. "I will. I promise."

Matsen suddenly announced to Plenty Trees in a loud voice, "Chief, you keep your braves out of my country. If I find them down there trying to steal—"

"Matsen!" Hunter interrupted. He'd had more than he could stand of the man. "Close your mouth, get your string, and get out of my sight."

Matsen looked as if he were considering a snide remark, but when he saw Hunter's eyes, he changed his mind. With a nod to his men, they took the horses and rode away.

"Despicable man," Hunter murmured. Turning to Plenty Trees he said, "Chief, I'm very sorry for this incident. However, the law is very clear about situations like this. I'm supposed to arrest the men who stole those ponies, even though they were originally yours, but as a sign of good faith I won't do that today. Enough has happened." His stare moved to the ones who probably did the stealing. "But you need to let your braves know that horse thievery is a very serious offense. The next time, the law may not be so understanding. Is that clear, Chief Plenty Trees?"

"Yes, it is clear, Stone Man. I thank you for letting my braves be free, and I will speak with them. But your law is not fair to the Blackfoot. We have our own law, and it is fair to us."

Hunter nodded, his face stony. "We must work together, Chief. You and I."

"Yes, I agree."

Hunter looked down at Reena and reached out for her hand. "We're very busy at the fort right now. I don't know when I'll get to see you again."

"That's all right. We're about to do our spring planting anyway, so I'll be pretty busy myself."

He passed the back of his hand lightly over her cheek. "Are you feeling okay? Everything all right . . . anything you need?"

"No, but thanks for asking." Reena pressed his hand in hers and kissed it. "Be careful."

"Always."

———

It was every bit as bad as Dirk Becker expected. After receiving permission from Superintendent Irvine, he'd taken three men with him and gone from house to house checking on the sick children that Dirk knew about.

Almost everyone was sick, even the parents in most cases. Stuffy heads, fevers, deep coughs, chills—all the signs of a flu epidemic.

Growing up in Mississippi, Dirk had never witnessed the horrors of an epidemic, but many people in one county in the state had mysteriously contracted the same thing he was seeing now, and forty-five people had died from it. By the time the governor had declared the county under quarantine, the citizens had already isolated themselves.

Forty-five people, Dirk thought with a shake of his head, *and of course there were children among them.*

"Something wrong, sir?" asked Constable "Duke" Dillard. He was relatively new to the force, arriving the year before. Duke was a nice, intelligent young man who was liked by everyone. He and Dirk had hit it off instantly, since Duke was from a state neighboring his own, Arkansas. Together they endured endless teasing about their soft southern accents and similar names— Dirk-'n-Duke-from-Dixie, they were inevitably tagged.

"I don't like this, Duke."

"Me neither" was the gloomy reply. It was a rare occasion when Duke was sullen, and that only darkened Dirk's mood further.

"After this next house—I think we know what we'll find— we go straight back to the fort to report this. Someone has to get a doctor out here."

"More than one, maybe. We've already seen, what, six families sick? If *everyone* has it, that would be a mighty big challenge for one doctor."

The late afternoon sun was behind them, warm on their backs. They wouldn't get back to Fort Macleod until after dark, but Dirk felt the need to drop in on the Packard family. They had six children, from an infant up to the age of sixteen. Dirk liked and respected Seymour Packard and his wife, Elmira. Seymour had been one of the first settlers to establish himself on the vast prairie and felt the need to father every other settler who had arrived after him. If anyone lost a barn due to lightning or tornado or fire, if a family's crops happened to be destroyed by prairie fire, Seymour Packard was the first person to offer a helping hand. Dirk sincerely hoped he and his family were immune to the flu that was spreading like a prairie fire out of control.

When they topped the shrub-ridden rise to Packard's farmhouse, Dirk's heart sank.

"Oh no," Duke breathed beside him.

To the north of the log and stone house, beneath a copse of lodgepole pine, Seymour Packard was working with a shovel. As they watched, he paused, pulled a red handkerchief out of the back pocket of his pants, and blew his nose. Then he went back to work digging.

Dirk spurred his horse, hating the knowledge that was waiting for him beneath the trees. Who was it? One of the children? Elmira? The loss of any of them would be a severe heartbreak to the kind man. Dirk didn't see anyone else around and wondered if the rest of the family was too sick to come outside. Thinking about how quickly this flu had spread, Dirk abruptly realized for the first time that no one was immune from this sickness—not even him. Or Jenny, who was in the schoolhouse all day surrounded by sneezing and coughing children.

Packard looked up at their approach, and Dirk could see red-rimmed eyes even from a distance. The farmer was a tall man with a broad, kindly face, but right now the only emotion showing was grief. Dirk tried not to look at the body wrapped in blankets a few feet behind Packard.

"Mr. Packard," Dirk greeted, then he had absolutely no idea what to say in a situation like this. He found himself unable to meet Packard's eyes, so he looked down at the grave. It was about four feet deep, and the dirt was a deep rust-red. Then he looked over at the shrouded body that would be the occupant. From the size of it, Dirk knew it wasn't a child.

"It's my Ellie," the farmer informed them, his voice faltering on the name. "We been married twenty years on the coming Tuesday." He looked at his wife's body, then pulled his gaze back to Dirk. He seemed confused. "She was doing her quilting the other day, then said she didn't feel good and went to bed. She never got out of it."

"I'm sorry, Mr. Packard," Dirk said gently. "We all are." He nodded to Duke and the other two men, and they dismounted. "Do you have any more shovels? We can do this for you."

"Two of my kids are sick, Sergeant!" Packard cried, his pain and fear showing through plainly. "What are we going to do? What am I going to do without my Ellie?" His legs began to tremble, and he collapsed by the grave sobbing.

Dirk squatted down beside him and placed a hand on his shoulder. "We'll help you, Mr. Packard. Everyone has to pull together at a time like this."

Dirk and Duke comforted Packard the best they could while the other two finished digging the grave.

What are we all going to do? Dirk asked himself. Then it came to him what they *weren't* going to do: go back to the fort. They'd been exposed to whatever this was all day, and he wouldn't risk spreading it to the only law enforcement establishment within hundreds of miles. The only comforting thought was that he would still be able to see Jenny without fear of exposing her, since she already was in danger.

Oh, Lord . . . help us all.

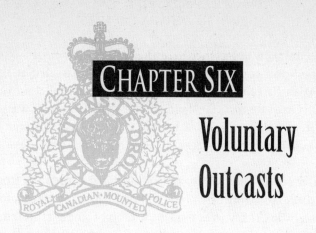

CHAPTER SIX

Voluntary Outcasts

Vic could have divided half of his journey traveling on a steamer barge, but with all the stops the barges made along the way, he figured he would make better use of time by riding. Besides, ever since he was a boy growing up in England he'd loved riding. The feel of a powerful animal beneath him was much preferable than a shaky, rattling barge.

On his second day out, he came across an Indian hunting party. Through sign language they managed a trade: a few of Vic's potatoes for a small satchel of wild strawberries they'd found. Vic was craving fruit but didn't feel he had the time to search for it. Also, Vic traded some flour to one of the braves for his warm-looking fur moccasins. The night before, Vic's feet had been so cold he'd had to don his boots, which caused a restless night of sleep. He sensed colder weather in the air and wanted to be sure to avoid the same thing happening again. The Indians were tracking a small herd of buffalo and invited Vic to come along—a high honor—but he had to refuse. Every day spent away from Megan only increased his loneliness for her.

As Vic traveled over the broad prairie, he stayed to the west of the Saskatchewan River, where the water was a little better and more wood could be found for fires. He marveled at the broad, expansive plains and thought how different it all was from his native Great Britain. The land he had ridden through was so endless it sometimes took his breath away, the sky so huge it seemed he could feel the weight of it on his shoulders, pressing him down.

Sometimes he sang to himself and his horses, anything from careless ditties to favorite hymns. The horses didn't seem to mind if he was a little off key. When he grew tired of singing, his mind would inevitably return to his mission, and he would talk to himself about what it was going to be like having a son.

"How in the world am I expected to be a *father*? I can no more raise a son than fly to the moon!" The magnitude of the responsibility that soon would be his was enough to make him shudder at times. Just when the doubt would become so overwhelming as to make him turn back to the safety of the fort and familiar surroundings, he would hear the voice in his head.

All things are possible with Me.

"That's right, Father. I forget that sometimes, as I'm sure all of your children do. Silly of us, isn't it? I *know* I can be a father, with my Father's guidance. Who's a better teacher than God?" Praying always made him feel better, so he would cast his worries on the shoulders of the One who could carry them.

On the third day he reached the trading post at the fork of the Red Deer and Saskatchewan Rivers. Knowing he was roughly halfway to Battleford, he also knew that the most dangerous part of the journey lay in front of him, with fewer rivers and lakes and mostly small scrub with which to make fires. Armed with that knowledge, he was tempted to buy more supplies than he could carry. However, what he worried about most was water, so he purchased two extra skins to carry an ample supply.

He would have enjoyed staying in the small boardinghouse near the trading post. Just one night in a feather bed with clean sheets, a hot bath, and a meal prepared by someone other than himself would refresh his tired body. But it was only noon, and he could make twenty or thirty more miles before dark, so he decided to just take the bath. He *did* allow himself the luxury of lingering in the hot suds until the water became cold.

Starting out again, with the sun revealing itself only rarely through quickly gathering clouds, Vic looked up at the sky and said simply, "Keep me in your care, Lord."

Then he and the two horses waded out into the brown grass and the endless, broken prairie.

Blue Bear had never been so angry in his life. To watch the Mounties *steal* the ponies from his people after he'd rightfully gained them back was almost more than he could stand. The temptation to strike out at the Mounties was overwhelming, and it was only because of Plenty Trees' presence that he did not fight them.

While watching a rabbit cook on his fire, the brave seethed with hatred for the Mounties for taking what was rightfully theirs. He'd left the village immediately after the Mounties rode off, ignoring the cries from his friends and chief to come back. He'd briefly entertained the idea of going after the red-eyed American named Matsen, stealing the ponies back, and killing Matsen so he would never steal Blackfoot horses again. Indeed, he'd even begun to navigate in a wide circle toward the border to do just that when he remembered Stone Man's stern warning about hanging from a rope. What an inglorious way to die! Blue Bear feared a humiliating demise more than anything in the world. Things were much simpler before the white man came. Stealing was an art, something to be admired and praised.

Blue Bear and his friends had traveled all the way down to Montana to retrieve what belonged to them in the first place. Now the ponies were gone again, and the tribe would lack steeds for the buffalo hunt that was almost upon them.

"Plenty Trees knows that," he muttered to himself, savagely tearing a leg from the rabbit. It was hot and burned his fingers.

He tossed it in the air a few times to cool, which only made him more angry.

Suddenly, a new look came over Blue Bear's face—one of craftiness and cunning. As he bit into the rabbit leg heartily, he realized what he must do.

————

Dirk Becker and his men were silent all the way from Becky Dodd's farm to the fort. They'd covered almost a twenty-mile radius around Fort Macleod checking on settlers and families. Nearly every home had at least one person who was suffering from the flu or the early symptoms of it. The implications were greater than any of the Mounties wanted to consider, so they didn't speak of it. With all that had to be done to help those who were sick, there seemed to be no time for inane conversation, certainly not for the teasing and joking that was common among patrols. Therefore, silence reigned.

Dirk's mind was occupied with his own responsibility, both for duty and the men under his care. He let his gaze pass over those under his command. Young Billy Strom was almost asleep in the saddle. Duke's eyes were bloodshot and tired. Hank Smith-Penny, a rail-thin man of thirty, stared straight ahead with glassy eyes. Dirk was startled to realize that the man was asleep with his eyes open.

When they reached the town of Fort Macleod in the purple twilight, Dirk sensed a stillness he hadn't known since he'd come to the Territories. The town seemed to be holding its breath, waiting to see where the flu would take itself next and who would awaken with a sore throat or sniffle.

Duke grunted beside him. "I guess we missed the party; everyone's already gone home." His voice was raw and cracked and rang hollowly through the empty street.

Dirk didn't reply. *Where is Jenny? Is she all right?*

To his right, on the other side of Duke and Smith-Penny, Billy Strom coughed from deep inside his chest. The other three looked at him and saw alarm in his smoky-blue eyes.

"Just trail dust—it's not anything but trail dust, so stop looking at me like that."

"It's okay, Billy," Dirk assured him.

"No, it's not. I see that look in your eyes."

"What look?"

"The same one you've had for three days now whenever you look at all those sick people. It's pity, and I'll not have it."

"Billy, there's a difference between pity and concern—"

"I'll not have it from none of you," Billy finished moodily, then coughed again without meeting their eyes. He looked at Smith-Penny. "How about one of those smokes, Hank?"

Smith-Penny glanced at him in surprise but didn't answer.

"Well? How about it?"

"But you don't smoke, Billy."

"I reckon I have a time or two. Settles the nerves."

Smith-Penny shrugged and reached into his tunic for rolling papers and tobacco pouch. "Suit yourself."

Dirk knew the boy was only doing it to cover up any future coughs. And, then again, maybe it *was* trail dust. Dirk hoped so, but the fear of him and his men coming down with the flu haunted his thoughts constantly.

They passed Jenny's boardinghouse, and he eyed her window closely. The lamp was lit, and he imagined her in there, reading as usual. A nagging thought tugged at a corner of his brain that said *Maybe she's lying on the bed, unable to get up from weakness from the flu.* Dirk shoved the thought away and said a quick prayer.

As if reading his mind, Duke murmured, "She's all right, Sarge."

Dirk acknowledged the comment with a grateful nod and smile. The smile didn't last more than an instant before he remembered the spreading epidemic the community was trying to deal with.

Stopping their small party a good distance from the fort's gate, Dirk hailed the guard and asked to see Superintendent Irvine. What Dirk was about to do was distasteful but fully

79

necessary. He glanced over at the men with him and saw they didn't relish the idea, either. Billy looked more pale than he had a few minutes before.

The gate opened and out stepped the superintendent. "What's the meaning of this, Sergeant? You're interrupting my dinner."

As usual, Dirk couldn't tell if the man was being serious or not. Superintendent Acheson Gosford Irvine was an old-school militia man, not given to levity where duty was concerned. But since his promotion to commander of Fort Macleod, the men had seen a break in the stiff demeanor a few times. Hunter said that he actually saw Irvine smile once. Dirk didn't know how he could have *seen* it, since the entire lower half of the superintendent's face was covered with a bushy brown beard. His mustache grew over his mouth, so that it was sometimes unsettling to hear the man talk and not see lips move. Maybe that's what he intended.

"I'm sorry to bother you, sir," Dirk said, "but I didn't think you'd want me and my men inside the fort after you've heard what I have—"

"I'll be the judge of that, Sergeant," Irvine said curtly.

Dirk had his answer about what sort of mood he was in. It was almost fully dark and impossible to see Irvine's eyes as anything but cold, lifeless buttons.

"Now climb down off those mounts and come in for supper." The superintendent half turned back toward the parade ground inside the gates.

"No, sir, we can't."

"You—? Excuse me, Sergeant, did you say—?"

Dirk was tired, dirty, and felt as though he could have easily been drawn into an argument or fight with someone like this; however, Irvine was not the man to challenge. So he took a deep breath and said with more calm than he felt, "Sir, if you'll let me explain. It's the influenza, and it's much worse than we thought. We've traveled all around the community and found that it has affected almost every family. It's bad, sir."

"So, Sergeant, does that mean you can't dismount and have a hot meal? I'm sure you and your men are tired."

Irvine's tone held a surprising note of compassion in direct contrast to his frozen remarks only a moment before. For some reason the empathy touched Dirk, and he found himself sorely tempted to accept the offer. He was so tired, and the thought of a nice feather mattress and . . .

Irvine took a few steps toward them, breaking Dirk out of his reverie. He held up a hand in warning. "I wouldn't come any closer, sir."

"Whyever not?" But he did stop at once.

Dirk glanced at Duke, who gave an almost imperceptible nod. Looking back to Irvine, he said, "I know it's not a popular idea, Superintendent, but Constable Duke Dillard and I have been considering the . . . um . . . implications of what we've seen, and we think it would be best if we stayed away from the other men. This flu is—"

Irvine snorted. "Oh, come now, Sergeant Becker! Aren't you an educated man?"

"Yes, sir. Graduated third in my class from the University of Mississippi."

"Then you can't possibly subscribe to that wives' tale about these sicknesses being spread just by being *around* someone who's been *around* another who has it?"

Again Dirk glanced at Duke and this time received a small shrug as if to say, "We tried, you're on your own now." Dirk was the superior officer here, and it was up to him to convince the superintendent. He closed his eyes for a few seconds, wishing he'd already won the argument, had already eaten, and was lying in his blanket almost asleep right now.

Billy Strom saved him. He coughed deeper and longer than before, then looked at Irvine and said, "Sorry, sir."

Irvine actually took a step back, his black eyes glittering with suspicion. The movement made Dirk smile. If the unpopular contagion theory was so ridiculous, why was Irvine reacting that way? It was time to drive the nail home. "Superintendent, both

Duke and I have seen this kind of thing before, back home after the war. Everyone was poor, and there was even some malnutrition that led to many people getting sick. These things spread, sir. We may not know exactly how, but if we can cancel out one of those possible ways, we're willing to do it."

With one more wary glance at Billy, Irvine asked, "What are you suggesting?"

"That the four of us stay outside the gates and away from the other men. We could be of help out here with the townsfolk and possibly stop any other Mounties from getting this flu." Dirk decided to press further. "I know it may sound a bit extreme, sir, but these are unusual circumstances. We can't let the only law enforcement in the Territory come down with sickness. That wouldn't be very prudent, would it, sir?"

Irvine cleared his throat and shook his head quickly. The urge to be away from Dirk and the others was palpable. "Good thinking, Sergeant. I'll arrange for some tents and a hot meal to be placed outside the gates. Just leave the horses . . . um, do the horses carry. . . ?"

"No, sir," Dirk answered, stifling the urge to laugh out loud. "They don't get influenza."

"No, of course not. Just leave the horses here, and we'll get them tended to."

"Yes, sir."

After Irvine had gone back inside, Duke asked, "What do you think about that fella?"

Dirk shrugged, then got of his horse and stretched tired, stiff muscles. "I don't know. Haven't been around him enough."

The other three dismounted, Billy and Hank with groans. Duke looked as though he could climb back up on a fresh horse and do the whole three days all over again.

"I know one thing," Hank commented, "and that's that Irvine's not a Macleod. Macleod would have thought up something to do right now except eat dinner." His eyes ran over Duke critically while the younger man immediately began performing deep knee bends to loosen up. "Don't you ever get tired, kid?"

Duke paused in his exertions and thought a moment. "Not really."

"And what about you and that horse?" Hank said, shaking his head in amazement.

"Sam? What about him?" Duke moved closer to the big bay as if someone even mentioning him was threatening.

"You know what I mean. You won't let anyone even touch him, just like the sergeant and his horse, Egypt. What is it about you southern boys and your horses?"

Duke glanced at Dirk, who gave him a secret grin in the dark, and then told Hank, "We were born in the saddle, my friend. When we're out of it or away from our horses, it just doesn't feel . . . natural." He shrugged. "And we just like taking care of our own."

Billy made a scoffing noise deep in his throat. "You sound like you're talking about family, for crying out loud."

"I am." Duke grinned as he stroked Sam's neck. "I am."

———————

When Dirk finally laid his head down that night after a meal of roasted pork, beans, and biscuits topped off with cherry cobbler, he groaned with pleasure. "I'm sufferin' with comfort," he drawled to the top of the tent. He began saying his nightly prayer, but didn't manage to finish before sleep overtook him.

"Dirk?"

Sleeping soundly, Dirk didn't hear the call, even though it was right outside the tent.

"Hey, Dirk!"

This time, the harsh whisper brought him out of his well-deserved slumber to the light of a lamp burning low. "What?" he said caustically, shielding his grainy eyes. "Can't you see I'm trying to sleep here?"

"Yeah, I see you need it, too."

"Hunter?" Dirk came up to a full sitting position, then he

remembered why he *was* sleeping in a tent and scooted to the far wall. "Get out of here, Hunter! Don't you know why we're out here?"

Grinning, Hunter came inside and nonchalantly plopped down across from him. "Who are you kidding, Dirk? If we're meant to catch that flu, we'll catch it."

"Hunter—"

"Besides, do you really think I'm going to hide in that fort with all the trouble around us? Not hardly. And neither would you."

Dirk thought a moment. "But *someone's* got to stay healthy."

"There's plenty of able-bodied men in that fort to chase the whiskey traders and law dodgers. We've got other problems."

"Like what?"

"Well, you tell me. You're the one who's been wandering all around the countryside for three days."

Dirk recounted the sickness they'd seen, the burial of Seymour Packard's wife, and the general hysteria that seemed to be mounting among the settlers. "And what about getting a doctor?"

"I have no idea."

"If we do find one, he'll have his hands full. Have you seen Jenny, Hunter?"

"She's working hard taking care of sick people. They just gave up on school when the attendance dwindled down to a few."

"What have you been doing?"

Giving him a wry look, Hunter said, "You don't want to know."

"Try me."

Hunter told him about the incident with the albino Matsen, and he was unable to keep the bitterness out of his voice. "Matsen probably stole those horses in the first place, and I had to turn around and take them from Plenty Trees. How's that for justice?"

Dirk grunted. "Kind of different where I come from. If

someone steals your horses, you go get them, then string the thief from the nearest tree."

"That's justice in Mississippi?"

"Absolutely."

Hunter stared at him for a moment, the said grimly, "If that's true, then I think Matsen had better keep his toes out of Mississippi."

CHAPTER SEVEN

Jaye

Just before dawn, Megan stirred uneasily in her sleep. Kicking off the covers, her face gleaming with a light sheen of perspiration in the murky gray light, she moaned softly and turned on her side. Her bedclothes were tangled around her legs, and she kicked at them, too.

Heart pounding, her eyes popped open. The dream was back. It was not exactly the *same* dream, but all the similar elements were there. It was just a different calamity. Megan buried her face into the feather pillow and tried desperately to forget it, banishing it from her mind like an unwanted thought. But it wouldn't leave her.

In the dream, Vic and the little boy had been traveling in an arroyo. Some danger had forced them to follow the dry riverbed, whether it was hostile Indians on the vast prairie or a mountain lion, it didn't matter—they were in it, and that's where the trouble came from.

In the two similar dreams they'd been on the prairie when something bad happened to them. Once a fierce tornado had formed out of the clear blue sky and whisked them away. In the other one a prairie fire had roasted them alive. The terrain didn't matter, not now.

As father and son crossed the arroyo in a jerky dreamlike motion, Vic with Jaye's reins in hand, Megan heard herself screaming "Get out! Get out of there!" But it was to no avail. Just before the storm hit, she thought the faceless boy cocked his head to the side just an inch or two, as if he'd heard her. Then the rain began.

It didn't begin slowly. The heavens burst and a deluge filled the riverbed with terrifying speed. The horses began flailing about frantically, white-eyed, and the boy lost his grip on the saddle horn. Vic reached out to grab him but missed. Jaye tumbled into the churning water and disappeared. Without hesitation, Vic dove in after him and vanished from sight also. In horror Megan watched them bob up once, gasping for air, then go down again. That's when she awoke.

"Oh, Lord, please take these dreams from me," she whispered, close to tears. She shivered, cold now, and drew the covers over herself all the way above her head. "Please . . ."

———

For the last twenty miles to Battleford, Vic fell in with a trapper named Minor. Middle-aged and raw-boned, Minor had been out trapping for a while, from the smell of him. But Vic didn't mind; it had been a long five days with only the prairie animals and birds to keep him company.

The morning had turned cloudy, and Vic thought he could smell rain in the air. He hoped it would hold off until they reached town, and he said as much to Minor.

"Nah, it ain't gonna rain," Minor said evenly, glancing at the sky. "It's over to the east there."

"But we're headed east."

"*Way* over to the east." Minor removed his beaver-pelt hat and hung it over his saddle horn. Then, with a surreptitious glance around the empty prairie, he produced a small brown jug from one of his saddlebags. With a wink he took a pull from it, then offered it to Vic. "Care for a snort?"

"I don't drink," Vic returned, doing his best to hide a grin. Casually he added, "You know, that's illegal in the Territories."

"No, it ain't. Sellin' it to the Indians is, but this is my own private stock, y'see."

"I don't mean your private stock. I mean offering a drink to an officer of the law."

Minor almost choked on his next pull from the jug. "Law! What do you mean, law?" His dark eyes raked over Vic's chest, looking for a badge, then narrowed. "Hey, wait a minute! You're one of them Mounties that don't wear a pretty jacket and try to catch us innocent folk doin' something when we—"

Vic had to chuckle. "Relax, Mr. Minor, I'm off duty. On vacation, I suppose you'd say."

Minor relaxed visibly, then smiled. "Vacation, huh? And the best place you could think of to go to is Battleford? Where you from, anyway? That's quite a fancy accent you got there."

"Originally from England, currently from Fort Macleod."

Minor took this in with a furrowing of the forehead. "Macleod? Why, that's way down south, almost in Montana Territory."

"That's right."

"So what brings you way up to these parts?"

With pride Vic answered, "I'm going to Battleford to find my son."

More brow furrowing. "Well . . . how'd you come to lose the little feller?"

Vic laughed and found that it felt exceptionally good. His spirits were high, and his son was within a day's ride. "It's a long story, Mr. Minor. What brings you to Battleford?" He eyed the saddlebag that had quickly swallowed the brown jug after its owner discovered he was riding with a Mountie—albeit an off-duty Mountie. "Going to replenish your 'private stock'?"

"Naw, I'm going for this!" He produced a well-worn flyer from an inside pocket of his jacket and handed it over.

Vic read: " 'The Mounted Police Star Minstrel and Variety

Troupe / Performance at 8:00 in the evening / April 14, 1877.' "

"Biggest thing around these parts in a while," Minor stated. "Me, I was in the U.S. States' War, and we'd get together and clown like these boys when we weren't chasin' Bobby Lee." His bearded face split into a mischievous grin. "Hey, you know what my name woulda been if I'd made major?"

Vic was surprised Minor waited for an answer, but he did. "Major Minor."

The trapper laughed heartily. "Hey, Mr. Mountie, you're pretty smart. Most fellers I ask that don't have a clue."

"Just a lucky guess," Vic said with a smile, then reflected on the stunning lack of intelligence among Minor's friends. *If he is the smart one, then that's a bit frightening.*

"Hey . . . what was your name again?"

"Vic."

"That's a mighty short name to carry around. Anyways, why don't you tell me that story about your boy? We got plenty of time, and I just *love* to hear a good story. How 'bout it?"

"Of course, if you'd like to hear it."

"Would I? Fire away, pardner!"

Vic took a quick sip from his canteen and began. "Her name was Fran—I called her Frannie in the short time I knew her, and—"

"Wait, whose name was Fran?"

"My son's mother."

"And what do you mean her name 'was'?" Minor asked suspiciously. "I don't take to no sad stories, mind you. I only like those with happy endings, Vic."

Inclining his head, Vic said, "Then we're very much alike, Mr. Minor. I, too, detest unhappy endings. But surely you'd be so kind as to agree with me that all good stories have both happy *and* sad elements to them?"

Minor held up his thumb and forefinger barely half an inch apart. "Just a *few* sad . . . um . . . whatever that was you said. Okay, Vic?"

"Agreed. So, Frannie and I met on a snowy, cold night . . ."

The town of Battleford surprised Vic a great deal. He'd heard that of all the settlements that had sprung up around Mountie posts, Battleford had grown the most. This was a bustling place sprawled at the foot of the Eagle Hills with not only one hotel, but two, according to Minor. Even more new construction was taking place as Vic and Minor rode into town from the south, and Vic was fairly certain more buildings were being raised at the north end, too.

They passed children playing hopscotch on the boarded sidewalk while their mothers or parents flittered in and out of various shops along the main street. The general store was swarming with people, and Vic said, "What's going on?"

"What do you mean, what's going on?" Minor asked, puzzled. "They're gettin' supplies. What's wrong with that?"

"But there are so *many* of them!" Vic returned.

Minor eyed him with mirth. "Not too many folks down Fort Macleod way, huh?"

The last big city Vic had visited had been Winnipeg on his way west, but the amount of sheer activity in Battleford seemed to rival even that great metropolis. The population wasn't without the sordid few, however. Two men leaning against the side of a hardware store followed Vic's progress down the street for a few moments with steely eyes, then dismissed him as a non-competitor. The sound of rowdy laughter and what was either a small caliber weapon discharging or a firecracker came from one of the hotel saloons.

"This is where I get off," Minor said with a wink.

"How's the other hotel?" Vic asked carefully. The last thing he needed was a noisy saloon beneath his room when he needed sleep badly.

"Oh, it's not as fun as this one," Minor said.

"Then I suppose that's where *I'll* get off."

Minor nodded. "Just up the street, then. The Palace Hotel. Livery's just beyond it for those tired ol' nags of yours." He paused and gave Vic a gauging look, then held out his hand. "It was nice travelin' with you, Vic. I hope you find your boy."

"Thanks, Minor. May God be with you."

The trapper seemed surprised, then greatly pleased. "Why, thank you, Vic. Thank you very much." With that, Minor dismounted, tied up his horse, and made a sheepish beeline for the saloon.

Vic nudged his horse forward, shaking his head, then grinned when he thought about a hot bath, an even hotter supper, and a warm feather bed.

———

When Vic stepped out of the hotel the next morning, he was surprised to find that it had rained during the night. The hard-packed streets were muddy, and the morning sun reflected brightly from puddles of water here and there. Vic had slept so soundly that he hadn't even heard the rain.

Taking a deep breath of humid air, he tipped his hat to a lady walking by and made his way toward the Mountie station. He was dressed in his uniform—scarlet jacket, blue trousers with the yellow officer's stripe down the side, and white gauntlets—in order to appear more official to the superintendent in charge. Vic would be counting on the man's help and needed to make a good first impression.

When Vic walked through the door, Superintendent Jackson Reed eyed his muddy boots with a critical glare. Reed was an older man with iron-gray hair and a stout build. A monocle rested in his right eye socket. After running his gaze down Vic's lean frame once more, he asked in a surprisingly high-pitched voice, "And what can I do for you today, Sub-Inspector?"

"Sir, I'm Jaye Eliot Vickersham, and I need your help. I've come to Battleford to find my son. I've heard he's being cared for by a woman named Stella Smith who may be in the area."

Reed waited, his steady gaze unwavering. "And?"

Vic looked at him. "Well . . . that's all, sir. I was wondering if you—"

"Vickersham, do you honestly expect me to know the name of every person in this district?"

"No, sir, but I'd hoped—"

"I'm not aware of any such woman, but you're free to ask some of the men about her." Reed removed his monocle and began polishing it on his sleeve. His uniform was immaculate, not a trace of lint to be found.

Vic took the act of polishing the eyepiece as a dismissal. "Thank you for your time, sir."

"Good luck, then, Vickersham."

The enlisted men of the fort proved to be much more courteous than their leader. The third man Vic questioned, whose name was Golden, was more than helpful. "Stella Smith? Sure, I know where she lives." Golden was a short man, with merry blue eyes and sandy blond hair. He leaned toward Vic in a conspiratorial manner. "Strange woman, that one."

"How do you mean?"

"Keeps to herself, just her and that boy out there all alone."

A chill ran up Vic's spine. "Is the boy all right? Do you know him?"

"I've seen him a time or two when they come to town to get supplies. Fine-looking kid." Suddenly Golden looked at Vic more closely. "Say, you wouldn't be related somehow, would you?"

"You could say that. I'm the boy's father."

"Well, whadaya say! You mean you and Miss Smith. . . ?"

"No, no. The boy's mother is dead. Miss Smith is her cousin."

They were standing outside the stables when they heard a commotion from inside. Golden grinned and said a bit sheepishly, "That's probably my Bess. When she hears my voice she tends to raise a ruckus because she wants out of there. The only horse I ever had that *wanted* to be rode. Say, you want me to take you to the Smith place? I need to exercise Bess anyway, and it's only a few miles from here."

Vic was surprised and pleased. "That would be wonderful!

93

Are you sure Superintendent Reed. . . ?"

Golden waved a hand dismissively. "The old man barely knows what goes on around here. The *real* boss is Inspector Yancy, and I'll clear it with him, no problem."

"Thanks, Golden."

From the stable came another huge bang—obviously a horse kicking a wall—and a yell. "Hey, Golden, would you come get your silly mare before she breaks the whole place down?"

———

Golden proved to be a real talker. He had plenty of opinions on the government, the running of the Mounted Police, the weather—any subject that was broached was fair game for the young man's brutal honesty.

Vic was content to let Golden prattle on. His own private thoughts intensified with every yard they gained toward the Smith place. He found himself nodding absently to Golden, throwing in an occasional "Mmm" or "Oh, really?" just so he could entertain his concerns at the moment.

What if the Smith woman was crazy? Wouldn't that have a dire effect on Jaye? What if the boy had been neglected his whole short life, so much so that he was totally incapable of communication or normal behavior? Or what if the woman was abusive? Vic had seen what that did to a child, thinking of Jenny Sweet. Once away from her vicious father, it had taken her almost two years to feel comfortable around anyone but Dirk Becker. Her recovery had been slow and painstaking.

The one fear he had was that the woman wouldn't give him his own son. He had Fran's diary for proof of his being the father, but what if—?

All things are possible with Me.

The thought came from nowhere, jolting Vic out of his gloomy reverie. "All things . . ." Vic whispered.

"What's that, sir?" Golden asked. "Did you say something?"

Vic was surprised the boy had even heard him through his expounding on something or other. "I said, all things are possible with God. Did you know that, Golden?"

"Uh, sure. If you say so." Golden looked around the vast prairie, as if just realizing that he was all alone with this total stranger who was older, stronger, and outranked him.

"It's all right, Golden, I'm in my right mind. I just like reminding myself, and anyone who'll listen, of God's strength."

Golden shrugged, relieved. "If you say so, sir."

The country became more hilly, with large copses of lodgepole pine and aspens. Vic breathed deeply of the cool air, enjoying the quiet for the first time. Apparently Vic's comment about God had dampened Golden's need to talk so much. Then Vic remembered something he'd meant to ask the younger man. "Golden, what does my son look like?"

Golden, wide-eyed, asked incredulously, "You mean you've never seen him?"

Vic didn't answer, for he didn't feel like going into the details of the whole thing.

"Well, let's see . . . he's got brown hair . . . uh . . . he's a handsome little devil—er, tyke—and he's got big brown eyes that are kind of the first thing you notice when you look at his face, you know? Kind of like . . ."

"Like what?"

"If you don't mind me saying, sir—kind of like you. The boy looks a lot like you."

Vic tried to picture a miniature version of himself but couldn't.

"We're almost there, so you can see for yourself, sir."

Butterflies began racing around in Vic's stomach. The most horrible question of all, one that he'd avoided at all costs over his whole trip, popped into his mind. *What if he doesn't want to come with me?* He saw himself snatching Jaye from Stella's embrace while the boy screamed that he wanted to stay with her, but he knew he couldn't do that. He didn't know *what* he'd do, but he wouldn't do that. *Oh, enough of this!* "Golden, didn't you say that nag of yours liked to run?"

Golden grinned boyishly. "Like the wind, sir."

"Then let's make her happy, shall we?"

"Yes, *sir!*"

They broke into an all-out run, and the spirited and well-rested Bess easily outdistanced Vic's tired mount. Vic didn't care. He just wanted to get to his son.

Bursting over a hill, well behind Bess and Golden, Vic saw him. His boy. His firstborn. His heir. And even from a distance, Vic could see that Jaye *was* a miniature of himself. His heart soared, and he told himself that the tears in his eyes were from the strong wind of the wild ride.

Outside a modest cabin, little Jaye was attempting to chop wood. The ax was almost as tall as he, and the boy could barely lift it, but he was giving it a valiant try. Around him strutted a few chickens pecking in the dirt. Vic stopped his horse beside Golden, who was watching expectantly.

"What do you think of him, sir?"

"Think of him? He's . . . he's . . ."

"Something, eh?"

"Incredible!" Vic breathed.

At that moment a woman came around the side of the cabin holding a hoe. She wore a bonnet that hid her face, and the long apron over her dress was soiled with dirt. When she saw what Jaye was doing, she immediately dropped the hoe, went to him, and rudely snatched the ax from him. Then, with much more force than necessary, she grabbed his arm and spun him around toward the door of the cabin, shrieking something unintelligible.

Vic took off as if he'd been shot from a cannon and covered the distance in a matter of seconds. When the woman heard hoofbeats, she turned, holding the ax with both hands as if to ward off an attack. Beneath the bonnet he saw coal-dark eyes and gritted teeth.

"What do you want?" the woman shouted, brandishing the ax. "I ain't done nothing to bring the Mounties on me!"

Vic dismounted and walked right up to her, scattering chickens from his path. "Stella Smith?"

"Yes," she replied as she backed away from him, leaving the false bravado behind.

"The Mounties *should* be on you for the way you're mistreating that child." He reached out and tore the ax from her grip, then buried the head into the stump.

Still in the screeching, sharp voice, Stella said, "Who are you to tell me how to raise my child? I'll treat him any way I want!"

"First of all," Vic returned in a low, ominous whisper, "he's not your child. Second, I'd stop a complete stranger, no matter who they are, for jerking on a child's arm like that. You could have broken it!"

"How do you know he's not my child?"

"Because he's mine."

Stella took yet one more step back, almost falling over some of the split wood behind her. "He's . . . he's *what*?"

"You heard me. Your cousin, Fran, who gave you that child to raise, would be as appalled at your treatment of him as am I."

Incredibly, a smile crept over Stella's face, though her eyes remained steely. "You're Vickersham? Jaye Eliot Vickersham?"

"I am."

"Well, how about that! You come here to get your boy, did you?"

"I did."

"Good!" Stella crowed, marching toward the cabin. "That's one less mouth around here to feed. Jaye, your daddy's here to take you away! Get yourself out here! I'll go get your stuff."

Vic couldn't believe the callous behavior of the woman and didn't know whether to be grateful or furious. He was definitely going to get his boy, anyway.

From the cabin door Jaye peeped at him. Vic could hear all kinds of racket coming from inside, where Stella was slamming things around in her haste. Vic called to the boy, who had run inside. "Jaye? It's all right. You can come out here. I won't hurt you. What Stella said was true—I'm your father, and I've come to take you home. Didn't anyone ever tell you about me?"

97

The boy stayed inside. Vic turned to Golden, still mounted a few yards back. "What do I do?"

Golden shrugged and said, "I don't have any kids and never been around them."

When Vic turned back around, Jaye was again peeping around the doorway. "Come here, Jaye," Vic called gently, motioning. "Come here and shake my hand. My name's Jaye, too. Did you know that?"

Jaye started out the door, but only because Stella was pushing him, carrying a small suitcase. "Here's his things in this case. Never had enough money to buy him many clothes, but he's never gone around naked. Go on, now, Jaye. That there's your daddy I told you about." She stopped when she saw the boy wasn't following. "Come *on*, this is your daddy. There's nothing to be afraid of."

Not meeting Vic's eyes, Jaye came over slowly.

"The boy dawdles when you want him to do something," Stella informed him wisely, "but when you *don't* want him to do something, he goes about it like a cyclone. Come on, boy!"

Vic squatted down and tried to get Jaye to look at him, but the boy wouldn't. His eyes, which were exactly the same color as his father's, were staring at the chickens. Vic held out his hand. "Glad to meet you, Jaye."

As if in a dream, Jaye reached out and placed his hand in Vic's. Feeling something like an electrical shock at his touch, Vic closed his fingers around the small ones. Then, unable to help himself, he pulled the boy toward him to give him a hug, but Jaye cried out and hid behind Stella's skirts.

"He's a bit shy," Stella said, "but he'll get used to you. Here, do you want this suitcase? I got work to do."

Vic handed the suitcase to Golden, who tied it behind his saddle.

Stella motioned to Jaye and said, "Get up on your daddy's horse. Your goin' with him today."

Jaye looked up at her and shook his head.

In a more stern tone Stella said, "Go on, now."

The boy threw his arms around her legs and began to cry.

Vic couldn't stand it. "Miss Smith, maybe it would be better if the boy got used to me before I take him—"

"Nope! You're so all fired up about how I treat him, and think you can do so much better, *you* take him! And that's final." She lifted the sobbing Jaye easily and hoisted him on the back of the horse and into the saddle. "Watch you don't fall off, now." Then she stepped back and waved.

Vic, not believing that the woman could be so unfeeling about letting Jaye go, swung up onto the back of the horse behind Jaye and whispered, "It'll be all right, Jaye. Don't worry."

"Bye, now," Stella called, as if she would be seeing Jaye later that evening.

Vic turned the horse, seeing Jaye twist around and watch the only security he'd ever known being distanced from him by two strangers. What could be going through his mind, Vic couldn't imagine. He was still sniffling, but he had stopped outright crying.

When they were almost at the crest of the hill that would take them out of sight, Vic turned back to find that Stella Smith had already gone back to her work. *What a strange, lonely woman*, he thought with sadness.

He heard Jaye make a small snuffling noise and said, "You all right, Jaye? I know you're sad, but we're going to get along famously, you and I. Famously."

Jaye made another noise.

"What was that, son? What did you say?" Vic realized that he hadn't heard Jaye say a word yet.

"Home" came the soft reply.

"I know that was your home, son. But I've got another one for you just as fine, and you'll even have a new mother, how about that?"

"Home."

Vic felt tears come to his eyes when he heard the pain behind the simple word. Then he, too, whispered, "Home."

CHAPTER EIGHT

A Matter of Trust

Reena stopped the pinto and patted him on the neck affectionately. "Good boy, Orion. Thanks for not throwing me." The horse was black with patches of white here and there. On one side of him were fairly large spots, but on the other were small ones that looked identical to the constellation Orion. Reena had explained this phenomenon to Orion's owner, a Blackfoot brave by the name of Sleeping Hare, and ever since he'd been afraid of the pinto. "How could a horse have the markings of the night sky?" he'd asked superstitiously, and even though Reena tried to explain to him the meaning of coincidence it did no good. From that day, Sleeping Hare hadn't ridden him. So whenever Reena needed a mount, she would ask to borrow Orion, and he never turned her down.

Another strange thing that Sleeping Hare didn't care for was the fact that Orion always tried to throw him, but never Reena. Sleeping Hare believed the horse was possessed of haunted, angry spirits that cared more for the white woman than for him. He would gladly have given Orion to Reena, but he was gathering three horses to offer to Raven for his daughter. Let Raven

ALAN MORRIS / WINGS OF HEALING

deal with the cursed mount while Sleeping Hare lived happily with his offspring.

Reena grinned as she thought of this, but when she raised her head, the smile trickled down into a frown. The Tice home was worse than an eyesore—it was a travesty. Reena dismounted and walked through knee-high grass that carpeted the yard all the way to the door of the house, which stood askew. Around the yard lay broken tools and farm implements, long since untouched by their former owner. A wagon wheel with spokes missing leaned against one corner of the house. Off to the side, a mule with its ribs clearly showing searched through the high grass for something better to eat.

"Oh, Judy," Reena breathed, "you poor woman."

After tying Orion to the hitching post near the house and retrieving the sack she'd brought, Reena knocked on the door. The door itself almost came off the hinges with her less-than-firm knocking, and Reena said a quick prayer that someone would answer her summons.

The door opened with a loud grating, revealing Judy Tice. "Reena! What are you doing here? Come inside, honey."

The smell hit Reena first. It was the unmistakable odor of sickness. "Judy, I came as soon as I heard. Amanda's sick?"

"Yes, she must have brought it from the school." Judy's lusterless eyes, with black half-moon bags riding beneath, focused on Reena's sack. The stark stare of a famished predator briefly crossed her gaunt face, then she smiled a weary smile. "I'm sorry about the house. I just haven't had the energy to keep it up since . . ."

Since Ira's been gone, Reena mentally finished for her. Unwashed dishes were piled in the kitchen, and a fine coat of dust covered everything. "It's fine, Judy. You have a lot more to worry about than your house. How's Amanda? Can I see her?"

"Of course! She's sleeping right now, but I'm sure she'd like a visit from you."

"No, let her sleep. Let's warm up this soup first."

Judy couldn't contain her delight. "You brought soup?"

"And fresh bread."

"Oh, thank you, Reena. It seems that I just haven't had time to cook for us like I should."

While Reena prepared the soup, they talked about the spread of the flu throughout the community. Since Judy was mostly housebound, she wasn't aware of the severity of the epidemic. "You mean it's everywhere? Reena, what are we going to do?"

"I don't know," Reena answered grimly. "Pray harder, I suppose."

"Oh, that won't do any good!" Judy commented bitterly.

Reena was shocked, for Judy was a fine Christian woman. They'd shared some Bible study times together, and Judy's knowledge of God's Word was impressive. To hear a comment like that come from Judy's lips was unthinkable.

Reena turned to her. "Judy, are you all right?"

"I'm just sick of it, Reena!" Judy cried, collapsing into a battered wooden chair and covering her face with her hands. "I'm sick of struggling. I'm sick of feeling horrible all the time. I'm sick of Ira being gone. What will happen to Amanda if I . . . if I . . ."

"Shhh, don't think like that, Judy," Reena said, going to the woman and placing her hands on shaking shoulders. Hating to ask but knowing she needed to, Reena said, "Are you feeling worse? More pain?"

Judy wiped her eyes and visibly tried to take hold of herself. In a very soft voice she said, "It comes and goes more often now. When the pain's here, I have trouble even getting out of bed, much less taking care of Amanda."

Reena suspected that Judy suffered from some form of stomach cancer. She'd seen Judy when the pain was great, and it would indeed almost incapacitate her. Reena couldn't imagine the pain growing worse than what she'd witnessed in the past. "I'm sorry, Judy," she whispered.

Judy stood and faced her, trying to smile reassuringly. "That wasn't me talking earlier, you know that. I'll never stop trusting the Lord. It's just that . . . some times are harder than others."

"I understand," Reena said, but she didn't. She couldn't imagine how a person lived with that kind of pain.

"Let's take some of this soup to Amanda, Reena. Enough of this dreary talk."

When Reena went into Amanda's room she couldn't believe it was the same girl. Gone was the active, boisterous child who'd wandered so far one day that an Indian had found her. For a brief, terrible moment Reena thought the girl might have died while they were in the kitchen.

Amanda lay on her back on the bed. Heavy quilts, tattered but intact, fully covered her. Above them, the girl's face was a white mask, with only the barest of color to the cheeks. Sweat beads glistened on her forehead in the dim light from the heavily curtained window of the room. Amanda was normally a pretty girl, but at the moment she looked much older than her eleven years.

"Amanda?" Judy called softly, touching her shoulder beneath the quilts. "Wake up, honey. We've got some nice hot soup for you."

The girl stirred, and lines of fatigue creased her forehead. "Not hungry . . . thirsty."

"Reena's here, darling. Don't you want to see her?"

"Reena?" Amanda opened her eyes, but a deep coughing spell closed them again.

"I'm here, Amanda," Reena said when the coughing stopped. She sat on the edge of the bed and began wringing out a cloth from a bowl of water on the side table. Gently applying the cool cloth to Amanda's forehead and cheeks, she said, "The last time I saw you it was Valentine's Day, and you were having a snowball fight with some young man. Was he your valentine?"

Amanda thought a moment. "Yes."

"Shouldn't you be trying to get a kiss from your valentine instead of having a snowball fight with him?"

"That's how the fight started."

"He tried to kiss you?"

"No, I tried to kiss him. He didn't like it."

Reena chuckled and said, "Well, it looked like you were winning the fight. Did you ever get your kiss?"

"Didn't want it. Besides, he was all wet and yucky by then." A smile crossed Amanda's lips that Reena was glad to see. It vanished very soon, however.

"How about some soup? I made it myself, just for you and your mother."

"I'm not hungry, and my throat hurts. Can I have something to drink?"

"Of course, but you have to eat at least *some* of my secret recipe soup, or you won't get the present I brought you."

"What present?"

Reena wiggled a finger at her. "Soup first."

Amanda made a face, but when Reena had propped pillows behind her and set the tray of soup and crackers in front of her, she proved to have a pretty good appetite. Reena encouraged her to eat more, but she would have none of it.

"What about my present, Reena?"

"Amanda!" Judy scolded. "Don't be greedy. And mind your manners. Thank Reena for her wonderful soup that you just gulped down like a field hand!"

"Thank you, Reena."

"You're very welcome. And I'll be right back."

While Reena was gone to get the sack she'd brought, Judy went to Amanda's side and resumed wiping her face with the damp cloth.

"Mama, I don't feel good at all."

"I know, baby. I know." Despite herself, Judy's eyes filled with tears, and she kept her gaze averted so Amanda wouldn't see.

"When will Daddy be home?"

"I don't know, Amanda. Soon."

After a brief pause, she said, "You always say that, Mama."

Reena returned and took the spot on the other side of Amanda's bed, placing the sack beside the girl. "This is your get well present from a beautiful little girl named Sun Flower. She made it for you."

Amanda, looking more animated than at any time since Reena had arrived, opened the gift. "Oh, Reena, please thank Sun Flower for me!" She held up the doll so her mother could see. "Look, Mama, it's made out of . . . what *is* it made out of, Reena?"

"Mostly straw, wrapped with deer gut. And Sun Flower painted the face herself."

Amanda inspected the doll more closely, then asked, "What did Sun Flower name her?"

"She said for you to name her," Reena said, smiling.

After thinking it over for a few seconds, Amanda announced, "Her name is Sun Flower."

"Sun Flower it is, then."

Amanda abruptly nestled herself beneath the covers. "We're going to take a nap now."

Judy and Reena exchanged glances and, by unspoken agreement, decided to wait until Amanda fell asleep. It didn't take long. Soon she was breathing deeply, and Reena was glad to see that the hot meal had caused some color to come back in her cheeks.

Reena looked over at Judy. Whatever a mother felt for a sick child, Reena couldn't fathom. Lately she'd found herself wishing for a child of her own, and the intensity of the sudden longing would take her by surprise at times. Now, looking at Judy's tight expression as she watched her very sick daughter sleep, Reena wasn't so sure she wanted to have children. *Who was it that said a wife and children are hostages of fortune to a man? Milton? Frances Bacon? Whoever it was, I'm witnessing the truth of it right now.*

Her thoughts turned to Hunter. He'd made no mention of marriage to her, and she wondered if he ever thought about it. What would she say if he surprised her by asking one night? If she said yes, then *she* would be a hostage of fortune. Somehow that thought frightened her.

"Reena," Judy whispered, her gaze still on the sleeping Amanda. "Why?"

"Why what, Judy?"

"I've thought about it over and over. I've prayed for an answer, but I don't get one. It's driving me crazy."

Alarmed, Reena asked, "Judy, what are you talking about?"

"This!" came the answer with vehemence and a gesture at Amanda.

When Judy turned to her, Reena was struck by the combination of outrage and pain on her friend's face.

"Why, Reena? Why do bad things happen?"

"I . . . I don't know—"

"I just don't understand it," Judy whispered. When she looked back down at her daughter, a tear fell on the sleeve of Amanda's nightgown.

Reena stayed a while longer to comfort her friend, but Judy became very quiet and sullen. When Reena left on Orion, she was ashamed to feel relief that she was able to escape witnessing so much personal pain.

————

When Reena reached Fort Macleod she asked for Hunter. She hadn't planned on stopping there, but the time spent with Judy and Amanda had depressed her as she'd ridden along, despite the beautiful spring day. Besides that, she hadn't seen Hunter in days, and though she wouldn't want to admit it to him, the extended times away from him were becoming more tedious than ever before.

Recognizing that her thoughts seemed to be going to him more and more over the past few months, she'd begun praying for God's guidance. Was He telling her it was time to settle down with a God-fearing man and raise a family? Or was she merely becoming more infatuated with him, contrary to God's wishes? She didn't know what to do. God hadn't revealed any answers.

But from the Bible Reena knew that the greatest gifts come

when one waits on the Lord. Whatever happened, if she trusted, believing that her life was in His hands, then everything would work itself out.

"Reena?"

She turned to find Hunter walking toward her with a curious look on his face. He was dressed in his uniform trousers, but no scarlet jacket. His three-button cotton shirt was soaked with sweat around his suspenders and along his broad shoulders. "Hello, Hunter. It looks like I'm interrupting some hard work."

His white teeth flashed in a grin. "Yes, and thank you for that. How can I make it up to you?"

"Take me for a walk?"

"At your service, milady. Please allow me to change shirts and leave orders with these dunces I'm supervising, and we'll be on our way."

He wasn't gone long and returned in a clean dark blue shirt and leather vest. Reena said, "That shirt really complements your eyes. I don't want to see you wearing it around any other women."

"You mean you want me to go shirtless? I'd think that would be—"

Reena took his arm and pinched. "You know what I mean, silly."

"Yes, ma'am. Any other orders?"

"Not at the moment, but give me time."

He leaned down and kissed her cheek.

"My, aren't we bold and ornery today?"

"Excuse me, but I'm not the one who showed up unannounced and shamelessly asked me to go for a walk. Brazen behavior for a lady, isn't it?"

"Are we going to walk, or are we going to talk?" Reena asked, tossing her head in defiance.

"Which way?"

"The river."

"Old Man's River it is."

They began walking, and Reena enjoyed the sight of the

colorful flowers in the green carpet of grass, with tiny butterflies darting all around them. She could smell freshly cut grass from the other side of the fort, where men were binding the shavings for hay. Sighing deeply, she squeezed Hunter's arm.

"That sounded like a deep sigh of contentment," he commented.

Reena smiled up at him. "Did you know that just ten minutes ago I was about to fling myself into this river?"

"Any particular reason?"

"Oh, I've just had a dreary morning and was feeling sorry for myself. But you always make me feel better."

"I'm glad of that, but what's wrong?"

They reached the river and began walking beside it. A bee came a bit too close to them, and Hunter swiped it away. Now Reena could smell the rich mud of the riverbank and the river itself.

"Reena?"

She stopped and bent down to pick a white lily with a golden middle. "Do you ever doubt the goodness of God, Hunter?"

"What? Of course not! You *have* had a bad day, haven't you?"

"Don't try to joke about it, Hunter, please." She looked him directly in the eye. "Have you? Ever doubted?"

He thought a moment, then shook his head. "I can't say that I have since becoming a Christian. He *loves* us, Reena, more than we can imagine. How could you doubt that?"

"I'm not doubting His love. I've just been wondering about . . . not *goodness*, really, but . . ."

Hunter reached out and ran his hands up and down her arms gently. "What happened this morning?"

It all came out in a rush. "I went to visit Judy and Amanda Tice, never mind Ira, he's barely in the family anymore. Can't you catch him peddling his whiskey and show him he's got a family and responsibilities? Anyway, Amanda's really sick with the flu—you already know about Judy—and we were sitting there, Judy and I, and it all just seemed so *horrible*, what with both of them being sick, and we started to wonder why all these bad things had to happen to good people—innocent people who've never hurt a soul—"

"Shhh, that's enough, slow down," Hunter said gently, taking her in his arms and resting his chin on the top of her head.

Reena remembered Amanda's pale, sickly face and dull eyes, and she buried her face in Hunter's shirt. "Judy's weakening, Hunter, both in health and in her faith. She asked me what would happen to Amanda if Judy ... if she died, and I don't even remember what I said because we *know* what would happen. That worthless Ira would put her in some horrible orphanage. What's fair about that? Where is God in that?"

"I don't know—"

"And I *hate* doubting like this, but ... oh, it's just one of those days, I guess."

Hunter held her at arm's length and said, "It's hard to ignore things like that. We're always trying to apply logic to the things that happen in the world, but sometimes there *is* none. If you dwell on it, you'll drive yourself crazy worrying about every little thing. Why did the American states go to war with one another? Hundreds of thousands of young men died in the span of a few years."

Reena nodded slowly. "Please don't bring up that war. I don't even want to think about it."

"I don't either. But whenever I read in the Bible of someone who is in a lot of trouble, or a great wrong has been done, the word 'trust' always enters in. 'Trust in Him, trust in the Lord.' The way Jesus taught it was 'While you have light, trust in the light, that you may be children of the light.' Don't you see?"

Reena passed her arm through his and started back in the direction of the fort. "I think so."

"And don't forget the granddaddy of them all."

"What's that?"

"Proverbs 3:14: 'Trust in the Lord with all your heart—' "

Reena smiled and joined him, and together they finished the passage. " 'And lean not unto thine own understanding. In all thy ways acknowledge Him, and He shall direct thy path.' "

Hunter said, "Don't try to understand it, honey. There are some things we may never understand, but God wants us to trust Him anyway. What do you think?"

Reena stopped him and locked her arms around his neck. "I think you're a very smart Christian man who also happens to be fairly nice looking."

"I think I'm going to ask your opinion more often. I like the way you think."

Reena kissed him, impulsively at first, then with more ardor. *Hostages to fortune* passed through her mind, but she quickly banished it and enjoyed his warm lips and embrace. There had been enough gloom and doom for the day. She was in the arms of her beau, the day was fine and sunny, and God was on His throne. What more could she want at this moment?

When she slowly pulled away from him, he said, "Now I'm supposed to go back to work after that? Let's stay out here all day, take our shoes off, put our feet in the water, and just look at each other."

"Just look?"

"Well, maybe I could steal a kiss or two?"

"And what about Superintendent Irvine?"

"Hey, don't drown my dream with logic."

"I have things to do, Sub-Inspector Stone, though it's a tempting offer."

Suddenly, Hunter reached for her and kissed her with more fervor. "I love you. Do you know that?"

Reena, breathless, saw that he was serious and really wanted an answer. The playful mood was gone, and the tone had about-faced into a completely different direction. *Oh my*, she thought, then answered, "I do know that, darling. And I thank God that you do."

He kept looking at her, his clear eyes holding a curiously intense passion. "Reena . . . will you—"

"Stone!"

They both twitched at the shout and turned to see Superintendent Irvine halfway to them from the fort.

111

"Stone, I need you!"

Reena turned back to Hunter, desperately hoping that the mood hadn't been taken from them, but she could see from his face that it had. With a boyish grin and shrug he said, "Duty calls."

"Hunter . . ."

"Yes?"

She wanted to tell him to ask whatever he was going to ask, but that would be wrong. "Nothing. I just wanted to tell you thanks for the advice. I really needed to hear that."

"Anytime. But I can't promise that I'll always have the right things to say."

"Who can?"

They turned and started toward Irvine. Reena glanced back one more time to where they'd been standing and decided to memorize the spot. Without really knowing why, she sensed that something important had almost happened there, and she didn't want to forget it.

"Sorry for the interruption, Stone," Irvine said when they approached. "I understand the need for privacy, but after all, you were standing right out in the open. Not very advisable, son, if you don't want a kiss ruined. Miss O'Donnell, how are you today?"

"Fine, sir, thank you for asking."

Irvine's features hardened. "Stone, I've got to go back East. My wife's taken badly ill."

"Sir, I . . . I'm very sorry. What can I do?"

"Take over the fort."

"Sir?" Hunter asked in a small voice.

"You heard me. I have to leave immediately, and my temporary replacement won't be here for a few days. The fort's yours."

Hunter shifted his weight from foot to foot twice. "But, sir, isn't there anyone more *qualified* to take—"

"Stone, I don't have time to stand here and argue. Come with me, and I'll show you the duty rosters for the next three days. We've got work to do. Miss O'Donnell," he said, tipping his hat.

"I hope your wife gets better as we speak, Superintendent."

"Thank you, young lady. By the way, would you mind sending some prayers heavenward for her?"

"I'll be glad to."

"Make it quick, Stone," Irvine said with a mischievous grin. "Oh, by the way . . . a new doctor will be arriving in two days from Montana. Watch for him."

"We certainly need him, sir."

Irvine hurried off, and when Reena turned to Hunter she saw that he was still in semishock. "Darling, relax! You know as well as I do that you're more than qualified to do this."

"I'm . . . I just . . ."

Reena shook his arm. "You'll do wonderfully! I'm so proud of you."

Taking a deep breath and letting it out slowly, Hunter nodded. "All right. I guess I should take my own advice and trust the Lord on this one, eh?"

"That's exactly what you should do."

"Where are you going, Reena?"

She gave him a quick kiss on the cheek and a confident smile. "I'm going straight back to Judy's house and preach my friend the same sermon you gave me."

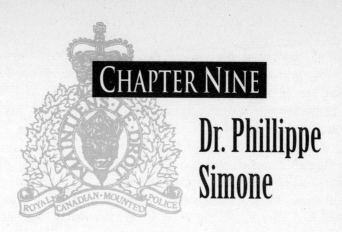

CHAPTER NINE

Dr. Phillippe Simone

Two days after Superintendent Irvine left, Reena knocked on Megan's door in anticipation. She hadn't seen her sister in almost a week. Even after living close to each other for nearly two years, Reena still had trouble believing they got along as well as they did. They had spent their childhood attempting to adhere to finely drawn battle lines, carefully maintaining an indifferent attitude toward each other. However, inevitably one of them would cross a forbidden line, and the battle would begin in earnest. Megan, robust and strong, had little trouble overpowering the younger, thinner Reena in their physical fights.

Then, when they were older, Megan had become a master of manipulation. Reena lost many boyfriends to Megan's charms or to her convincing words. Sometimes Reena's homework mysteriously disappeared on the morning it was due. Megan would enlist the dreaded younger brother, Liam, to her side to play pranks on Reena, such as scaring her in the middle of the night or placing frogs or garter snakes in strategic positions in Reena's room. Many a night Reena would go to sleep in tears, vowing never to forgive her evil sister as long as she lived.

While waiting for Megan to answer the door, Reena couldn't help but grin to herself. She was actually looking *forward* to seeing Megan.

Just when Reena was beginning to think that Megan wasn't home, the door opened. "Hi, Megan."

"Reena, what a nice surprise! Come in."

Though it was almost noon, Megan was still in her nightgown and robe. Her hair, normally lustrous and carefully prepared, hung down in uncombed simplicity. Her face held a pale, sallow look that Reena didn't like. "What's wrong, Megan?" she asked as she stepped inside.

"Oh, just a little under the weather, I guess."

"Sis, the weather's grand. Now, what's really wrong?"

Megan chuckled and waved a hand. "Just a touch of—"

"Oh, Megan, not . . ." Reena couldn't even bring herself to say the word.

"No, no, not the flu. Just some stomach problems." She gestured for Reena to sit on the sofa, and Megan took a seat in a walnut armchair.

"You're pale, Megan."

"I'm having trouble keeping food down."

Reena gave her a stern look. "You're worrying about Vic too much, aren't you? Worrying yourself sick."

"No, *Mother*, I'm not. I just caught something nasty."

Suddenly, Reena gasped. "Megan, you're not . . . pregnant, are you?"

"Reena!"

Excited now, Reena clapped her hands and asked, "Are you going to make me an aunt? I'd just love to have a little niece or nephew to bounce on my knee!"

"Settle down. I'm *not* pregnant. I've already got one on the way, so to speak. If you want a baby so much, then get married and have one yourself."

All the animation left Reena's face as she averted her eyes.

"Oh, Reena, I'm sorry—"

"No, don't apologize. It's true."

Megan leaned forward and asked quietly, "What is it? Did you and Hunter have a fight?"

"No, nothing like that. It's just that . . . lately I've been having some strange thoughts in that area."

"What area? Marriage?"

"Yes."

"What kind of thoughts?"

"Megan, what do I do if Hunter asks me to marry him?"

"Asks you. . . ? Reena, is he going to?" Megan's pale features lit up at once.

"I don't know. I've just had this *feeling* lately that . . . that . . . oh, I don't know! Maybe I'm just being silly."

"What if you're *not* being silly, and he asks? I couldn't tell you how to answer. You know that. But to me it looks like the best of all worlds. A handsome, intelligent Christian man like Hunter, who's stable in every way." Megan spread her hands and chuckled. "How could you say no?"

Reena reached down and plucked lint from the sleeve of her deep blue gingham blouse. How *could* she say no? Everything Megan said was true, with a hundred other things Reena could add. But something still nagged at the back of her mind like a worrisome blister.

"Reena?"

"This *is* silly, Megan. He hasn't even asked me yet, and here I am worrying about it. Besides, I wouldn't have to give him an answer that second, would I?"

"Of course not."

Reena asked quietly, "Did you know? When Vic asked, did you know?"

"Yes, but that was different from your situation, I think. Vic and I were saved together, and from that point on everything just clicked together like a puzzle. We both knew it was God's will for us to be together for the rest of our lives."

Reena said nothing, but her face fell.

Megan moved over to the sofa and sat down beside her, placing a hand over hers. "That doesn't mean that it's not His will for you and Hunter. Not at all. If you're confused about it, yet it's still on your mind, try to pray whenever you get anxious. God will listen, and maybe one time He'll give you a clear-cut answer."

"I know." Reena nodded. "I'd already thought about that, and here I am still stewing about things. Thanks, Megan."

From the back door came the sounds of boots stomping and men's voices.

"Who's that?" Reena asked.

"Del and Uncle Faron. They were in back tending to the horse and buggy. I think I had a wheel come loose."

As the two men came into the room, Faron was saying, "I have to admit me mistake—I don't do that often, mind ye—but I sure thought God gave ye the sense to know which end of a horse was the dangerous one, Dekko."

"I *do* know!" Del answered vehemently.

"From the looks o' that arm, I'd have to disagree with ye."

"Well, I been kicked more times than I been bit! 'Sides, I wasn't doing anything to her, she just reached out and took a plug outta me."

"I'll wager that first part isn't true," Faron returned. "A nag won't kick ye unless you're back there pullin' on her tail—least a normal one won't—but they like to take a nip at ye whenever they're of a mind."

"You ain't got any more idea of what you're talkin' about than the man in the moon. You just make things up as you go along—"

"Ah, Reena, me darlin'," Faron called out when they entered the parlor. "What brings ye here?"

Reena stood and gave him a hug, bracing herself for his strong squeeze that would almost take her breath away. "Just a visit, Uncle Faron."

"Hi, Miss Reena," Del said. He was holding one forearm gingerly.

Megan asked, "Did Juniper bite you, Del? Here, let me look at it."

"Aw, it's just a scratch, Miss Megan."

"Let me look!"

Del uncovered his arm. The spot was already swollen an angry red and purple, but the skin hadn't been broken.

Faron made a noise that could have been interpreted as either surprise or ridicule. Del chose the latter. "What are you laughin' at? It hurts!"

"I'll get an ice wrap for that, Del," Megan said, then went into the kitchen.

"Now, don't bother, Miss Megan, what with you feelin' poorly and all—"

"No bother!" came the call from the kitchen.

Del gave Faron another sullen look, daring him to make another comment.

"What happened, Del?" Reena asked as she inspected the nasty wound more closely.

"I guess ol' June was just in a bad mood this mornin'."

Faron, who was now innocently staring out the window, said under his breath, "Tends to happen when ye mess about with her feed bag before she's done."

"Now, how would you know?" Del roared. "You weren't even there. You were pretendin' like you were fixin' that wagon wheel!"

"Well, *somebody* had to fix it! I didn't see where it was in any danger of gettin' *your* attentions, seein' as how you were playin' with the mare's oats!"

"Enough, both of you!" Reena exclaimed. If she didn't know better she'd have thought they were having a serious argument. "Don't you two ever stop arguing?"

Del and Faron exchanged glances for a moment, then shook their heads and answered in unison, "No."

Megan returned with ice wrapped in a small towel. "Haven't you figured that out by now, Reena? They'll go to their graves arguing and loving every minute of it." She began tending to Del's bite when someone knocked on the front door. "Would you get that, Reena?"

"Great heavens, no!" Faron said. "I'll get it. Dekko needs both of your attentions, what with that massive scrape he has."

Del shook his head as Faron walked off. "I hate to tell you, girls, but you've got one mean skeleton in your closets in that man. He's so mean he makes a hornet look cuddly."

Megan showed Reena a grin that Del couldn't see and commented, "That's a strange thing to say, Del, considering you spend almost night and day with the man."

"Cain't get away from him! He follows me ever'where."

"Wasn't that you calling Uncle Faron a one-armed bandit the other night during one of your poker games you think I don't know about?"

"Yep."

"Don't you think maybe that's a bit mean?"

Del looked at her, all surprise and pure innocence. "Why, he *is* a bandit! What's wrong with that?"

Faron opened the door to Jenny Sweet. "Ah, little one, yer as radiant as the mornin' itself."

"Hi, Uncle Faron." She stepped inside and announced, "You've got to come to the fort."

"What's wrong?" Reena asked, immediately thinking of Hunter.

"Nothing's wrong . . . the new doctor's here."

———

Dr. Phillippe Simone rose from his chair in what was temporarily Hunter's office when Reena, Jenny, and Del entered. Megan had begged off, wishing instead to lie down for a nap, and Faron had been sidetracked by a growing game of gin in one of the enlisted men's quarters.

Jenny's first thought at seeing the new doctor was *Oh my.* She'd never seen such an interesting face or more incredible blue eyes. Simone was about six feet tall, dressed in a white derby sack coat, unbuttoned, with black shirt and black trousers. His oval face held an aristocratic, thin nose over a generous mouth surrounded by a neatly trimmed goatee.

Taking Reena's hand, Simone said, "From your appearance you must be the lovely Miss O'Donnell."

"Why, yes. How did you know?"

"Your Superintendent Stone has a habit of bragging about you behind your back."

"*Acting* superintendent," Hunter corrected as he stepped through the door. He touched Reena's arm as he went by her to his desk. "But I do have that bad habit."

Simone took Jenny's hand in both of his. "And you'll be Miss Sweet."

"Please—" Jenny had to stop to clear her throat. "Call me Jenny."

"Jenny it is, then. I've heard rumors about you, too. It seems you've been quite the nurse around here."

"I've . . . I've done what I can." Jenny was flustered. Dr. Simone was caressing the inside of her wrist with his thumb. Combined with those intense blue eyes, she could barely speak.

"I think you're being modest, Jenny. Perhaps you could assist me in my rounds? I can always use a good nurse."

"Of course." At last he released her hand, but the soft inside of her wrist still tingled where he'd touched her. Did he know he was doing that?

Simone stepped up to Del. "And you are?"

"Del Dekko. Glad to meetcha." He held out his hand, still holding the cloth to his horse bite.

"What seems to be the problem there, Mr. Dekko?"

"Horse nipped me. It'll be all right."

"Let's have a look."

While Simone inspected Del's arm, Jenny stole a quick look at Reena. She, too, seemed to be fascinated with Simone's looks and bearing. Hunter was watching him also and didn't notice Reena's inspection. Reena suddenly glanced at Jenny, then actually blushed and looked away. *Yes, she thinks he's handsome, too,* Jenny thought.

"That's quite a nasty bite," Simone commented. "But there's nothing to do for it except pack it with ice as you have."

He turned his indigo eyes on Jenny. "Your work?"

Jenny felt herself blushing just as Reena had done seconds ago, then felt silly. *What's wrong with me? He's just a man, probably with a pretty wife somewhere.* "No, I can't take credit for that. It was Megan Vickersham, Reena's sister."

"By the way," Reena said, "Megan's sick with a stomach ailment. Could you look in on her later? She's napping right now."

"Of course. It seems we have our work cut out for us, Jenny. I hope I won't be taking all your time from a husband or beau."

"I have a beau, but he's very busy, too."

"Oh? What does he do?"

"He's one of my sergeants," Hunter said.

"Really?" Simone grinned good-naturedly. "I'd better mind my p's and q's, then."

Hunter didn't return the smile. "Any reason you wouldn't?"

Simone's brilliant smile faltered.

"Sit down, Doctor. Let's all get acquainted."

Del told them he had things to do and left. The rest of them took chairs in a semicircle around Hunter's desk.

"Where are you from, Doctor?" Reena asked.

"Summerton, a small town north of Dufferin. I'd heard about your trouble and tried to recruit more doctors to come with me, but it was a losing battle. Seems back East they still believe they can be scalped out here in the Territory," he finished with a chuckle.

Hunter smiled faintly. "And from the information we're getting, they may be right. Sitting Bull and his followers are moving across the border into the Cypress Hills area."

"Then I have to say I'm glad I wasn't aware of that fact, or I might not be here."

"Why is Sitting Bull doing that, Hunter?" Reena asked.

"Tired of the American government hounding them, I suppose. Now it looks like he's our problem."

Jenny noticed the tightness around Hunter's mouth when he said this. Ever since the Custer massacre at the Little Bighorn the year before, the name Sitting Bull was synonymous with the word "fear." Hunter and Reena had been in the area of the massacre when it had happened—had even endured an encounter with some Sioux warriors—and considered themselves lucky to have lived to tell about it. The Sioux were a fierce, proud people, and Hunter obviously didn't relish the thought of having a great number of them only a hundred miles away.

Dr. Simone didn't seem to be overly alarmed by the prospect of it, however. Jenny thought that his flippant comment about the situation was probably his attitude toward life—meeting it head on with a wry twinkle in his eye. He tended to use his hands when he talked, and she noticed that his fingernails were well cared for, much like the rest of him.

"Are you a family man, Doctor?" Hunter asked.

"No, I'm not."

"What are you—twenty-seven, twenty-eight?"

After a glance at the ladies, Simone answered, "Let's just say that I'm a bit older than I look."

Hunter arched a brow but said nothing. Jenny had the distinct feeling that he didn't like the doctor, but she couldn't imagine why.

"What's the plan of action, Super—I mean, Mr. Stone?"

"I've got a few sick men I need you to see to first. Just because an epidemic comes to the community doesn't mean crime stops. I need every healthy man I can muster."

"Very well."

"Jenny can tell you which families need the most attention, and we can go from there."

Simone stood and opened the door for Jenny. "Shall we?"

Jenny nodded to Reena and Hunter and went out the door into the library, very aware of the presence behind her.

"He's got a tough exterior, doesn't he?" Simone said with unmistakable amusement.

"Who?"

"Mr. Stone."

"He's a wonderful man. I think he's just been under a lot of stress while waiting for the new superintendent. Hunter is a leader, without a doubt, but not when it comes to paper work and things like that."

"Mmm. He seems right snobby to me."

"You just have to get to know him."

They stepped outside into the sunshine, and Simone waved a theatrical hand over the parade ground. "Show me the way to the sick and hurting, Jenny. Our duty calls."

Jenny gave him a weak smile, but inside she thought, *What a pompous man!*

———

"So what do you think?" Hunter asked after Simone closed the door.

"Hey, it doesn't matter what *I* think. You're the boss around here."

Hunter pointed a finger at Reena in mock anger. "The next person who calls me that will get swift punishment."

"Ooooh, you've got me scared! What are you going to do, arrest me?"

"That, or turn you over my knee," he grinned, then he rubbed his face vigorously and the smile was gone. "This job is driving me crazy. Can you imagine baby-sitting a hundred men who have the most *petty* complaints you've ever heard?"

"I *did* baby-sit a man for a couple of months, and that was plenty of experience," Reena teased.

Hunter looked blank for a moment, then he smiled and shook his head. "How quickly we forget, huh? But I wasn't *that* bad, was I?"

"You were a perfect angel when you were asleep." When she'd met Hunter, he'd been a breath away from death. His wife had been killed by a renegade Indian, who'd also been responsible for Hunter's wounds. In truth, Hunter had been a handful to nurse, but not because he'd been pitiful and whining—much the opposite. Every time Reena turned around, he'd been trying to do too much too soon in order to go after the renegade and seek revenge. *Those days seem so long ago now*, she thought.

"You didn't answer my question," Hunter said. "Or rather, you dodged it very well. What do you think about Simone?"

Reena shrugged. "If he can help people, I don't care about his character."

"So you think he has a bad character?"

"I think he's arrogant. Anyone can see that after spending five minutes with him."

Hunter gave her a sideways glance. "But you didn't mind looking at him, did you?"

"He's a handsome man," Reena agreed. "But he doesn't hold a candle to you. Not even close. So don't try that jealousy thing with me, Hunter Stone. And don't try that innocent look, either."

"I can't get anything by you, can I?"

"No, but you can keep trying," she answered sweetly.

They talked about Megan and wondered about Vic and little Jaye, then Reena said, "You do look tired. When's the new man supposed to be here?"

"We're looking for him tomorrow or the next day."

"You don't sound like you're looking forward to it. Why not? I thought you were more than ready to hand over the reins to him."

"It's just awkward breaking in a new officer."

"Breaking in? *You* have to break *him* in?"

Hunter stood and stretched, then yawned. "We all do. I mean, the other officers and sergeants. It's always an adjustment when a new superior officer comes in. Takes time to gauge him."

"And how do you do that?"

Hunter perched on the side of the desk and gave her a lop-sided grin. "Test him."

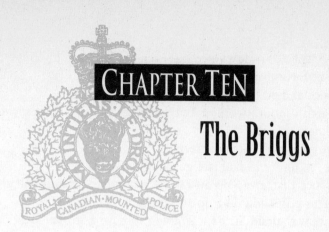

CHAPTER TEN

The Briggs

Sergeant Preston Stride was in fine form.

"You tubercular, epileptic, neurotic, asinine progeny of misbegotten anthropoid apes! You're a disgrace to the Mounted Police! You stand at attention like a string of giggling schoolgirls waiting their turn to read *Her Scarlet Sin*! Your tunics look horrible, your boots look disgusting, and your quarters look like pig sties!"

Dirk Becker hid a smile as he watched the men cringe. Stride's voice, strong and clipped in regular conversation, now rang through the early morning air like the clang of crossing swords. The men had piled out of their quarters expecting an Indian attack when Stride had bellowed, "Guard! Turn out!" and a few of them were only half dressed. Those unfortunate few felt the full heat of Stride's tirade.

"Did your mommies not finish dressing you this morning? Am I interrupting your beauty sleep?" He stopped directly in front of Charles Hatch, who wore only trousers and one boot. "Do you know what time it is, Hatch?"

"Um . . . about six-thirty, sir?"

If possible, Stride's voice was even louder when he shouted, "It's six-forty-five! What in blazes are you doing wearing only one boot and no tunic in the middle of the day?"

Hatch's mouth worked, but nothing came out. The silence was almost palpable.

"Answer me!" Stride screamed.

"I . . . um . . . I had late guard duty, Sergeant!"

"Does that give you an excuse to lounge around half the day? This post should be up and running by six! SIX!"

Dirk was afraid Stride was going to have a stroke. His normally ruddy face was now past red and turning blue.

"Now, back to the pig sties! Were any of your mothers pigs? Is that where you learned your sanitary habits? Sergeant Becker!"

"Yes, sir!" Though they were both of the same rank, Stride had many more years of experience than Dirk; therefore, the "sir."

"Do you see anything *porcine* on any of these faces?"

"Now that you mention it, sir, there may be a few who have that look."

"Aha! I was correct, then, in assuming that there may be some questionable heritage in our midst." Stride glared at each man in turn as he slowly walked through the ranks. "We have a new superintendent arriving at any time. He may be outside those gates as we speak, and if he is . . . well, I hope you're all religious men, because there will be no one to save you except God."

The tirade went on. Dirk noticed Hunter emerge from the library and start toward the stable. A hint of a smile came to his lips when he looked over at Stride's antics.

"Now, I'm only going to say this once!" Stride bellowed. "This fort will be clean enough so that the queen herself would be proud to stay here for an extended vacation. Do I make myself clear?"

"Yes, sir!" answered sixty throats.

"Good! Your enthusiasm is admirable—now get to it!"

Dirk watched the mad scramble toward the barracks, finally allowing himself a grin.

"Becker!"

"Yes, sir."

"What are you smiling about?"

"Nothing, Sergeant, I just—"

Stride was suddenly in Dirk's face, fixing him with his dark glare. Then, ever so slowly, the barest tinge of a smile tugged at the corners of his mouth. "Do you think it worked?"

"Absolutely, Sarge. That is, if the whole force doesn't desert out of pure fear."

"What was that about desertion?" Hunter asked from behind them.

"Just a joke, sir," Stride told him quickly.

"I know that, Stride. You *are* allowed to smile, you know. Even laugh if the moment takes you."

"Thank you, sir."

Hunter shook his head at the man's incessant military discipline as he pulled on his gauntlets.

"Are you off for somewhere, sir?" Dirk asked.

Hunter's relaxed look faded into a tight expression. "To Plenty Trees' village. We just got word that they're to be put on a reservation."

"What? The Blackfoot tribes?" Dirk was stunned. Not just Plenty Trees' people, but nearly all the Blackfoot tribes were considered nothing but the most well-behaved of all the Indians in the North-West Territory. The only thing Dirk could think to ask was an emphatic "*Why?*"

Hunter fixed him with a grim stare. "I don't know. They didn't consult me."

"But . . . but how can they. . . ? What's the thinking behind . . . ?"

"I don't *know*, Becker! So stop stammering around and asking *me*. They didn't send along an explanation for this stupid order." He took a deep breath and looked skyward for a moment. "Sorry. I don't mean to take it out on you."

"No, it's all right. But why don't you let me or Sergeant Stride tell them?" Dirk paused, then added, "And Reena."

Hunter shook his head. "Thanks, but it has to be me. I kind of wish the new boss were here so *he* could do it."

Dirk and Stride exchanged knowing glances. Dirk said, "No, you wouldn't. You'd want to do it yourself even if Commissioner Macleod was here. For Reena's sake."

"Has anyone ever told you you're a know-it-all, Becker?"

"I'll second that," Stride agreed.

"No, I think you two are the first," Dirk grinned.

"Enough of this," Stride growled. "I've got to go check on the babies and make sure they're straightening their rooms in the right way."

"Stride?" Hunter said.

"Yes, sir?"

"Keep a sharp eye out for the new superintendent. It might even be wise to post a man at the other end of town to watch for him."

"That's a good idea, sir. I'll do it straightaway."

"I wonder what kind of man he is?" Dirk pondered.

"So do I," Stride said. Turning to Hunter, he said, "Beggin' your pardon, sir, but I've served under some . . . shall we say, incapable officers in my time."

"You mean lousy," Hunter corrected.

"Well, that too."

Hunter sounded wistful when he sighed and said, "I wish Irvine hadn't left. At least you knew where you stood with him and what was expected. Let's just hope our new man isn't like some of the ones you mentioned, Stride."

"I'll go you one better, sir. You'd better *pray* he's not like those others."

———

Reena's reaction would have been comical had the matter not been so serious. Mouth open, her unbelieving gaze swept from Hunter to Plenty Trees to her friend Raindrop over and over in turn.

Hunter waited, cringing inwardly, for the explosion he knew was coming. Reena was a fine, caring woman, but she possessed a fairly healthy temper, one that he'd been unfortunate enough to feel the full force of a few times over the years. They stood outside Plenty Trees' tepee, just the four of them, but Hunter knew that if Reena began yelling, they would have company very quickly, which Hunter didn't want.

He looked at Plenty Trees, the faithful chief who cared absolutely nothing about the white man's politics and only wanted the best for his people. The hard, flat gaze was trained steadily on Hunter with an intensity he could almost feel.

But it was the meek, rotund Raindrop, wife of Plenty Trees, who found her voice first. "No! We will not go!"

This outburst apparently freed Reena's tongue. "Hunter, are you *insane*? There's absolutely no reason to place these people on a reservation! They're self-supporting, they're peaceful, and they help the Mounties more than any other tribe in the Territory! Of *course* they're not going!"

"Reena, it's not for me to decide—"

"Then who's responsible for this?" she demanded, placing her hands on her waist.

"The Canadian government—her *Majesty's* government."

"Well, then, I'll just take it up with you, then maybe Commissioner Macleod, then maybe Her Majesty herself!"

"Reena, calm down, you know there's—"

A slim, shaking finger was suddenly in his face, with blazing blue eyes behind it. "Don't you tell me to calm down like you would to some little schoolgirl, Hunter Stone! I've lived with these people for years. They're my *family*, and I won't allow some stupid, nonsense law to cheat them out of their way of life!"

Hunter spread his hands helplessly and endured more of her tirade. Glancing at Plenty Trees, he was surprised to see not defiance or determination, but a spark of defeat in the black eyes.

This was the last reaction Hunter had expected from the proud chief. But then he understood. Plenty Trees was very intelligent, and he was well aware that his people were at the mercy of the Mounted Police and the "Great White Mother's" government. If they were told to go to a reservation, they would have to go, and Plenty Trees had already grasped that which neither Reena nor Raindrop had. Hunter felt a great sadness envelop him. Suddenly he wished that he *had* let someone else bring this terrible news to these peace-loving Indians.

"—and we'll find a way to fight this, no matter what it takes!" Reena promised as she finished having her say. She took a deep breath and pushed a lock of hair back from her flushed face. By then, a small group had gathered around them, whispering questions to one another about what was going on. A number of the tribe understood English, and when the word spread, Hunter was faced with hostile glares and indignant faces.

Raindrop nudged her husband gently, whispering, "Tell him we will not go." He looked at her sharply, and she physically backed away a step with eyes averted. Plenty Trees was an honorable man, but as was the Blackfoot custom, he wouldn't be told what to do by any woman, even his wife.

To Hunter he asked, "Where do they want us to go?" Not "We will not go," not "We will fight this," only a tone of resignation. Raindrop looked up at him curiously, but he didn't acknowledge her.

Hunter was hating this meeting more every second. "I don't know, Chief. Somewhere to the east, I would think."

Plenty Trees looked off to his right at the smoky blue Rocky Mountains looming in the near distance. "East is away from the mountains?"

"Yes, I'm afraid so."

"Why east? Why not here, where we already are?"

Hunter shook his head. "I'm sorry, it's just not done that way. The government decides where you go, and usually that's toward *them* in Dufferin."

"Dufferin?" Reena echoed. "Hunter, that's hundreds of miles away!"

"I didn't mean Dufferin itself. I just meant in that direction, probably no more than a hundred miles."

"Oh no!" Reena breathed. "A hundred miles away?"

"How far is that?" Plenty Trees demanded.

"About four days' ride," Hunter told him reluctantly.

Plenty Trees couldn't hide his shock. Once again he looked over at the Rockies, and his broad face became stony. In the barest of whispers he said, "I've lived here all my life—near the mountains."

Reena suddenly grabbed Hunter's arm and pulled him around the side of the tepee, away from all the eyes and ears. With her face considerably more calm than before, she held on to his arm and said, "I'm sorry I blew up at you like that. That was wrong. I know it's not your fault. I was just raging at the uniform, I suppose."

"I know that."

She smiled her thanks at him, then said, "You and I both know that this is wrong. But how am I supposed to explain it to those people? They don't understand what's going on, or why they're being told to leave the place where they've been living for centuries! *I* don't understand it. Could you please explain it to me?"

Hunter took her hand and walked them toward the shade of a pine tree. "I don't know for sure, but the only thing that makes sense to me is it's because of Sitting Bull."

Reena stopped, eyes round. The memory of their close call at the hands of the Sioux was plain on her face. "What does he have to do with it?"

"He's coming to the Territories with a lot of his people. They're tired of the American government and want to settle around the Cypress Hills."

"So? What does a hostile Sioux chief have to do with these peaceful Blackfoot? Why are *they* being punished for *his* crimes?"

"It's just mistrust, Reena. Those politicians back East don't know Plenty Trees and his people. All they know is that they're of the same race as Sitting Bull, and Sitting Bull makes them very nervous."

"So don't let him in the country!"

"That's what I think, but how can we stop him?"

"With an army! How else do you stop an army? You and I both know that Sitting Bull *does* have an army."

Hunter shook his head. "He says he's coming in peace, with his guarantee that he'll abide by Canadian law."

"Oh, posh!" Reena cried, making a slashing gesture with one hand. "Are we really supposed to believe that? Do *you* believe that?"

"Reena, it doesn't matter what either you or I believe. Don't you see?"

Her shoulders slumped. "So what can we do, Hunter? We have to try something, writing letters or—"

"Remember Macleod? He's the most powerful man in the Mounties now. If we can get him on our side—which should be absolutely no problem because he knows and likes Plenty Trees—maybe he can do something."

Glumly, Reena said, "Maybe. If you say so."

He took her by the arms and looked into her eyes. "Try to stay upbeat and positive for them, darling. They're going to be scared and angry, so you need to try to keep them from doing anything stupid, like talking about war. That would only make things doubly worse. Do you understand?"

"Yes." She gnawed her bottom lip, then asked, "Hunter? What am I supposed to do if *I'm* scared and angry?"

He grinned crookedly. "Then you have to do what I do in my job."

"What's that?"

"Don't let them see it."

———

Irene Briggs looked around the room, and gradually her upper lip curled in distaste. At forty-two years old, she still sported an hourglass figure proudly and could still manage a blush when complimented on it. Irene liked to use her blush. She'd discovered when she was younger that the talent could open many doors that would have otherwise remained shut.

Now, however, she wasn't blushing in the face, but a crimson flush crept up the back of her neck above her lace collar. Hearing movement behind her in the doorway, she said in a tight voice, "Cameron, you really don't intend for us to actually stay here, do you?"

Major Cameron Briggs squeezed by her and dropped their suitcases on one of the two small beds, causing dust motes to fly in every direction. He was a small, balding man, standing an inch or two shorter than his wife, with dark brown eyes and a broad nose. "My dear, this is a palace if you've ever slept on the ground in a thunderstorm."

"Well, I haven't *slept* on the ground, thunderstorm or no, thank you very much. And I *don't* intend to sleep here." Irene's voice was clipped and precise from her Eastern American schooling, and it dripped with the indignation she felt at the moment.

Cameron's usual stern expression softened, creating a surprising contrast. "What would you like for me to do, darling? This is the only way station on the prairie before we get to Fort Macleod. It's only one night. We'll be there tomorrow."

"*Only* one night?" Irene demanded, beginning to pull off her tight lavender gloves finger by finger. Her day dress was pale stone-colored silk, trimmed with blue satin piping, and combined with her dark hair, green eyes, and finely chiseled features, she seemed as out of place in the dismal room as the queen in a lean-to shack. "*Only* one night, Cameron? How am I supposed to sleep in this . . . this . . . *pit*? Tell me that, Cameron."

"Now, now," he said soothingly, placing a hand on her shoulder. Irene stiffened the tiniest bit at his touch. "I'll ask that fellow in there—Tyler, that was his name—to change the bedclothes and—"

"Changing the bedclothes won't make a difference. Taking a torch to the place *might*."

Tyler himself appeared in the door, rail thin and bony. "Ev-er'thing all right in here?"

Cameron's iron demeanor returned instantly when he saw the man. In a low, menacing voice—the one his wife called his "military tone"—he growled, "No, everything is *not* all right. Change these bedclothes immediately and sweep the floor. This room is filthy, and I won't have my wife subjected to it."

"Sub . . . what?"

"Do as I say, man! At once!"

Tyler ran his hollow gaze up and down Cameron's smaller form deliberately, then said calmly, "Now, hold on here. Don't get your dander up at me, mister. I don't think you realize who you're talking to here."

Cameron advanced on Tyler slowly with his fist clenched behind his back. His eyes glowed with a dangerous intensity that Tyler didn't see.

"I'm the only shelter on these here plains for a hundred miles, maybe more. It don't do yourself any good to get on my bad side, if you know what I mean."

Cameron didn't stop until he was standing toe to toe with the taller man, his head only reaching to Tyler's chin. Tyler looked down at him smiling easily, then he saw Cameron's eyes. The amusement left his face at once.

"Now you listen to me, you arrogant goat-herder!" Cameron barked. "If you ever—*ever*—try to threaten me again, I'll stick your head on a pike and leave it for the buzzards! *No one* talks to me that way. Do you understand?"

Tyler had taken a step back during the speech, but Cameron had matched it. Now Tyler brought his hands up between them but didn't dare touch Cameron or push him away.

"*Do you understand?*" Cameron roared.

Tyler flinched and took another step back, nodding vigor-ously. "Yes, sir. Yes, sir, I understand. I'll get the missus on it right away. You and the lady are more than welcome to go to the kitchen for some coffee while we see to your . . . um . . . request."

"I don't suppose you have tea? My wife only drinks tea."

"Um . . . no, sir, Mister Bri—"

"*Major* Briggs."

"Right, right, *Major* Briggs, sure . . . I'm surely sorry, but we don't have no tea around the place. Most folks just want coffee."

Irene came up to them with a smile fixed on her face and said sweetly, "Coffee will be fine, Cameron. After all, it's just one night, correct?"

Cameron looked at her, hearing the double meaning that no one else could and seeing the flash in her eyes meant solely for him. "Of course, Irene. I'll be happy to pour you a cup with lots of sugar—"he stopped and fixed Tyler with another beady glare—"you *do* provide sugar?"

"Oh, yeah, we got loads of it." Tyler seemed very happy to finally be able to say yes to a question.

"Good." Cameron's face made the amazing transformation to devotion again when he looked at his wife. "With lots of sugar in it to settle your stomach. Come along."

Irene gladly took his offered arm, which she rarely did. She loved it when he made a fuss over her, even though it was usually at the unfortunate expense of others. When Cameron was out of uniform—which was rare—people often misjudged his small stature for weakness. Usually they discovered their mistake when it was too late. Irene would never forget the time a man had let the door of a clothing store slam back almost in her face. The man had made a scoffing gesture at Cameron when he'd called out to him. Cameron had hauled the man outside and beaten him senseless. Irene had been especially kind to her husband that night, even going so far as to baking him some pastries. She'd had to ask their cook where everything was and how to do it. In the end, the cook had actually done all the preparation and handed the platter over to Irene, but in Irene's mind she'd done the whole thing.

When she saw the kitchen, she lost her good mood. There was no copper cookware, no chromolithographed tins of tea, coffee, and spices. No custom-crafted, handsome cupboards. No glass-front cabinets. Irene actually gasped. "You mean someone actually cooks in here?"

Cameron chuckled softly and shook his head while pouring their coffee from the wood-stove hot plate. "Irene, people cook under these conditions, and sometimes worse, all the time."

"I'm glad I don't have to."

"Darling, you don't cook at all," he reminded her with a smile.

She started to throw off a retort about the pastries she'd just been thinking about but decided not to. They'd already had a little row about staying here, and she was tired and just wanted some sleep—if she could sleep in that horrid bed.

They sat down at the small wooden dining table with countless dents and scratches in it. Cameron handed her the sugar-laden coffee, and she blew on it to cool it down. "Cameron, will they have tea at this fort?"

"I don't know."

She fixed him with a look that made his eyes widen, then he patted her hand reassuringly. "If they don't, I'll search the Territory until I find some for you. How's that?"

"Am I going to be the only lady for thousands of square miles?"

"Of course not! Irene, there's a whole *town* around this fort. There'll be other women."

"I didn't say women. I said ladies."

"I'm sure there'll be ladies also. Maybe they'll even have some sort of social gathering every once in a while."

Irene sipped her coffee and grimaced. "Cameron, you've absolutely *saturated* this with sugar! How much did you add?"

Major Cameron Briggs set down his own cup, which he'd been enjoying very much, and immediately prepared another for his wife. He didn't complain. In fact, it never even crossed his mind to do so.

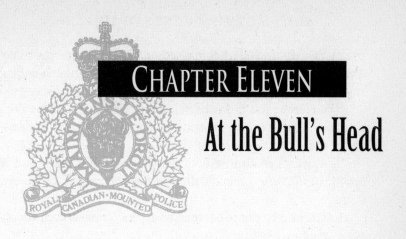

CHAPTER ELEVEN

At the Bull's Head

The aroma of bacon mixed with burnt toast filled the small dining room as Vic watched his son pick at his breakfast. Vic hadn't been around many children, but Jaye was definitely the quietest boy he'd ever seen.

It had been uncomfortable for both of them since the previous day when Vic had taken him away from the only home he knew. The responses Vic received from his attempts to start a conversation—if he received any at all—were mostly monosyllabic. Only once had Jaye strung two sentences together, and that had been, "I had a dog. She died from a snakebite." Vic had tried to get him to talk more about it, but to no avail.

Vic had gotten a small cot for Jaye to sleep on from the hotel owner, a friendly man by the name of Jeter. After a hot bath, Jaye had fallen asleep almost immediately. Vic wasn't so lucky. He'd tossed about for nearly two hours before he finally dozed off. During the night he awoke to the sound of sniffles from Jaye, and he'd gone to him at once, only to find he'd fallen asleep again. Vic didn't know how long the boy had been crying.

Now, watching Jaye shift his scrambled eggs around on his

plate, Vic felt an overwhelming compassion for the boy. "Jaye? I'm sorry you miss Stella so much. I heard you crying last night."

Jaye didn't look at him, but Vic saw the tiniest of shrugs.

"You know, you and your new mother are going to get along famously. She's very loving and also happens to be very pretty."

"What color are her eyes?"

The question surprised Vic, both in its abruptness and its strangeness. "Why, they're the most lovely green you've ever seen."

Jaye took a bite of toast, then said, "I ain't never seen anyone with green eyes before."

Vic started to correct his grammar but decided against it. At least Jaye was talking to him. There would be time later for proper schooling. The thought of school hit him hard, but pleasantly. *I'm going to have a son in school! I'm going to be helping with homework, and meeting his new friends, and passing on my knowledge to him—*

"Is she fat?"

Vic had to keep himself from bursting out laughing. "Why, no, she's not fat."

"Is she skinny?"

"No, she's not skinny, either. She's, um . . . just right. She's not tall. She only comes up to my shoulder. She has beautiful golden hair and a tiny, dainty nose. And her laugh . . . oh, my boy, if you could only get her to laugh. It's like the sound of fine crystal tinkling together."

"What's crystal?"

"It's a very brilliant kind of glass. When we get home I'll show you a crystal goblet we have."

"Will it hurt me?"

"Will what hurt you?"

"The crystal goblet. Stella told me once that if I was bad, a goblet would come and punish me."

This time, Vic did laugh out loud. "No, son, you're talking about a *goblin*, not a goblet. A goblet is a glass that you drink out of." Vic's good cheer died when he realized what Jaye had just revealed. Leaning forward to make eye contact with the boy, he said, "And Stella was wrong to tell you that. Very wrong. There's no such thing as goblins. Neither Megan nor I will ever let anyone hurt you. Do you understand?"

"I guess so," Jaye answered quietly, pulling at the collar of his shirt.

"Is something wrong with your shirt?" The few belongings that Stella had sent along had been a few items of clothing that weren't much more than rags. Vic had taken Jaye to one of the busy general stores in Battleford and purchased some sturdy outfits for him that were suitable for their long journey.

"My neck itches."

"Here, let me help." Vic reached across to unbutton the top button of his shirt, but Jaye flinched back uncertainly. "I'm not going to hurt you, Jaye. Don't you know that?" Vic had noticed how he'd avoided contact with the general store owner, and the man's wife had ended up fitting Jaye's clothes for him. The boy hadn't allowed Vic to help him into his bedclothes the previous night, either.

Jaye continued looking at Vic uncertainly. Vic withdrew his hand, studying his son intently, then he was overcome with an enormous sadness. "Oh, Jaye," he said in a whisper, "what have they done to you?"

———————

Vic purchased a sturdy wagon for them from the livery. While the team was being hitched, he loaded their gear into the bed, and they left Battleford without delay. Now that he finally had his son, he wanted to get him home as soon as possible to begin their new life together.

Throughout the morning's ride, despite long periods of silence, Vic questioned his son about everything. There was so much Vic wanted to know about his life, but by midmorning there was only one issue he was leading up to.

"Have you had many friends, Jaye?"

"No."

"None?"

"Well . . . I think I had one, but I can't remember him very good."

"What was his name?"

Jaye was silent for a long time. "I don't remember."

"Do you remember anything about your mother? Fran?"

"No." He turned to Vic suddenly. "Why didn't you stay with her? Why couldn't we have been a family?"

Vic knew the question would have come out sooner or later, but he would have preferred later. "Well . . . that's a long story, Jaye. For now let's just say that it didn't work out that way. I'm sorry, but it didn't."

"Did you leave my mother for Megan?"

"No! It wasn't like that at all. I met Megan long after your mother and I . . . separated." Vic sighed, thinking, *Now or never, I suppose.* "You see, for whatever reason, your mother chose not to tell me about you. I know that probably doesn't make sense— it doesn't to me, either—but that was her decision. But when I *did* find out about you, I started looking at once. And now I've found you," he finished with a smile.

They rode in silence for a while. Vic wanted to give Jaye the time he needed to digest all this new information at his own pace. When Vic finally decided there would be no new questions coming, he said, "Jaye, I want to ask you one more thing. I know you don't remember friends, but what about Stella? Did she have friends? A man, perhaps? Sort of like a husband for a while?"

"Yes" came the answer quietly.

"Look at me, Jaye. Did he treat you and Stella nicely?"

The boy's head bobbed along with the movement of the wagon, but his gaze didn't waver. Vic saw a flash of something behind his chocolate brown eyes, then he answered in a voice so low that Vic could barely hear. "No."

"I'm sorry to hear that, son."

Jaye's lower lip began to tremble, and he looked away.

Vic was glad to finally see some emotion from him, though

he felt angry at what his son must have suffered. "Let's stop for a minute, what do you say? Stretch our legs for a bit."

Vic tied the horses to an aspen tree, then reached up to help Jaye from the wagon. Getting him in and out of the wagon had been the only times he'd been allowed to touch him, so Vic took his time, enjoying the brief moment of holding his son. Once he was on the ground, Jaye moved away.

"Let's take a walk," Vic said, and Jaye fell in step with him as they made a path through the tall grass. "Jaye, was he a bad man?"

"I don't wanna talk about him no more."

"We have to, son. I need to know about it."

"Why?"

"Because I'm your father, and in order for me to be a father to you, I have to find out how you've been treated. Now, was he a bad man?"

There was no response.

Vic touched his arm and squatted down in front of him face-to-face. "Tell me, Jaye. I promise you'll feel better if you tell me about it. Did he strike you?"

Jaye wouldn't meet his gaze, and took a half step back.

"Jaye?"

"Why are you askin' me this stuff?"

"Well, I've already told you that I—"

The boy walked a few steps away and kicked at a dirt clod. "I don't wanna talk about it no more."

Vic began to realize that he was probably asking too much of Jaye right now. If there was something in his past that needed to be dealt with, then Vic would have to let his son decide when he was ready to talk about it. The only thing he was accomplishing at the moment was to further alienate the boy. Vic stood and said in a careless tone, "What would *you* like to talk about then?"

"I dunno." He gave another clump of dirt a big kick, sending powdery granules into the sunshine.

"The fine art of kicking dirt perhaps?" Vic grinned.

A smile touched the corners of Jaye's mouth, but he didn't look up.

"Ah, a smile! I was beginning to wonder if your mouth could work that way."

Embarrassed, Jaye's smile turned into a full-fledged grin.

Vic went to him and ruffled his hair gently. "Come on. Let's have a few of those luscious apples we got this morning. You know, I do believe the color of those apples matches your face right now."

With a small giggle, Jaye quickly turned his blushing face away, then followed his father back to the wagon.

———

Jenny watched Dr. Phillippe Simone as he took the woman's pulse. His bedside manner was exquisite to the point of perfection, and from observing the comfort and care he brought to the patients, she frequently wished she could be a doctor. To bring so much relief to sick people must make a doctor feel great satisfaction in his work.

"Now, Mrs. Townsend," he was saying to the sick woman, "I want you up and around as much as possible. You need rest, I know, but I don't want all that nasty phlegm going into your chest if we can stop it. I'll come back and check on you in a couple of days, all right?"

Mrs. Townsend, like every other female who'd been under the doctor's care, smiled and batted her eyes at him. No matter how sick the patients were, they couldn't resist Phillippe's good looks and charm. They always seemed to manage a "batting" at him, as Jenny had privately come to call it.

Outside in the late afternoonsun, Phillippe loosened his tie and let out a long breath. "That is, if I have time," he muttered.

"What?"

"I said I'll be back if I have time. How many more to see today?"

Jenny looked down at the list of people Dirk had given her to go see how they were. "The Kirschners, they live over by the

Dawsons we saw yesterday. Sam Weems, he lives way out by the old Blood Indian encampment—"

Phillippe threw his bag behind the buckboard seat and cursed. "There's just too many, Jenny, and only one of me. I can't run all over the Territory to find these people."

Jenny had been waiting for this. Over the course of two days she'd taken him miles and miles to visit the sick, and she'd seen it wearing on him. She was tired, too, but he didn't seem to be accustomed to the traveling as she was.

Waving his hand and making a disgusted sound, Phillippe helped her into the wagon, then climbed up beside her. "I'm starved. Let's go get something to eat at that restaurant. What was the name of it?"

"The Bull's Head."

"How about it?"

Jenny hesitated. They hadn't dined out yet, since most of the families would feed them when they were hungry. But the last three places they'd been to had housed sole occupants, and they'd been too sick to offer a meal. But the Bull's Head was close to Fort Macleod, and she worried that she might accidentally run across Dirk.

"Jenny? Aren't you hungry?"

"Not really. I think I'll just go home if you're too tired to see anyone else for the day."

Phillippe's dark eyes bored into hers. "Nonsense, you've got to be just as hungry as I am. I've seen you eat more at one sitting than me." His eyes scanned down her petite frame quickly and efficiently. "For the life of me, I don't know where you put it all. You're as trim and pretty as a teenager."

I am a teenager, she thought with amusement. *Well, almost . . . just twenty.*

"Jenny, I'm wasting away from hunger as we speak—"

"All right, I'll go." Why should she be afraid of meeting Dirk accidentally? It was only a friendly dinner between a doctor and his "nurse." Besides, despite what she'd said, she was hungry.

The Bull's Head was almost deserted for a Friday night. There was a table filled with Mounties, but Dirk was not among them. It didn't matter even if he did walk in. Jenny knew word would get back to him from these men present. Every Mountie knew Dirk and Jenny had courted. *And why am I still worried about it?* she asked herself. A few of the policemen nodded to her when they caught her eye, then naturally they filed away the looks of the man she was with who casually held her arm while she sat down.

"Ah, it smells good in here," Phillippe said. Rubbing his hands together he asked, "What do you recommend?"

Jenny kept her head down, pretending to scan the one-page menu, aware that the Mounties were glancing over at them and whispering. Suddenly she didn't have an appetite. "Well, the mutton is really good, and of course the steak. They have a good beef stew also—"

"Mutton it is, since that was your first suggestion." Now Phillippe noticed the curious stares from the policemen, and nodded to them. "Gentlemen."

Two of them nodded back, but there was no return greeting.

"Well, that was less than cordial," he commented, and when his ebony eyes came to rest on Jenny they widened. "Oh, now I see! Your beau is a Mountie, right?"

"Yes, but that's not—"

"So that's why they're staring! To see who's stealing their friend's lady. The talk will be very interesting at the fort tonight, don't you think?"

Jenny didn't like the amused tone he was using and gave him a hard look.

"I'm sorry, Jenny, I don't mean to upset you. But you see, this dinner is very innocent—that's why I can make light of it. Would you like for me to go speak to them?"

"No, no. That's not necessary."

"Are you sure? I'd be happy to set things straight and save you any embarrassment later."

"No, thank you."

After Phillippe ordered the mutton, Jenny told Frank Twillinger, the owner, that she'd have a small steak.

"A *small* steak?" Twillinger asked in amazement. He was in his mid-fifties, with a pencil-thin mustache and bushy eyebrows. Frank had a strange way of holding himself stiff and slightly cockeyed, as if gravity affected him differently from anyone else. "Since when do you only have a small steak, Jenny? When I saw you come in, I was prepared to give you the largest steak in the kitchen."

"I'm not very hungry, Mr. Twillinger. How is Alicia?"

"She's fine. I consider myself a very lucky man, Jenny. Neither me nor my wife has this horrible flu, and my daughter and her newborn son are fine. Alicia has been driving us crazy ever since you had to shut down the school because of the sickness." He leaned down closer, and the smell of garlic was strong on his breath when he whispered, "Nothing against Megan, you understand, but you're Alicia's favorite teacher. She actually *misses* going to school!"

"That's nice, Mr. Twillinger. Let me introduce you to the new doctor—Phillippe Simone."

"Ah, the doctor!" Twillinger exclaimed, reaching for Phillippe's hand. "No, please don't get up. We've heard you were here, and we also hear you've been very busy visiting those who've come down sick."

"Word does get around this community, doesn't it?" Phillippe smiled.

"Oh, yeah. I remember once about . . . oh, six years ago, that a rumor started—"

"Mr. Twillinger?" Jenny interrupted carefully. "Dr. Simone is very hungry. We haven't had anything to eat since—"

"Of course!" Twillinger said. "I'm so sorry. I'll go get your meals right now. We've got to keep the doctor fed and healthy, eh?" He lurched off in his strange, sloping gait.

"If I hadn't interrupted him, he would have talked your ear off, and we'd never get anything to eat," Jenny explained.

"Thank you, Jenny. Taking care of me? Seeing that I don't starve to death?"

Jenny looked down at his hands clasped in front of himself, avoiding his eyes. Sometimes when he looked at her, as he was doing now, she felt as if he were inside her head, searching her thoughts, and finding exactly what he *expected* to find. It made her feel uncomfortable.

The Mounties at the table across from them prepared to leave. One of them—Jenny remembered the face but not the name—stopped to ask if she was all right, directing a scarcely disguised look of suspicion at Phillippe. After Jenny assured him that she was, introduced Phillippe, and explained their mission, he seemed to relax.

When they'd gone, Phillippe said, "It seems I've stumbled upon a particularly fierce fraternity here."

"They're lawmen," Jenny shrugged. "They're trained to notice things out of place or different. Naturally suspicious, I guess."

"Mm-hmm. Or naturally protective."

Twillinger came back a few minutes later carrying two plates heaped with food, but for once he didn't stay for idle gossip. Despite Phillippe's claim of being famished, he ate his food leisurely, carefully slicing into the mutton with surgeonlike precision. He even cut his boiled potatoes with the knife when he could have easily done it with the fork.

"So, Jenny," he said after taking a few bites, "tell me about yourself. Where you're from, your family . . ."

"I don't really like talking about my past, if you don't mind," she said as she sliced the large steak on her plate.

"Not even your family?"

"I don't . . . I don't have any family."

"None?" His fork stopped halfway to his mouth.

"I was raised by my father, who is dead. I never knew my mother."

"Jenny, I'm so sorry. Everyone should have *some* family to speak of." Phillippe chewed thoughtfully for a moment. "I have a multitude of aunts, uncles, and cousins. I wish I could loan some of them to you."

Jenny gave him a smile. "That's kind of you, but I have plenty of friends who keep me company."

"And one special Mountie?"

"Yes." The mention of Dirk made her wonder what sort of story he was hearing from the other Mounties by now. Surely one of them would have told him where she was and with whom. She just hoped they didn't embellish the story to the point of making him jealous.

Phillippe did most of the talking while they finished dinner. He had several amusing stories of people he'd treated over the years and told about some of his quirky relatives. When Twillinger cleared their table, he asked if they wanted coffee. Jenny declined, saying that she had to be getting home.

When they were outside, Phillippe said, "You know, Jenny, we live in the same boardinghouse. Maybe we could have that coffee when we get there?"

"No, thank you. I'm pretty tired. I think I'll just go on to my room and read."

Phillippe inclined his head. "As you wish." He offered his arm to help her into the wagon, but Jenny didn't take it.

"I think I'll walk, Phillippe. It's only a couple of blocks." She saw definite disappointment cross his features, then disappear quickly.

"In that case, I'll put the horse to bed and see you in the morning, bright and early."

"All right. And thank you for the dinner."

His white teeth gleamed in the night. "My pleasure, and thank *you* for the company and the mutton recommendation. It was excellent."

"Good night."

"Good night, Jenny."

On her walk she reflected on Phillippe Simone. Beneath the good looks and charm, the stylish manners and magnetism, Jenny sensed something more. *Dangerous*, she thought. *No, not*

149

dangerous, but something close to it.

The hoot of a distant owl startled her, and she quickened her step. "Who are you, Dr. Simone?" she whispered. "You've spent two full days with me, and now you want to spend the evenings with me, too?"

When she reached the steps of the boardinghouse, the owl hooted again. Quickly she climbed the steps with a shiver. She'd never liked the sound of owls in the night. They reminded her of funerals and graveyards for some reason.

"Hello, Jenny."

"Oh!" she cried, putting a hand to her heart. "Dirk, I didn't see you!"

He came out of the shadows at the end of the porch where the swing was. By the dim light thrown from the window he passed, she could see that he was in uniform, though the top two buttons of his tunic were unfastened, and he wore his easy grin. The scar that ran down his face glowed white.

"I didn't mean to scare you."

Jenny laughed softly with relief. "If I didn't know better, I'd say that was a lie. What are you doing here?" *Oh no, here come the questions. He's heard about the dinner, and he wants some answers.*

Dirk leaned down and kissed her cheek. "I haven't seen you in two days. Is that a good enough reason to be here?"

"Sure it is," Jenny answered quickly.

"Are you nervous about something? Is this a bad time?"

"No, just tired, I guess."

He touched her arm lightly. "How's it going with the good doctor? You two been all over the countryside?"

"Yes, it's been really hectic."

"And the doctor?"

"What about him?"

Dirk chuckled. "My, you're acting strange tonight. Are you getting along with him? Does he know what he's doing?"

Jenny searched his face, then asked, "What have you heard, Dirk?"

"Heard? What do you mean?"

"It was just dinner, nothing more. We were hungry, okay?"

"What in the world are you talking about?"

He really doesn't know, she realized, then she noticed the tired cast to his face and the dust on his trousers and boots. "Where have you been?"

"I had to take a prisoner across the border to the Americans. I just got back. Now, what's this about—"

Jenny smiled and shook her head. "It's nothing, but I'm sure you'll hear about it when you get back to the fort. Dr. Simone and I had dinner at the Bull's Head, and there was a table of your fellow Mounties there. You're probably in for some serious teasing tonight."

Dirk raised his arms and stretched, yawning hugely. "Is that all? For a minute there I thought you were going to tell me that he proposed to you."

"Of course not!" Jenny exclaimed, relieved that he was so understanding. She slipped beneath one of his arms and said, "I know someone who looks like he's about to drop, and here I am complaining about being tired. You're exhausted, Dirk. Why don't you go get some rest?"

"Trying to get rid of me?" he asked, then yawned again, and they both laughed. He kissed the top of her head and started down the steps. "I don't want to hear about you eloping with this handsome doctor I've heard about, Jenny Sweet."

"Get some sleep, Sergeant. You have nothing to worry about."

She watched him disappear into the night, reflecting that she'd been silly to think Dirk would misconstrue an innocent dinner with another man. He wasn't the jealous type.

Jenny took a long, hot bath and washed her hair in the bathroom at the end of the hall. It felt so good to have scrubbed the road grime from her body that she laid her head back and actually dozed off for a few minutes.

When she returned to her room, she found a note had been

pushed under the door. *Breakfast downstairs at seven sharp! Sweet dreams—doctor's orders. P.S.*

Phillippe's handwriting, like everything about him, was neat and masculine. Jenny smiled and said softly, "He's just a nice man. Why are you trying to read more into this, Jenny? He feels sorry for you because you don't have any family, and he's trying to be an uncle to you or something. Nothing more."

She tucked the note away in the drawer of her small bedside table. She didn't know why, but she wanted to keep it.

PART TWO

THE FIRST TIME

We shall not cease from exploration
And the end of all our exploring
Will be to arrive where we started
And know the place for the first time.

T. S. Eliot
Four Quartets

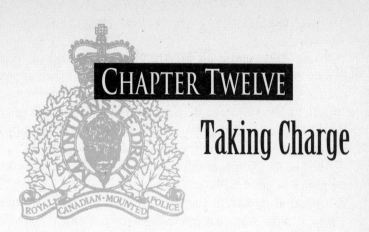

CHAPTER TWELVE

Taking Charge

"Cameron, you can't be serious!" Irene exclaimed as they drove their carriage through the town of Fort Macleod. "We can't live *here*!"

"It's just temporary, Irene. I've told you that." The major's tone was growing more gruff with her by the hour. He loved his wife dearly, but after four long days with her—and only her—in the carriage, his patience with her complaining was growing perilously thin.

Two little boys playing marbles on the boardwalk were the only human beings in sight. Cameron called out, "You there! Yes, you, the blond-headed boy. Where is everyone? This looks like a ghost town."

"Sick" came the shy answer.

"Sick? What do you mean?"

The boy pointed at the sign above his head that read:

I. G. BAKER STORE
CLOSED DUE TO FLU

Irene gasped. "Let's get out of here, Cameron! Right now."

Cursing softly under his breath, Cameron flicked the reins hard over the two horses' backs, and they doubled their speed.

"Cameron! What are you doing? Home is the other way!"

"Irene, I have a job to do here, and by thunder I'm going to do it! No one told me about any sickness before we left. If I'd have known, I wouldn't have allowed you to come."

"Allowed me? You *made* me come with you! And now look—we're going to get sick!"

Through gritted teeth Cameron told her, "We're *not* going to get sick! Now stop that infernal whining, woman!" He felt bad at once for losing his temper with her, but what he was really thinking was that she could be right—they definitely *could* get sick. Irene often struggled with colds in the spring, and here they were in a strange new area with all kinds of different species of vegetation. If she caught a cold and got worse . . .

He cursed again, louder this time, earning himself a disapproving look from Irene. He didn't care. Someone was going to pay for not informing him about this flu outbreak.

Fort Macleod came into sight. Irene let out another audible gasp but said nothing, thankfully. She knew how far she could push him, and once she reached the point where he raised his voice to her, she kept her mouth shut. He certainly didn't like yelling at her, but sometimes it had its advantages.

Cameron saw a flurry of activity at the gate as he crossed the small river. The sentries must have spotted his scarlet jacket from afar. *Good . . . maybe these men won't need much of my famous training.* Cameron liked things to go smoothly and by the book. In fact, he *insisted* upon it.

The activity at the gate of men scuttling about produced a tall officer who stepped forward from the crowd. Cameron liked the cut of his trim figure and the way he seemed to carry himself with a confident air. *By george, this might actually be a crack outfit, one that could carry my reputation further.* Feeling much better now that his duty post was in sight and seemed ready for his arrival, Cameron said, "Don't you worry, Irene, my dear. I'm going to set things straight around here and make you

156

comfortable. I can promise you that. And I think I'm looking right at the gentleman who'll help me do it."

———————

Hunter's nerves were raised another notch when he saw the look of his new commanding officer. If anyone seemed to have been born to wear a uniform and command men, it was him. Hunter was reminded of General George Armstrong Custer, whom he'd met before his untimely demise at the hands of Crazy Horse and three thousand Sioux and Cheyenne the previous year. Though Hunter hadn't liked Custer personally, he couldn't deny that the young general possessed the natural talent of leadership and demonstrated unquestioned bravery.

The new superintendent racing toward him in the carriage had a look on his face of almost maniacal anticipation, like a thirsty man in the desert finally reaching an oasis. What this meant, Hunter didn't know, but it gave him a strange feeling of uneasiness. He suddenly hoped he'd left the paper work he'd been responsible for in official shape, and all the quartermaster's manifests were in good order.

The woman in the carriage beside him was a rare beauty who was capable of lighting up a social room. The almond-shaped eyes were visible even from a distance. She held her parasol as if she'd carried it from birth. Her pale, oval face boasted perfect symmetrical features. Her eyes were on him, gauging in a cool, unattached way.

The carriage came to a stop in front of Hunter, and he had to choke back a cough from the cloud of dust it brought with it. The superintendent didn't seem to notice the discomfort he'd brought. Hunter saluted and said, "Welcome to Fort Macleod, sir, ma'am. My name is Sub-Inspector Hunter Stone. I've been Acting Superintendent since Superintendent Irvine left."

The man squinted at him. "Didn't they tell you my name, Stone?"

"No, sir. We didn't get that information."

"That figures," he muttered loud enough for Hunter to

hear. "I'm Major Cameron Briggs, and this is my wife, Irene."

"I'm glad to meet—"

"What's all this about a flu, Stone?"

"I'm sorry to inform the superin—"

"Major."

"Sir?"

"My official title is major, Stone. You and your men will do well to remember that in the very near future. Now, go on."

To Hunter's knowledge, there wasn't a rank of major in the North-West Mounted Police. What was that all about? "I'm sorry to inform the major that the epidemic is pretty bad here."

"Epidemic!" Cameron glanced at his wife in disbelief, and she fully mirrored his look of concern. "No one said anything about an epidemic."

"It hit pretty fast, sir. One of the first victims was the town doctor, and—"

"*Victims?* Are you telling me that people are *dying* from this flu?"

Hunter was already tired of being interrupted by this bullying man, and he'd only been talking to him for two minutes. *Give me strength, Lord*, he prayed quickly, visualizing the long days ahead with Briggs. "I'm afraid so. We did have a doctor come in from the East . . ." He trailed off when he saw that Briggs wasn't listening to him but was clambering down from the carriage, cursing audibly. Then he helped Mrs. Briggs down.

"Show us our quarters, Stone. I want to get Mrs. Briggs settled before we go to work and straighten this mess out."

"Yes, sir, right this way. The men who aren't on patrol duty have turned out on parade for you."

Cameron grunted and said irritably, "They'd better be in tiptop shape, Stone. I've got enough to worry about without having undisciplined troops."

Hunter was leading them, so Cameron couldn't see when he rolled his eyes and stifled a sigh. "If I may say so, since the major is British, he might be pleased to know that these troops were trained by a pretty good British Regular Army sergeant by the name of Stride."

"Well, you can't go wrong there, I suppose," Cameron grunted in reply.

The men were standing in ranks three deep, stiff at attention. Hunter was pleased to see that they looked sharp and fit. When they reached Sergeant Stride, he clicked his heels together and saluted crisply.

Hunter sincerely hoped that having a fellow British Regular Army man would appease Briggs, so he stopped them in front of him. "Major Briggs, I'd like to introduce Sergeant Preston Stride, formerly of the British Army."

"Ah, now here's a man in the know," Cameron said, obviously pleased. "Did you see any action, Stride?"

"Yes, sir!" Stride shouted in the traditional British way. "In New Zealand, the Second Maori War, the year of sixty-four, sir!"

"Excellent, Stride, excellent. I'm glad to know there's a man around here I can depend on without hesitation."

"Thank you, sir!"

Hunter ignored the barbed insult, intentional or not, and sneaked a glance at Mrs. Briggs. She was inspecting him with appraising eyes and met his gaze directly, then her violet-flecked eyes boldly moved down to his mouth and back again. He saw a mature beauty, definitely high-society, that would probably have a hard time adjusting to the rustic setting of Fort Macleod. A hint of a smile played at her full lips, and Hunter quickly brought his attention back to the major. He sensed a lurking danger in the woman's eyes.

"Africa was the place to be for Her Majesty in the sixties," Cameron was saying. "The Peshawar Valley, Bhutan, places like that for a man to cut his teeth on in battle."

Hunter concentrated on Cameron's balding spot at the crown of his head. The major barely reached Hunter's shoulder and Stride's chin. He looked like a schoolboy standing between the two of them. Still Hunter felt Mrs. Briggs' continued inspection of him and wondered just how bold this woman could be. He decided that he didn't want to find out.

Cameron began walking down the rank of men with Hunter and Stride following, nodding here and there, sometimes scowling. Watching the major's gait, Hunter was reminded of a peacock. Suddenly, Cameron stopped in front of a man and peered down at his feet.

"That's a poor excuse for a shine, son. Sergeant Stride, I proceed by the demerit system. Give this man one demerit." He peered directly into the face of the constable. "Nine more and I promise you there'll be a flogging."

Hunter had to bite his lip to keep from objecting. Flogging would be used only if the major could get through Hunter first.

Cameron turned to Stride and said, "I don't have time for a full inspection, Sergeant. Frankly, I'm afraid of what I'd find if I did. See to it that none of these other poor souls receive any demerits when I *do* have an inspection."

"Yes, sir!"

"Carry on." He turned to Hunter. "My quarters, Stone?"

"This way, Major."

They crossed the parade ground, passing by the twin nine-pound cannons.

"I trust these field pieces are in working order, Stone?"

"Yes, sir, though we've never had to use them." *And I certainly hope you're not thinking of using them.*

"But there are men trained to work them?"

"Yes, sir." Hunter was beginning to think Briggs could force a major conflict with a bunch of priests if he set his mind to it. He'd seen a few men like the major before: warlike in nature and always spoiling for a fight.

Irene Briggs spoke for the first time, surprising Hunter with her husky voice.

"Are there any other ladies around this area, Mr. Stone? At least some who aren't sick and taking care of ten children?"

"Yes, there are, and I'm happy to tell you that we've planned a special dinner for tonight in honor of your arrival. You'll meet a few ladies there." He stopped in front of the superintendent's quarters and waved a welcoming hand toward the door. "I hope you like your new home, Mrs. Briggs."

Cameron opened the door for her and then nearly ran into her as he followed. She'd stopped just inside the door and inspected herself in the Florentine gilt-wood mirror in the small hallway. "Very nice," she murmured.

Hunter didn't know if she was commenting on the mirror or herself. He wouldn't have been surprised at all if it were the latter. He said, "Commissioner Macleod used to occupy these quarters, and whenever his wife came out to join him, she added a few feminine touches."

"Quite unexpected," Irene said over her shoulder, and she sounded pleased.

Hunter followed them into the sitting area, where there was a mahogany sofa with matching chair and a fireplace across from them. Irene breezed straight through to the dining area and kitchen, then about-faced to inspect the bedroom.

Cameron went over to the fireplace to peer at the simple items on the mantel. "What's this, Stone? A painting of a buffalo hunt on bark?"

"Yes, one of the chiefs in the area made that for Commissioner Macleod. He was fascinated with the buffalo—their size and strength."

Cameron's eyebrows raised. "These Indians around here bring gifts?"

"Of course. They're a very kind people."

The major grunted but said nothing more.

Irene came back into the room and announced, "It's not really what I'm accustomed to, but I suppose it will do for a while."

Cameron smiled at her, the first show of kindness Hunter had seen from him.

"I'm glad you're satisfied, my dear."

"I didn't say 'satisfied,' I said it will do."

Hunter made a sidestep move toward the door. "Major, the dinner is planned for six o'clock, if that's all right."

Cameron gave a curt nod. "Where do you think you're going, Stone?"

"I wanted to give you and Mrs. Briggs time to get settled, sir."

"Have someone bring our things. My wife can 'get settled,' as you call it. You and I have work to do. Show me my office."

Hunter had hoped to get out of the man's presence for just a few minutes to collect his wits and prepare for the onslaught that Major Cameron Briggs was sure to bring about, but it wasn't to be. He was already beginning to dread the next few days he'd have to spend in close contact with Briggs.

———

Dirk was waiting at the gate for Reena and Megan when they arrived for the dinner. Reena wore a moss green dress with black buttons up the front and she carried a black fan. Megan had chosen a white dress with a large black bow at the hem.

"You both look fine tonight, ladies," he commented.

"Why, thank you, sir," Reena returned in a Southern accent while curtsying. "That makes it worth the trouble of struggling into this corset." She turned to Megan with a giggle. "That's what's so nice about being a missionary among the Indians—no corsets!"

"Reena, please, you're embarrassing our gallant Southern gentleman. Look at him blush."

"Oh, stop it, Dirk! You're just like one of the family here. Why are you blushing?"

"I . . . well, I wasn't aware that I *was* considered part of the family here, to be honest with you."

Reena flicked her fan shut and slapped him on the arm with it. "Of course you are, and you know it. I consider you on the scale of Liam, my own little brother. You're just not as obnoxious."

Dirk flashed an easy grin. "Maybe I should try harder."

"You'll do nothing of the kind," Megan stated, stepping up and putting her arm through his. "Now, show us to the dining room . . . or do you call it the wolf-down-your-food-in-a-manly-way room?"

Reena took Dirk's other arm. "Or how about the let's-surround-some-grub room?"

Dirk sighed and shook his head. "Speaking of surrounded, I'm surrounded and outnumbered here. And by the way, we're going to the officers' mess."

"Mess?" Megan grinned. "That sounds appropriate."

"Very," Reena agreed.

A shadow passed over Dirk's handsome face. "That word won't be used around here while Major Cameron Briggs is here. The boys have probably scrubbed the floors enough so that we could eat off of them."

"Is he a tough one, this Major Briggs?" Reena asked.

"Tough? He could probably make a Texas Ranger cry."

"That bad, huh?" Reena spotted Hunter making his way toward them from across the parade ground and wiggled her fingers at him. "Here comes another tough one. But he's *my* tough one."

"I think he's about ready to strangle the major after only one day with him," Dirk said. "Briggs has had Hunter showing him every square inch of this place, and then there's the matter of all the paper work Hunter's been struggling with. Briggs wanted to see every report since Hunter took over, from the commissioner on down to the cook."

Reena could tell from the tight line of Hunter's mouth that he was under stress. Nevertheless, he smiled when he reached them.

"A sight for sore eyes, ladies. Hello, Megan, how are you?"

"Fine, Hunter, thank you."

He tilted his head and gave her a sideways look. "I'll bet that's not quite true. I'd say you're probably pretty anxious for Vic to get home."

"Of course I am," Megan said, but her pleasant expression faltered. "It's just hard not knowing where he is or if he and the boy are all right."

"It must be incredibly hard, Megan," Hunter said gently. "I'm sorry I haven't had the time to come around and see you lately. It's been a little busy around here."

Megan waved a hand dismissively. "You don't have to apologize to me, Hunter. I know you've had a lot of pressure thrown on your shoulders. Besides, Dirk here has been a regular mother hen to me, stopping by almost every day."

"Well, I want Vic back very badly, too, but for more selfish reasons. It's going to take more than myself to handle that major. The man's a maniac about details and cleanliness and order. He's . . . well, I'll let you see for yourself. It's time to have our little dinner that I wish I hadn't planned."

Reena took his arm and said, "He sounds like a regular ogre from the way you and Dirk are talking."

"Draw your own conclusions during dinner."

The officers' mess was located next to where the enlisted men ate, but instead of wood stoves for heat, it had a large fireplace that had a modest fire blazing. A large portrait of Queen Victoria hung on the east wall, and staring back at her from the west wall was a painting of Commissioner Macleod, a handsome Scotsman with dark, piercing eyes that the artist had captured perfectly.

Megan noted the empty room and asked, "Are we early, or are they late?"

Hunter consulted his pocket watch. "Six straight up. But I'd say that knowing Mrs. Briggs, they'll be fashionably late to make a good entrance."

Reena rolled her eyes. "Oh no, not one of them."

"One of them," Hunter nodded.

"That should make you happy, Megan."

"My society days are over and you know it, Reena," Megan said stiffly as she stared at the queen's portrait. "My, she looks regal, doesn't she?"

Dirk moved over to her to consider the queen. "If you ask me, she looks like she's had a prune or two too many."

"Dirk! You can't say that about the queen!"

"Why not? I'm an irreverent American, and so are you. We can say anything we want."

Hunter cleared his throat. "I'd like to hear you say that in front of Major Briggs. And I believe that I'm not the only one in this room to swear to uphold the queen's laws in this great land."

"Swear to uphold her *laws*, not necessarily the queen." He glanced at the portrait again, and Reena saw his eyes take in the queen's extra weight. "Now, upholding the queen—*that* would be a tough job."

"What would be a tough job?" came a booming voice behind them.

They all spun around, and the first thing Reena noticed was the beauty at the major's side. She, too, was looking at Reena with undisguised scrutiny. When she finished, her bold gaze went to Megan and did the same.

Hunter made the introductions, and when he came to Dirk, Major Briggs raised an eyebrow. "You're the Sergeant Becker who loves his beauty sleep so much, eh?"

"He got in very late last night, Major, after a trip across the border," Hunter informed him. "When that happens, Commissioner Macleod made it a policy to let them get a full eight hours' sleep, regardless of how late in the morning—"

"That was a former superintendent of this fort," Briggs countered. "Granted, he's moved on to the highest office of this police unit, but now *I'm* in charge here, and that policy will be rescinded at once. Only the men who regularly rotate on night watch will be allowed to sleep past the hour of six A.M. Make a note of it, Stone, and post it on the parade ground board."

Megan and Reena exchanged glances that said, "This is going to be a very interesting time for our men, isn't it?" When Reena turned back to the Briggses she was startled to see that Mrs. Briggs had seen the looks, as evidenced by the tiniest of smiles tugging at the corner of her full mouth.

Major Briggs looked around the room. "Where's Sergeant Stride?"

"He had other duties to see to," Hunter answered. Waving to the head of the table he asked, "Would you like to sit down, sir?"

After helping Irene to her seat at the other end of the table, Major Briggs took his own, with Hunter and Reena on one side, Megan and Dirk on the other. Before Dirk could take his chair, Briggs said, "Go see about our food, Sergeant, my wife says she's famished."

"Yes, sir, right away."

"Hold on there! You're an American, are you not? A southerner, I believe?"

"Yes, sir. From Mississippi."

"Then were you in—? No, of course not, you're too young. I was about to ask if you saw action in the States' war. What a magnificent contest that was, eh?"

Dirk's face tightened, and his scar turned a shade more pale. "I wouldn't call it that, begging the Major's pardon. I'd call it an all-out tragedy."

"Of course you would. You were on the losing side. The 'Lost Cause,' I believe you call it?" Briggs waved a hand dismissively. "The food, Sergeant."

Reena saw Dirk hesitate as if he were about to say something else, then with a glance at Hunter he left. Reena was horrified at Major Briggs' insensitivity concerning a war that had taken hundreds of thousands of lives.

Briggs unfolded his cloth napkin and placed it in his lap, saying casually, "All those southern people are still tender about that war. Of course, I wouldn't know how they feel because I've never been on the losing side of a battle, much less a war."

Reena couldn't stop her tongue and saw from the corner of her eye as she spoke that Megan was right behind her. "I'll tell you how they feel, Major. Very sad, since almost every family lost a loved one—sometimes more than one—and many lost their homes and property, too. That young sergeant's father and brother were both killed at Yellow Tavern near the end of the war. Doesn't he have a right to be 'tender?'"

The silence that followed was thunderous. Briggs glared at Reena with ill-disguised anger for having been dressed down by a woman. Hunter looked as if he wanted to crawl under the table. Reena detested having a conflict with someone she'd just met, but Briggs' cavalier attitude about the American Civil War was inexcusable.

Irene Briggs clucked her tongue and said quietly, "My, we have a little temper, don't we?"

"I'm not angry, Mrs. Briggs. Not at all." Reena gave her a dazzling smile.

"What exactly is it that you do here, Reena?"

"I'm a missionary to the Blackfoot Indians."

"A missionary! But you're so young and pretty. You must mean that you help your husband in his work."

"I'm not married."

"Reena was called of God, Mrs. Briggs," Megan told her.

"Oh? What was she called?" Irene asked, then burst out laughing with a look at her husband, who dutifully laughed with her.

Reena felt her face burning but didn't reply.

"That's a very serious thing to be joking about, Mrs. Briggs," Megan said tightly. "Very serious."

"I'm sorry. I don't mean to offend I was just trying to ease a tense situation, that's all." Her gaze went to Hunter. "What about you, Mr. Stone? You're a quiet one."

"What about me?"

"*You're* not an American, are you?"

Reena took a sip of water to hide her outrage at the bold woman. The jab had been well placed and well executed. With one seemingly innocent question, Mrs. Briggs had excluded Reena, Megan, and Dirk from the table. Now it was only her, Hunter, and Major Briggs.

"I was born and raised in Canada, ma'am," Hunter replied.

"Ah, a native son! I was beginning to wonder if I was the only one who was actually Canadian around here. Now we have something in common. Isn't that nice?"

Oh, very nice, Reena mused. *And very nicely done, too, Mrs. Briggs.* She looked over at Megan, who seemed suitably impressed also. Megan knew the games better than anyone, but now it seemed she might have met her peer. She was glad when Dirk came back with six enlisted men carrying trays of food.

———

Hunter halfheartedly cut up some of his roast pork. The food was excellently prepared by the fort's cooks, so Hunter was sure they had worked hard to avoid Briggs' ire for as long as possible with the impressive menu and delicious food. Hunter would hate to tell them that their careful work was probably in vain. If the Major wanted to rain down on them, he'd find a reason, no matter how farfetched.

Major Briggs was prattling on at Dirk about some obscure battle in Africa in which he'd supposedly led his troops to a resounding victory. Hunter ignored him for the most part while pretending to listen, which was difficult, considering Briggs was right beside him making sweeping motions with his hands that came very close to Hunter's head.

The dinner wasn't going well at all—much worse than he'd even imagined. He'd known that Reena and Major Briggs would clash over the reservation idea for the Indians. The subject hadn't even been broached and they were already in adversarial positions. And Hunter sat right between them. How could he defend Reena and not be thought guilty of insubordination by Briggs?

For all his worries at the moment, his dinner tasted like paper in his dry mouth.

And then there was Mrs. Briggs. He caught her looking at him quite a few times, and she would try to show him a shy girl's smile. Suddenly it hit him that maybe she thought she was catching *him* looking at *her*. What a mess. It was no secret that she'd been flirting with him when she singled him out for questioning a few times. No secret except maybe to Major Briggs, who acted as if it were perfectly acceptable behavior at a crowded dinner table. What bothered Hunter the most was that she did it right across Reena, as if she weren't even there. Didn't she know that Reena was his love?

Dirk was doing his best to show interest in Briggs' pompous stories of his military glory, but Hunter knew he was still angry over the comments about his country. Hunter didn't blame him at all, but if he wanted to keep his sergeant's stripes, he'd better learn to dance lightly around this powerful officer. Beside Dirk, Megan ate in a silence that could only be explained as troubled.

"So, Mrs. Vickersham," Briggs said loudly, suddenly reversing gear, "I hear your husband has taken himself a little vacation to find his boy. That's a very touching story, but when can we expect him back? There's work to do around here."

Megan finished the bite of boiled carrots she was eating before she answered. "I'm expecting him, hopefully, around Thursday."

"Well, that's not so bad. He can jump right in there and be my right-hand man, since he's an Englishman, too."

The barbed insult at Hunter drew defense from the unlikeliest source.

"Now, Cameron, Mr. Stone has done a fantastic job of welcoming us and showing you around the fort today. Give him some credit, won't you?" Irene smiled sweetly at Hunter and said, "The major tends to overlook subordinates. I have to remind him sometimes."

Briggs took a big gulp of water and nodded. "You're right, my dear. My mind tends to go in all directions every once in a while." Turning to Hunter, he said in a much colder tone, "Good job today, Stone."

"Thank you, sir."

Irene looked pleased as she cut some more of her meat. "Mr. Stone, what's the situation with the Indian problem in the Territories?"

Reena perked up at once and threw a glance at Hunter.

"The situation is that there *isn't* an Indian problem." Hunter said. "The Blackfoot and Blood tribes are peaceful, as the rest of them are. Every once in a while we have a renegade who steals a cow or something, but that's rare. The Indians get along with the whites—and the Mounties as the authority over them—very easily."

Major Briggs wiped his mouth with his napkin and fixed Hunter with a condescending look. "I see I shall have to change your thinking for you, Stone. Much like the tribes I fought against in Africa, there are no honest Indians, only ones that haven't been caught at thievery or the murder of innocent people yet."

Reena gasped audibly. "Sir, that's not true! I've been around these people for almost five years now, and there's never been—"

"Young lady, I know your occupation forces you to defend these savages, but I really must remind you—"

"But, Major—"

"*Don't* interrupt me!" Briggs took a theatrical moment to gather himself, as if Reena had thrown mud on him rather than merely break into his oratory. "I must remind you, Miss O'Donnell, that I am the commanding officer of this region now. Therefore I will set the policy concerning the savages."

Hunter winced at the word, and Megan said icily, "We prefer to call them Indians, Major, not savages. They're a very intelligent people who don't deserve that name."

A forced smile cut across Briggs' face like a scimitar. "Thank you for the lesson in local etiquette, Mrs. Vickersham, but I'm perfectly capable and in the right to use whatever words I choose, despite what 'we' prefer. Now, these savages are to be handled—"

Suddenly, Reena stood and placed her napkin beside her plate. "If you'll excuse me, I don't feel very well."

Hunter and Dirk stood with her, but Major Briggs kept his seat.

Megan stood. "I don't, either. Reena, maybe you'd like to come to my house to lie down?"

"Thank you."

Hunter had no idea how to douse this particular fire. It went beyond rudeness, but then again so had the major. "Sir, I'd like to see the ladies out."

Briggs nodded curtly. "Good night, ladies. I'm sorry you'll miss dessert."

When the door closed behind him, Hunter had them both in his face.

"That imbecile! How could he—?"

"Hunter, that man should be in an asylum—!"

He held up his hands and said, "Whoa, let's get away from the door before he hears you."

Megan tossed her head haughtily. "I don't care if he hears me, he should be more—"

"Megan, you'd better care. He's your husband's new superior officer, and he seems the type who would make it very hard on Vic if you insult his pride, especially in front of officers. You know the type."

Megan stopped with a look of dawning comprehension. "Oh no, you're right! What have I done? Should I go back in and apologize, or should I . . . Hunter, what do I do?"

Shaking his head, Hunter advised her, "If you go back now while he's feeling insulted, he'll just be harder on you. No, just wait a day or two and send a letter of apology. Reena . . ."

"I know," she said resignedly, "I will, too."

"No, I was going to say you don't have to."

"Why not? I don't want him doubling your work load or making trouble for you, either."

"We're not married, Reena. And besides, he has his own special place prepared for me, I'm sure, since I made out the guest list." He grinned at them and was relieved to see that they still had a sense of humor. "Are you staying at Megan's tonight?"

"Yes."

"Good. I'll try to get away from that monster sometime in the morning and come see you. We've got to draw up a letter together to send to Commissioner Macleod. Remember?"

Reena smiled. "Oh, I remember all right. And that buffoon on the other side of that door makes it all the more pleasurable."

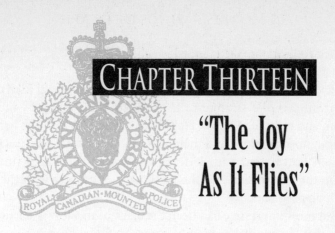

CHAPTER THIRTEEN

"The Joy As It Flies"

W e should be home tomorrow, Jaye," Vic told the youngster as they went zigzagging through some timber. The smell of wild strawberries and chokecherries permeated the stillness beneath the trees, causing Vic's mouth to water. But they were so close to home he didn't want to waste any time looking for them. The last few weeks had dragged, and he only wanted to be back at Megan's side and start being a family.

"Does Megan know we'll be there tomorrow?" Jaye asked.

"Why, no, I shouldn't think so. Why do you ask?"

"You mean we're just gonna surprise her?"

Vic laughed and asked, "What do you want us to do? Send smoke signals?"

Jaye's face brightened. "Do you know how to do that?"

"No, I was joking." During their time together on the trail, Vic had taken joy in passing along what he knew of nature to his son. *His son!* He still could scarcely believe he was a father. He could tell Jaye had led a mostly sheltered life with Stella, for all his curious questions only proved that he hadn't had the opportunity to get out and learn about God's beautiful world.

As they rode along, Vic taught Jaye about plants, flowers, birds, animals, and any other subject that came up.

Jaye saw his first prairie falcon, yellow warbler—he'd tried to imitate the bird's strange call, much to Vic's delight—blue heron, and red-tailed hawk. He'd been enthralled with the herd of pronghorn antelope and their wickedly sharp horns, the buck-toothed beaver that had skittered away from them at a small stream they'd crossed, and the small pack of coyotes with their small, yipping barks.

But most impressive had been the black bear. Vic was startled when they'd rounded a stand of aspens to find a bear in a small river only fifty yards away. When he reached for his rifle, Jaye, his eyes pleading, put his hand over Vic's before he could draw the weapon. Vic hesitated, testing the wind, and decided they were relatively safe being downwind of it. The fascination in his son's face as he'd studied the huge creature was worth more than money could buy.

Vic pointed out all the constellations he knew to Jaye when they'd lain awake at night. Those times were special for Vic as he got to know his son. It had been a perfect opportunity to tell his son about God and heaven and His incredible love and care. Jaye's young mind couldn't quite grasp all this, but it was a start that Vic would cherish and build on as the years went by. Indeed, Vic would hold the memory for the rest of his life.

"What do I have to do when I see her?" Jaye asked, breaking into Vic's thoughts.

"What do you mean?"

The small shoulders went up and down in a shrug. He was trying to be casual about the question, but Vic sensed that it was important.

"I mean, do I have to hug her? Or do I just shake her hand?"

"What do you want to do?"

Another shrug. "I dunno."

Covering a smile by rubbing his mouth, Vic answered, "I don't think you have to worry about it, because I think Megan will sweep you into her arms like you're her own."

"Really?"

"Yes. But that's only if you get to her before me, because she gives great hugs."

———

They stopped that night one more time, though Vic had been reluctant, since they were so close to home. But Jaye was obviously tired from their long journey, and Vic had to give the boy credit for showing surprising stamina for his age.

After a supper of prairie chicken and beans, they went for a walk in the late afternoon. Their camp was on a long, narrow ridge dotted with cottonwoods, the highest ground in sight. Vic always chose the high ground in preparation for one of the thunderstorms that seemed to develop out of nowhere on the plains. He knew God was watching out for them, because only one night had they had any rain, and it was only a light shower. Otherwise, the weather had been marvelous.

While they'd been eating, Vic had seen something from the ridge, and he led Jaye there now. "I've got a surprise for you, Jaye."

"What?"

"I can't tell you. I have to show you."

"Okay."

"But from here on, you have to be very quiet," Vic whispered. "Very, very quiet."

"Okay," Jaye whispered, all serious now.

"We're going to climb to the top of this little hill, but just before we get to the top, we're going to crawl and peep—very carefully peep—over the top. All right?"

Jaye nodded vigorously.

They began their short ascent, with Vic looking down at Jaye occasionally to put a finger to his lips. The boy was enjoying the game, but the prolonged anticipation was proving to be agonizing for him.

Finally they reached the crest and slowly raised their heads over the top. Vic heard Jaye's sharp intake of breath and looked

ALAN MORRIS / WINGS OF HEALING

over to see round, fascinated eyes.

Below them, only a hundred or so feet away, was a large, active prairie dog town. Interspersed among the scampering creatures busily gathering their supper was a herd of pronghorn antelope grazing on the rich grass. Also among them were meadowlarks and buntings, hopping here and there for insects. The scene, even though Vic had seen it before, was a picture of nature's tranquillity that he never tired of.

Vic whispered, "Quite a sight, eh?"

"Yeah!"

"All kinds of animals and insects are drawn to prairie dog towns."

"Why?"

"Well, they're constantly pruning the grass, making it the most delicious around for the antelope and buffaloes."

"*Buffaloes* like it here?"

"Oh yes, they love it. If you were very hungry and I offered you a biscuit or a nice juicy steak, which would you take?"

"The steak," Jaye said as he stared wide-eyed at all the activity among the prairie dogs.

"Animals are no different. They want what tastes the best, too."

Two of the prairie dogs had strayed nearer to their position, sniffing around busily for food. They both found something at the same time and had a short, intense brawl that was too quick for the eye to follow. When it was over, the winner was munching on the morsel while the other sat up on its hind legs and emitted a few guttural barks before continuing its search—this time a little farther away from the stronger one.

Jaye giggled into his hands. "They're cute! Can we take one home with us for a pet?"

"No, they don't make good pets. They're too wild. Besides, don't they look happy in their little town?"

"Yeah, I guess so."

"They tunnel underground and make little homes down there. The tunnels are very complex, and even though you can't see them, they're all over the place you're looking at right now."

"You mean it's like a bunch of little streets down there that go to every house?"

"Exactly like that."

"So they're kind of like people."

"Well, I wouldn't go so far—"

At that moment they heard a piping screech, and a small dog came charging out of one of the holes with a white-faced badger on his heels. All the other prairie dogs above ground gave out warning barks and chatters as they dove for the nearest hole. The antelope stirred uneasily at the commotion but weren't about to leave their good grazing spot for a minor fracas.

The prairie dog being chased gave it a valiant try, but the badger was almost upon it when they mercifully—for Jaye's sake—rounded the knoll and the kill was shielded from them.

"Awww!" Jaye wailed, frightening the antelope more. "Did that thing eat the little dog?"

"I don't know," Vic said. "Maybe it found another hole the badger couldn't squeeze into."

Jaye scowled. "You should have shot that badger."

"What for? He was only doing what's natural. A badger has to eat, too, you know. So do the hawks and coyotes—they like prairie dogs also. There's nothing wrong with it, Jaye. It's all part of God's program for nature."

"You mean God told that badger to eat that prairie dog?"

"He didn't *tell* him to, no. But He put it the badger's nature when He created him to like prairie dogs for supper."

Jaye thought about this for a long time—so long that Vic thought he might have forgotten about it. Then, in a low voice that was still filled with consternation, Jaye uttered, "I *still* hope the prairie dog got away."

————

"I don't know as I *asked* you atall," Stu Bryant said pointedly. "I believe I *told* you to come to my place and look after my missus and kids." He was a big man on a big horse, with threatening features and a snarl to his mouth.

In the wagon, Phillippe and Jenny looked up at him help-lessly. Phillippe didn't carry a gun, and Bryant's pistol was within easy reaching distance of the reins he was holding loosely. Phil-lippe rubbed a hand over his tired face. "Mr. Bryant, there are many people I have to see, and your place is fifteen miles away. I've got to see the people I'm closest to geographically rather than—"

"Geographically! What kinda doctor talk is that?" One leath-ery hand moved back to rest on his thigh, uncomfortably near the pistol. "My people are sick, and I want you to come see 'em. Now!"

Phillippe threw up his hands in disgust. "Very well—lead on, Mr. Bryant!"

Jenny hadn't seen Phillippe's anger yet and found it surpris-ingly petulant. "No, Doctor, we can't do that!" she whispered fiercely.

"Well, what do you want me to do, Jenny? Wait until he shoots me, *then* go?"

"Mr. Bryant," Jenny said in a calmer tone than she felt, "you've got to consider the other people around—some of them within a mile or two of where we sit—who haven't seen the doctor, either."

"I don't know them people, but I know my family, and they need help."

"You're being unreasonable, Mr. Bryant."

The big man cursed and pointed a gnarly finger at her. "You just keep your trap shut, little girl. This is between me and the Doc here."

Phillippe shook his head, his gaze straight ahead. "I don't believe this. Why can't everyone be in the same place?"

It took a moment for his rhetorical question to get through to Jenny, because when Bryant had pointed his finger at her and cursed, she'd had a horrible flashback to her father and fully expected Bryant to get down off his horse and begin raining blows on her head and face. With an effort she banished the vision from her mind. "What did you say?" she asked Phillippe.

He looked puzzled. "I said I wish everyone were in one place instead of spread out all over Canada."

"That's it! They can be in one place."

"Where?"

"The schoolhouse. It's large, it's heated, and it's close to town."

"Why, that's a wonderful idea, Jenny. If we could get the word out for the sick to come to *us* . . . Mr. Bryant, do you own a wagon?"

Bryant answered suspiciously, "Yeah."

"Then load your family into it and get to the schoolhouse in Fort Macleod."

"No, I done told you—you're comin' with me."

"No, I'm not!" Phillippe answered defiantly, surprising Jenny. "I've got a whole community to look after, not just your family. If you're going to shoot me, then that doesn't make a whole lot of sense, does it? Shooting the only doctor in town?" He picked up the reins and flicked them, then called over his shoulder, "The schoolhouse, Mr. Bryant! That's where I'll be."

Jenny expected Bryant to chase after them, but after a short distance, she looked back and saw that he was merely staring after them, his posture showing puzzlement.

Phillippe reached over and patted Jenny's knee, startling her. "That was a grand idea, Jenny. It'll keep us from crawling all over the countryside." His hand lingered after the pat for just a moment too long. She was about to remove his hand, when he withdrew it himself.

"We can't go back to the schoolhouse yet, Doctor. We need to—"

"When are you going to start calling me by my name, Jenny?"

"I don't . . . I'm not comfortable with that just yet. Now we have to stop by the Williamsons'. They have twin boys who might need treatment."

"Why can't we just go to the school?"

"Think about it, Doctor. The word's not out yet, and it'll take time for that to happen. I think I can get Dirk and some of the Mounties to help with that, though."

Phillippe looked at her with his cool, assessing blue eyes. "You think? I bet you could get young Mr. Becker to do just about anything you ask, hmmm?"

Jenny brushed a lock of hair out of her eyes and avoided his gaze. "Oh, I don't know about that."

"I do," he said softly. He reached over and moved the strand of hair back from her eyes that had fallen forward again. "I would if you were mine."

"Please, Doctor."

"Phillippe. Does your Mountie recite poetry to you? No? What a shame. One so young and pretty as you should hear a little poetry every day. I shall have to remedy that."

Jenny pointed and said, "Take this trail. The Williamson place is just around that bend."

> "He who binds to himself a joy
> Does the winged life destroy.
> But he who kisses the joy as it flies
> Lives in eternity's sunrise."

"Do you like that, Jenny?"

He suddenly seemed closer to her on the bench, though she hadn't noticed a shift in position. Jenny found that she couldn't tear her eyes away from his face. They were passing beneath a canopy of trees that caused shadows to quickly pass over his handsome features. Strangely, when his face was in shadow his smile seemed to be a leer, but in the sunshine it was just Phillippe. Jenny found the effect intriguing.

"Did you like the poem, Jenny?" he repeated.

Jenny's lips felt numb when she asked, "Who was the poet?"

His smile broadened. "So you *did* like it."

"Yes."

Phillippe leaned even closer. "Maybe I wrote it."

Breathless now, sure that he was going to try to kiss her and not knowing what her reaction would be, Jenny whispered, "Did you?"

The horses suddenly came to a halt, but Jenny hadn't seen him pull back on the reins. *How did he do that?* Now he was close enough where she could feel his breath on her lips.

A door slammed and someone called, "Jenny?" snapping her out of the moment. She looked up and found that the horses had stopped because they were practically on Jude Williamson's front porch.

"Jenny, that you?" Jude called out again.

"Yes, Mr. Williamson, it's me." She felt as if she'd been caught by her father sneaking her first kiss at sixteen and knew she was blushing terribly. "This is Dr. Simone, and we've come to see how you and your family are doing."

"Well, come on in! Just made up some coffee."

Phillippe kept his eyes on her as he helped her down from the wagon. "Remember, Jenny, 'he who kisses the joy as it flies.' "

"I'll remember," Jenny said softly. She felt almost dizzy as they climbed the porch steps.

———

"Well, it just don't make no sense to me," Del Dekko complained as he polished his saddle. "Our *saddles* got to be shiny? What for?"

Faron O'Donnell shook his head. "Never in me life have I heard a man complain so much as you, Dekko."

They sat outside the livery on benches in the early twilight. Usually that time of day found men lounging around, playing cards, gossiping—but not when they were under the watchful eye of Major Briggs. Most of the men were in their quarters polishing and shining like Del and Faron, while one group was going around and painting all the doors in sight a bright red.

"I ain't complainin'," Del continued. "I's just wonderin'."

Faron sighed. "When are ye goin' to learn, Dekko, that these military men have their own way of doin' things that us normal folk don't understand? All this scrubbin' and cleanin', maybe the major believes what someone said once, that Satan makes mischief for idle hands to do."

Del stopped polishing and squinted at him. "Who said that?"

"I don't remember."

"Why, that's the silliest thing I ever heard. I'm at my best when I'm idle. In fact, I'm downright cheerful when I'm idle."

"You ain't been cheerful since you left your mama, Dekko."

"Bah!" Del growled, waving him off. "You don't know nothin'. I tell ya, idle's good."

They kept at their work in sullen silence until Faron said, "Now, you take me for instance. If any one body's got the right to complain, it's me. Here I am, an old, one-armed man scrubbin' away on this here saddle like me life depended on it. I shoulda married me a nice woman to do all this for me."

Del made a pained face. "What woman in her right mind would have ya? You were a mountain man before you got shot and lost your arm, and mountain men are about as dependable as rattlesnakes. Nope, it's a good thing you didn't marry somebody and ruin their life."

"Well, that's a mighty fine thing to say!"

"But it's true, ain't it?"

Faron didn't bother to dispute it because he knew his friend was right.

"Say, Faron, did you get a look at His Majesty's wife? She'll catch your eye like a tin roof on a sunny day."

"Del, ye can't talk about another man's wife that way!"

"I's just admirin'! Nothin' wrong with that."

Faron leaned forward and whispered, "There's a rumor waftin' around that she's been eyeballin' Hunter."

"What!" Del slammed his polishing cloth onto the saddle and leaned back. "Well, it's official then. There's a yellow jacket in the outhouse."

"A what?"

"Trouble. We got a whole heap o' trouble here, mark my words. What with His Majesty tryin' to kill us all by workin' us to death, that flu's out there just waitin' to get us if he don't first, and now that hussy's set her cap for Hunter. Don't that strike you as trouble?"

"Well, when you put it that way . . ."

"Sure, it does. And that pretty-boy doctor takin' all o' Jenny's time from Becker—that's another fuse to a bomb. Not to mention that my buddy Vic might be lyin' out there on the prairie, dead as a peeled egg." Del paused and shook his head sadly. "I surely don't know how I get myself into these things."

"Do you wake up every mornin' with the weight of the world on your shoulders?" Faron demanded.

"Not *every* morning, but close."

"My stars, man, you've got no worries! The worst thing that might happen with all this work you're talkin' about is that ye might raise a blister on a finger. And you've already told me you've never been sick a day in your life, so ye don't have to worry about any flu. Why don't ye be thankful for what you've got?"

"No, now I'm depressed. Talkin' about all these problems has just plumb worn me out. I think I'll go to bed."

Faron looked at him incredulously. "It's seven o'clock in the evenin'! Ye just finished supper, for cryin' out loud!"

"Well, if His Majesty is gonna be comin' around at the crack of dawn to roust us out, that ain't too early. 'Sides, if I don't get my full share of sleep, I'm liable to wake up grumpy."

Faron shook his head in wonder. "There's somethin' wrong with you, Dekko. Somethin' very wrong."

183

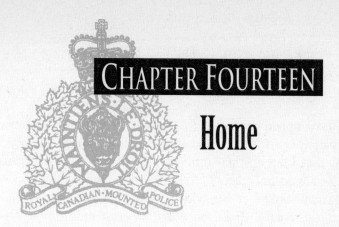

CHAPTER FOURTEEN

Home

Two days after the disastrous dinner with the Briggses, Megan and Reena had coffee on Megan's front porch. The morning was overcast and gray, with a definite threat of rain. The fort across the river was shrouded in a low fog, giving off the medieval effect of an ancient castle.

Because of the gloomy scenery, Megan had to double her prayers to fight off the depression she was struggling with daily now. It struck her as strange that she could be so dependent on another person when she'd been so *independent* her whole life. But she'd never felt for another like she did for Vic. She did know that in the future she'd fight with all of her being to keep him from leaving her for so long a period of time again.

Reena suddenly giggled beside her. "What is it?"

Pointing across Megan, Reena answered, "That squirrel over there. I think squirrels are so cute."

Megan looked over and saw a brown squirrel sitting up on its hind legs, vigorously chewing away at something. It watched them with black button eyes.

"Reena, when are you going back to your tribe?"

"Why? Are you trying to get rid of me?"

"Don't you worry about them when you're away for a few days?"

Reena sipped her coffee. "Not really. Why should I? They're completely self-sufficient and able to take care of themselves. I know they keep up their Bible studies while I'm gone because they've always got a list of questions for me when I get back."

Megan looked at her with a knowing smile. "You sound much too casual. I think you worry about them."

"Well, of course I worry about them some. They're like family to me. That's why this reservation talk makes me so angry. I can see putting Sitting Bull on one, but Plenty Trees? No."

Megan turned to see what the squirrel was doing, but it was gone. She did see something else, though. "Here comes Hunter."

"It's about time!" Reena declared with mock anger. "He snubbed me all day yesterday. Oh, I almost forgot," she said, rising from the chair, "I'll be right back."

"Where are you going?"

"To get what I forgot," Reena said over her shoulder as she went back into the house.

Megan shook her head and watched Hunter's approach. He took long strides through the now dissipating fog, a confident man who carried himself well. However, at the moment he had the look of a man who was preoccupied. Megan remembered when Reena was worrying about what to do if he asked for her hand in marriage and thought, *Give it to him, Reena. Give him your hand and never look back. He'll take care of you just as well as Vic takes care of me.*

Reena went back outside, and when Hunter heard the door slam, he looked up and waved. Megan looked down at what Reena was half hiding in her skirt. "What's that?"

"Oh, just a little something."

When Hunter was close enough he called, "You don't have

a lynching party in the house because I didn't make it yesterday, do you?"

"No," Reena said, "they're *behind* the house."

He removed his hat and sat down on the top porch step near Reena. "Good morning, Megan. Maybe I'll get a better welcome out of you."

"Good morning. You know you're welcome here anytime, despite what certain petulant young ladies say."

Reena tossed her head. "I've never been stood up before. I have a right to be petulant."

"Yes, you do," Hunter agreed, inclining his head, "and you have my deepest apologies."

"Thank you," Reena said at once, all traces of insolence gone. To Megan she asked, "There's nothing quite like a groveling man, is there?"

"Especially before breakfast."

"Kind of sets the tone for the day."

"Yes, it does."

Hunter hung his head. "I stand flogged at the stake."

"Since you're suitably humbled," Reena said lightly, producing the small gift-wrapped box, "happy birthday."

Hunter looked from her to the gift and back, perplexed. "It's my birthday?"

"No, yesterday was, but since you didn't show up . . ."

Megan, who was as surprised as Hunter, demanded, "Reena, why didn't you tell me? I would have gotten something for him."

"You've got enough on your mind, Megan, without having to rush around for a gift. Even I'd almost forgotten until I noticed a calendar in the general store the other day. Here, Hunter, take it."

He took the box, brushing the back of her hand lightly. "Isn't there supposed to be singing and bells tolling for this wonderful event in history?"

"The choir and bells were here yesterday. You weren't. You missed out, pardner."

Hunter inspected the box before opening it, and from the light in his slate-gray eyes, Megan was reminded of a small boy on Christmas morning. When he lifted the lid carefully and looked inside, he whispered, "Reena, you can't afford this."

Reena turned to Megan. "Is it just him, or does every man have to think about what a gift costs before he can enjoy it?"

"It's not just him—they've got to put a price tag on everything. What is it, Hunter? Let me see."

In a near state of reverence, Hunter lifted a sparkling gold pocket watch from the box.

Reena said, "I saw yours the other day, and I was surprised it still had a tick left in it. Then I saw this. . . ."

Hunter popped open the cover, still with a look of wonder on his face. "I can't wear this every day. It's too beautiful."

Megan said, "Now comes the part where he tells us how unworthy he is of it. Hunter, just say thank you!"

His face split into a broad grin as he gained his feet and gave Reena a delicate kiss. "Thank you, darling."

"You're welcome. Happy birthday."

Hunter withdrew his old watch, a bronze one with many dents and dirt in every cranny. Reena held out her hand. "Here, why don't you let me give that one a decent burial?"

"No, I'm going to give it to Del. He's always admired it."

"Well, I have to say that figures," Megan muttered.

Reena took Megan's coffee cup inside and returned with three fresh ones. Just as everyone sat down again, it began raining lightly.

"Where's your rain gear, Hunter?" Reena asked accusingly.

"Over there," he answered sheepishly, nodding toward the fort.

"A lot of good it's going to do you over there," she teased.

"I saw my chance to get away, and I took it. You two don't understand. Major Briggs is driving everyone crazy."

"Why wouldn't we understand?" Reena asked. "We couldn't even tolerate one dinner with him. I can't imagine having to live in the same general area and be under his authority. Did he say

188

anything after we left the other night?"

"Very little, but of course I could tell he was hopping mad. Then all day yesterday he kept me as busy as he could."

"Hunter, what about that order to put the Blackfoot on the reservation? Has he seen that yet?"

"Do you think if he had we wouldn't be rounding them up as we speak?" He sipped his coffee, and then one corner of his lip curled up in a sly smile. "Have you seen the superintendent's office? *Lots* of paper work."

"So where's the order?"

"I kind of buried it."

"Hunter! What do you think he'll do to you when he finds it?"

"The order stated that we have sixty days to get those Indians to the reservation, but then it didn't specify exactly where the land was! I think the order was just thought up by some politician who had a lot of time on his hands and dreamed this up without any sort of plan at all."

"I certainly hope so," Megan said with feeling. "Why doesn't someone come out here and see for themselves that the Blackfoot are peaceful?"

Hunter shrugged. "Your guess is as good as mine."

"That reminds me," Reena said. "I wrote that letter to Commissioner Macleod yesterday. You can add whatever you want and sign it."

Megan sighed. "And I've got that heartfelt apology to the major and his wife."

"Good," Hunter nodded. "I know it's not fair, Megan, but it's the right thing to do for Vic."

"It just seems so—" Megan stopped, suddenly not able to breathe. With trembling hands she placed her coffee cup on the tray between herself and Reena without taking her eyes from what she was seeing. Was she really seeing it?

"Megan? What's wrong?" Reena asked.

Through the misty rain and the sheen of tears that was forming in her eyes, Megan saw a wagon with two occupants emerge from around the west side of the fort. They both wore black slickers, but one of them was very small. Through the ringing in her ears she heard Reena ask again, "Megan? Are you all right?" and then she vaguely heard Hunter laugh out loud.

"Look over there, Reena," he told her.

Megan got up out of her chair on shaky knees.

Reena grabbed her arm to support her, then whispered, "Praise God, Megan. They're home!"

"There it is, Jaye. Your new home."

"There's people on the porch."

Vic squinted through the misty rain. "Indeed there are. Your eyesight is amazing, son."

"Who are they?" Apprehension had crept into the boy's tone.

"I'm sure Megan is one of them. What's wrong?"

Jaye looked incredibly small in the adult slicker. Vic had sliced the bottom half off of it, but that had still left Jaye looking as if he were wearing a tent. So Vic had tied knots in the back to make the slicker better conform to the small body. The only thing Vic couldn't fix had been the hood. Jaye looked like a tiny version of the Grim Reaper with the hood falling well forward of his face.

"They're waving," Jaye said in a small voice. "How did they recognize us?"

Vic's heart leaped toward his throat. *Home.* "I'd say it has something to do with the small person riding beside me and that star on my horse's nose. It looks exactly like a cross." Vic could feel excitement and anticipation humming through his body. "Are you ready, son?"

"I guess" came the glum answer.

"What's wrong?"

Jaye shrugged unexcitedly.

"Is it the other people? There are only two of them, and

they're probably the ones who will be your aunt and uncle. Don't you want to meet them?"

"Is that Aunt Reena you told me about? The missionary?"

Vic looked again to make sure it really was Reena and not Jenny. "Yes, that's her. I'm sure she's very anxious to meet you, along with my friend Hunter." Vic had talked to Jaye a lot about Reena, since she was so good with little children.

This seemed to convince him, because he looked at Vic with more confidence and said, "I'm ready."

"That's my boy."

Vic could see Megan clearly now, arms wide open and white teeth gleaming. She was a beautiful sight.

When they made it to the yard, the rain had picked up, but Megan apparently didn't care. She danced down the steps of the porch despite loud protests from Reena, reached Vic before he could even get down, and began tugging at him. "Megan, wait!" Vic cried through his laughter. He jumped down from the wagon and almost came down right on top of her.

Megan threw her arms around his neck and pulled him down to her, planting kiss after kiss all over his face, both laughing and crying at the same time.

"Megan, you're getting all wet!"

"I don't care!" she said between kisses. "You're home, and that's all I care about. Oh, I've missed you!"

Over her head, Vic grinned at Hunter and Reena. Hunter came down the steps, snapping off a casual salute, then motioned behind Vic. "I see you've got a partner. I'll help him down."

"Oh, my goodness!" Megan said, turning to look at Jaye as he sat quietly. "We've got to get him out of this rain."

Hunter reached the boy and said something to him, then held out his arms to help him down. Jaye didn't move and looked uncertainly at Vic. "Go back to the porch," he told Megan, "and I'll get him."

Vic shook Hunter's hand firmly, saying, "Good to see you, my friend. Don't mind the boy. He's still a bit skittish around strangers."

"Fair enough. From what I can see under that hood, he sure is a handsome little fellow. Good thing he doesn't look a bit like you."

Vic laughed and brought Jaye down from the wagon. Taking his hand he leaned down and said, "Don't be nervous, son. They're your family now." Together the three of them went to the porch. Vic greeted Reena with a hug, then turned to Megan as he began pulling the slicker off of Jaye. "Megan, my dear, may I present young Master Jaye Vickersham?"

Megan stood with her hands clasped in front of her, green eyes shining with pleasure. When Jaye was fully revealed, looking up at her shyly, her face softened and she said, "Hello, Jaye. You look just like your father—very handsome."

When Jaye didn't respond, Vic gave him a nudge. "What do you say, son?"

"Thank you," Jaye said, barely above a whisper.

Megan leaned down and held out her hand. "I'll bet you're pretty shy right now about hugs, but would you shake my hand?"

Jaye looked up at Vic, who nodded encouragingly, and then Jaye surprised them all by going into Megan's arms. He didn't wrap his arms around her, but he allowed her to hug him. Megan looked up at Vic with a sheen of tears in her eyes as she squeezed the boy. Jaye stepped back after only a moment to stand by Vic again.

Hunter said, "It looks like you two could use a change of clothes. I'll bring in your gear and take care of the horses."

"Thanks, Hunter," Vic said.

"But first I'd like to shake the little man's hand. My name's Hunter, Master Jaye. Welcome home."

Jaye tentatively shook his hand. "Thank you."

"And this beautiful lady here is your aunt Reena."

Reena took Jaye's hand, smiling warmly. "Hello, Jaye. Why don't you come inside, and I'll fix you a nice big breakfast while your silly mother dries herself off? Would you like that?"

"Yes."

"Good. Come with me."

Jaye cast an uncertain look at Vic over his shoulder as Reena led him inside. Vic nodded at him. "I'll be along in a minute. It's all right."

Megan moved into his arms and sighed contentedly when they were inside. "He's wonderful, Vic. I can't wait to get to know him."

"He's quite a boy." He tilted her face up to him with a finger under her chin. "And I can't wait to get to know you again. It seems like I've been gone for a year."

"Then let's get started, Mr. Vickersham," she purred as she raised her lips to his.

———

Megan felt much better after she'd dried her hair and changed out of her wet clothes. She did it in a hurry because she wanted to get in the kitchen and help make Jaye his breakfast. When Reena had offered, Megan had felt a moment of resentment—that was supposed to be Megan's job. But while changing clothes she could hear Reena talking to him in her easy way, and Megan reflected that she probably would have made Jaye uncomfortable from her own nervousness. Now she was glad that Reena and Hunter had been here when Vic and Jaye had arrived.

Brushing her hair at the dressing table, Megan smiled to herself. The boy looked exactly like Vic did when he was a young boy—she was sure of it. Straight, narrow nose, sharp chin, high, well-defined cheekbones—Megan didn't know what Jaye's mother had looked like, but she saw no one but Vic in the boy's face. "A little miniature of my husband around the house," she pondered out loud to her reflection. "What more could I ask for?"

She hurriedly put her hair in a bun and went into the kitchen. Reena was at the stove turning the bacon in an iron skillet, her back to Jaye, chattering about some of the games the Indian children played. Jaye, Megan found to her horror, was grinding pepper onto the dining room table into a large, neat pile.

"Jaye, no!" she ordered, knowing at once she'd spoken too harshly.

Jaye jerked back in his chair, dropping the pepper mill into the mess, scattering pepper onto the floor. His eyes were round and alarmed, and when Megan came toward him to begin cleaning up, he flinched away from her.

"Megan, I'm sorry," Reena said, "I wasn't paying attention—"

"Never mind. It'll clean up." To Jaye she said, "It's okay. You don't have to be afraid of me. I just spoke too loudly, that's all."

He continued to watch her uncertainly while Megan got a towel to wipe up. At that moment, Vic came in and asked, "What happened?"

A small accusing finger pointed toward Megan. "She yelled at me."

"I didn't yell at you, Jaye, I just—"

"She did," Jaye told Vic defensively. "She yelled at me."

Vic began helping Megan clean up the spilled pepper. "Even if she did, I'm sure she didn't mean to frighten you."

Megan looked up at him as she swept pepper over the edge of the table into her hand. "I *didn't* yell at him, Vic. I spoke sharply to get him to stop what he was doing, which was this."

"All right. No harm done. Jaye, would you apologize to Megan for making a mess?"

He continued staring at the tabletop when he uttered a "Sorry," which was barely heard.

"Now, you can do better than that, I know. Try again."

"I'm sorry, Megan."

"Apology accepted, young man. And I'm sorry I barked at you."

A shy smile came to Jaye's lips.

Vic patted him on the back. "Come on, pepper boy. Let's get you into some dry clothes before we eat."

Megan began setting the table and said quietly to Reena, "I hope he's not that sensitive all the time."

"He's got a lot of adjusting to do, Megan. You have to be patient with him."

"I know . . . but who's going to be patient with me?"

Reena set the plate of bacon on the table. "How about your husband? Won't he do?"

"Yes, you're right," Megan nodded. "I suppose he's in the worst position of the three of us. He's already had some time to adjust to Jaye and get to know him. Now Vic's going to be caught in the middle, so to speak, isn't he?"

"Don't let that happen, Megan," Reena said. "This is no place for choosing up sides, especially with you on one side and little Jaye on the other."

"I don't plan on that happening," Megan returned, more abruptly than she'd intended. Reena was only looking out for their best interests. "I'm sorry, Reena, I didn't mean to snap."

Reena placed a hand on her arm. "Just relax, sis. Make Jaye think that it's the most natural thing in the world for him to waltz in here and call it home. Go out of your way to make that happen, and things will become more natural and normal sooner than you think."

Megan smiled weakly. "How did you get to be so smart?"

"Among the Blackfoot, when the parents of a child die, a relative takes him in, no questions asked. I've seen it happen, and I know it's difficult. Just be glad you don't have any other children to throw into the situation. There's where the *real* problems start."

They finished setting the plates, silverware, and food on the table and sat down to wait. Megan couldn't help thinking that she'd already failed with Jaye, and he'd only been here for half an hour. Nervously she worried how things were going to work out.

"Megan, you'll do fine!" Reena whispered. "Do you want to know the most important thing to remember about children?"

"What?"

"It's ridiculously easy."

"So stop teasing me and tell me!" Megan grinned.

"They just want to know that they're loved, no matter what. That's it. Everything else just falls into place."

Megan heard heavy boots coming toward the kitchen. It seemed too simple, really. Just love them? If her sister was right, Megan would have no problems at all. Feeling a new surge of confidence, she nodded firmly and told Reena, "I can do that."

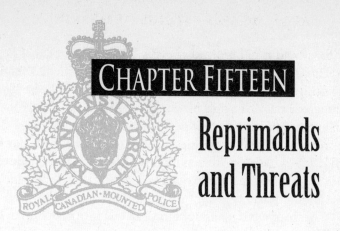

CHAPTER FIFTEEN

Reprimands and Threats

With the Mounties posting notices on the main roads and the message being passed by word of mouth, it didn't take long for news of the makeshift hospital at the schoolhouse to spread. The response was immediate and overwhelming. Sick families came in droves. Most of them were so weak it took all their strength just to make the trip to town. As they arrived, the lack of bedding and food became apparent, prompting Dirk and Jenny to go to Major Briggs and beg for help. To everyone's surprise, Briggs was remarkably sympathetic and ordered two wagons of supplies to be sent to the school. He also instructed Dirk to take five men with him to help get things in order.

Dirk drove one wagon with Jenny, while Duke Dillard and four other men followed in the other. Dirk was looking forward to finally meeting his "rival," as his pals called Dr. Phillippe Simone. Jenny fidgeted nervously beside him, and he wondered if it was because of that coming meeting. She'd been right about the amount of grief he'd endured at the hands of the men who'd seen her and Simone in the restaurant. Dirk was sure there was a great deal of embellishment thrown in, such as the "fact" that

Simone would take her hand at every opportunity, or that he'd even kissed her a few times. He'd laughed along with his friends, but nothing could stop the nagging, persistent doubt of *What if it's partly true?* Shaking off the thought, he asked, "How is Dr. Simone adjusting to fifty new patients all at once?"

"Fifty-seven and counting," Jenny corrected with a wry smile. "And we're both having trouble adjusting. I never thought so many people would come, and now the school doesn't look nearly as roomy as I thought it did."

"What happens if it fills up? How can you turn people away?"

"We can't. I guess we'd just have to set up tents outside."

He looked at her. "Is that wise?"

"What else can we do?" she asked, shrugging her shoulders.

Noticing the dark circles under her eyes, he said, "You look tired, Jenny. How much sleep have you gotten lately?"

"It's not the lack of sleep. It's being on my feet all day and night. I'm not used to it."

"Well, the boys and I can take some of that responsibility off of you. I'm not much of a cook, but I can sure boil soup and wash linens. How is the doctor treating these people?"

"He brought some sort of elixir with him from Summerton, which he's already almost out of. He sent Moss Gable to Fort Benton to see if he could find some more of it."

"Does the elixir seem to help?"

"It helps the coughing and fever a little bit, but this flu is pretty vicious—it doesn't help for long."

Casually, Dirk asked, "And how's the doctor treating you?"

"What does that mean?"

"I mean besides working you to death."

"He doesn't work me to death. I volunteered to do this. What have you heard now, Dirk?" Jenny asked. "That we were kissing on the porch swing?"

"Of course not! I haven't heard anything. I was just asking how you and Simone are getting along."

"Fine, thank you."

Dirk flicked the reins over the horse's back to speed her up.

This wasn't going as planned, and he didn't like his own feeling of suspicion. He and Jenny weren't engaged. He had no hold over her. But even though there'd been no talk of the future, he'd been under the impression—which he'd thought was mutual—that somehow they were meant to be together. It still disturbed him that Jenny hadn't learned to trust God. He'd prayed a lot about their relationship, but he hadn't sensed that God was telling him to break away from her. Jenny had had absolutely no Christian role model in all of her first seventeen years, and he wanted to show her the love and grace of God.

But why was she being so defensive about Dr. Simone? "Jenny, is there something I should know here?" She looked at him, and he saw a vulnerability in her face that he hadn't witnessed in a long time.

"I'm sorry, Dirk. I didn't mean to snap at you. I'm just tired, and I haven't . . . I haven't had time to even *think*—"

He reached over and patted her hand. "I understand. The first thing I'm going to do is have a talk with this doctor and tell him to give you some rest."

"Oh no, there's too much to do," Jenny protested.

"One day, Jenny, that's all I'm talking about. Take a walk in the woods, go fishing, take a ride, do anything but tend to sick people for just one day. Clear your head and come back fresh."

Jenny took a deep breath and let it out slowly. "Maybe in a few days when everything's—"

"Tomorrow," Dirk said firmly.

"But I've got to—"

"Tomorrow."

Jenny shook her head in an attempt to show exasperation, but he could see from her smile that she was pleased. "All right. All right. Tomorrow."

The mood had changed for the better between them, and they chatted about things that had nothing to do with sickness and death. When they reached the school, Dirk was shocked— though he knew he shouldn't have been—at the number of wagons parked on the south side of the school. "Where are the horses?"

"Sam Gatewood over at the livery made a corral for them out of rope in back of his place. That's another thing we're going to run short of—oats."

Dirk stopped the wagon in front of the school and helped Jenny down. She said, "Do you want to come inside and meet Dr. Simone?"

He hesitated, then said, "Sure." After he told Duke and the others to start unloading the supplies, he followed her up the steps and inside. The sour smell of boiled cabbage was strong, with the underlying aroma of chicken. Then his eyes adjusted from the sunlight and he was appalled at what he saw.

Lining both sides of the long room were cots of sick people. Some were merely lying on blankets on the floor. A few women, apparently healthy, flitted among the patients with water, soup, or wet towels. The four wood-burning stoves were all going, three of them with boiling pots of soup or broth steaming away. At the other end of the building a baby was crying, but otherwise it was unearthly quiet for a room so crowded with people.

A man spotted them from beside one of the beds and began making his way toward them. Jenny didn't have to tell Dirk who he was. It was obvious from the man's dark good looks and winning smile.

"A Mountie to the rescue," he said and touched Jenny's arm. "My dear, you've saved the day." He held out his hand to Dirk. "Dr. Phillippe Simone."

Dirk took his hand, which was surprisingly small. "Sergeant Dirk Becker."

"Ah yes, Jenny's spoken of you." He looked around Dirk toward the door. "No offense, Sergeant Becker, but are you the only one they sent?"

"I have five men outside unloading some things I'm sure you need. It's just a matter of where you want them put."

"Excellent! Things that can be stored can go in the shed out back. The perishables need to be brought in."

"I'll see to it."

Phillippe's eyes raked across Dirk's broad frame. "I'll bet you will. You seem to be a very capable young man and so young to be an officer."

Dirk didn't know what to say, so he merely inclined his head.

"Is there some great deed in your past that caused a promotion?"

He's toying with me. "We're both busy men, Doctor. Why don't we go about our business and help these people?"

Clucking his tongue, Phillippe said, "Such a modest young man! We'll just save the story for later, shall we?"

Dirk turned to go back outside. "I'll let Jenny tell it if she wants to." He knew she wouldn't, because the whiskey trader had been her own crazed father, who'd been killed in a massive explosion caused by the drink he peddled. It gave Dirk a small bit of satisfaction, however small the victory, to know that Simone wouldn't hear the story.

His pleasure was short lived, because he was fuming by the time he stepped out into the bright sunshine. Simone had been mocking him. If that didn't mean he was going after Jenny, nothing did. And why did he refer to Dirk's age three times? Was that supposed to demean Dirk in her eyes?

He stopped halfway down the steps, tempted to go back inside and somehow one-up the arrogant doctor. But that was childish thinking, and there were more important things going on here than his love for Jenny. Besides, maybe he was just imagining Simone's antagonistic approach.

But as the day wore on, Dirk became convinced that a challenge had been issued, as surely as if he'd been struck in the face with a gauntlet.

———

Blue Bear secretly watched from a few feet away as the news was given to the missionary woman, Reena. Her pretty face blanched, and a hand went to her throat.

"Oh no! Who?"

201

Raindrop said, "There are many sick. Some of the children, too."

Reena's hand went from her throat to her forehead, and Blue Bear thought she was going to faint. He'd been feeling smugly satisfied that the news hit her so hard. After all, it was the white man who'd brought this sickness, just as they'd brought small-pox, which had decimated Blue Bear's people twenty years before.

But it wasn't Reena's fault, he didn't think. She was the only white person who truly seemed to care for the Blackfoot, so he put aside his pleasure at her response and moved away. His anger—carefully nurtured and smoldering—didn't leave him, however. Ever since the horses his tribe rightfully owned had been taken away and given back to the Americans who'd stolen them in the first place, he'd felt shamed and ridiculed, as if people were laughing at him behind his back.

Then Stone Man, the one who'd ordered him to give back the horses, had come with the news that they were to move to a reservation. A reservation! Blue Bear believed that those places were only meant for the lowly, trouble-making tribes like the Sioux and Apache. Never would he submit to that dishonor!

And now the white man's sickness had come again. More of his people could die simply because they wouldn't be left alone by the intruding whites. Something had to be done to strike back for these wrongdoings.

And Blue Bear knew what to do.

———————

"Is this really necessary, Hunter?" Vic asked as they neared Major Briggs' office. "Couldn't I just hide out until he's gone?"

"Shrug it off, Vic. I think out of all of us, you'll get along with him better than anyone."

"Thank you so much, old boy," Vic returned with a pained look. "After you've told me about the wretchedness of the man, you say I'll be the one to get along with him..Lovely."

Hunter grinned and said, "You know, I take that back. He

seems to want to adopt Sergeant Stride."

"That sounds like a match made in heaven."

Hunter's smile faded as he considered what was coming. "What I'm worried about is why he's called me in. What did I do now?"

Vic looked at him. "Mighty strange talk coming from you. On the defensive, are we?"

"I believe I became his pet whipping boy after that disastrous dinner when Megan and Reena walked out. Lucky me."

To get to Briggs' office they had to go through the small library. Just as they reached the library door, it opened to reveal Irene Briggs. She wore a bright blue day dress with small pink floral-print bodice and skirt that suited her perfectly.

"Ah, Mr. Stone," she said, "so good to see you again."

"And you, Mrs. Briggs."

The penetrating green eyes turned on Vic. "And you must be the lost Mountie. We were beginning to wonder if you'd ever turn up."

"Jaye Eliot Vickersham at your service, madam." Vic took the daintily offered hand and squeezed lightly.

"My pleasure," Irene murmured. Turning back to Hunter she said, "I hope I've put out the fire for you somewhat with my husband. You came close to finding your head perched on a pike."

Hunter could tell this amused her. "What happened?"

"Now, you don't expect me to let the cat out of the bag, do you? It wouldn't be fair to steal my husband's thunder, either. I'll let you two gentlemen go. I know how anxious the major is to see you both." With a brilliant smile she passed by them, leaving a trace of sweet perfume in her wake.

When they stepped into the library Vic commented, "Good heavens, that was frightening."

"Very. I'd hate to get on her bad side."

"By the way she was looking at you, I'd say that's almost impossible."

"Don't try throwing *that* albatross around my neck along with everything else."

Vic raised his eyebrows. "She's a very pretty lady."

"I saw beauty the first time I met her. Now all I see is a gigantic warning sign."

"It's a pity how cynical you've gotten, Hunter."

"Just wait. Pretty soon we'll be able to start a cynical society around here, and I wouldn't be surprised if you were voted chairman."

"If I were a betting man, I'd take that wager." Vic stopped in front of the major's door and motioned toward it with a gracious nod of his head and tiny smile. "Be my guest. It's your funeral."

"Boy, I sure did miss you while you were gone," Hunter said sarcastically, then banged on the door with his fist.

"Come!" barked the major.

They opened the door to find Major Briggs behind his desk, wearing spectacles and writing. He didn't even look up.

Hunter cut a glance over to Vic, then said, "Sir, Sub-Inspectors Stone and Vickersham reporting as ordered."

Major Briggs continued with his scribbling as if they weren't even there.

Hunter asked a quick prayer of forgiveness for the contempt he was feeling for the arrogant, self-important little man. Briggs was from the British school of thought that respect was gained by ruling with a cruel iron fist. Hunter knew that it was only achieved in leading by example.

Finally Briggs finished the letter with a flourishing signature. Removing his glasses, he stood and looked at them for the first time. "So here they are! The lost little white sheep"—he looked at Vic—"and the bad little black sheep," he finished, turning to Hunter. "Be seated, gentlemen."

Hunter was fairly sure they were told to sit down because they both towered over Briggs, who remained standing with his hands clasped behind his back and looked down his broad nose at them.

"You'll pardon my finishing that urgent document before greeting you, but I felt it needed my immediate attention. Do you want to know what it is, Stone?"

Hunter hesitated, surprised at the question. "That would be at the major's discretion, sir."

"It's your official reprimand, Stone. It goes directly into your personnel file, never to leave."

Out of the corner of his eye, Hunter saw Vic look at him in shock. He clenched his jaw and willed himself to remain calm. "What am I being reprimanded for, Major?"

"This." Briggs reached down and plucked another document from the top of his desk.

Hunter recognized it instantly but didn't panic. He had suspected this was the reason he'd been called in.

"Or should I say, the negligence of bringing this order to my attention?"

"There were many orders on your desk when you arrived, sir."

"Ha!" Briggs barked, then reached for yet another set of documents and began thumbing through each one. "An order to expand the fort's garden. An order to count heads in the community. Here's one that says we're to better document our patrols so idiots in top offices may understand exactly what it is we do out here. And this one—oh, this is a dandy one here—we're to watch our flour intake. *Flour?*" Briggs slammed the orders down on his desk, picked up the one Hunter had "neglected," and waved it at him. "Are you going to tell me, Stone, that any of those orders hold even a candle of importance to this one?"

Hunter answered in a calm manner, "That order, Major, states clearly that we have sixty days to move those Indians to a reservation—"

"I can read, can't I!" Briggs bellowed.

"—and yet they don't even specify *where* the reservation land *is*. I took it to mean that—"

"*You* took it to mean? Are you the commanding officer of this fort?"

"I was when those orders were received by mail, and I interpreted it for what it is: the plan of some lazy politician who decided to draw up an order, no matter how ridiculous." Hunter watched the buildup of anger in Briggs' face by the cherry red rise of his color. His mouth worked, but nothing came out. "The Blackfoot are a peaceful nation, Major. They don't receive any help from the government because they don't need it—they grow their own food and hunt their own game. There's absolutely no reason to place them on a reservation, and that's why I've written Commissioner Macleod about the matter."

"You *what*!" Briggs' color was still high, but in a deadly calm voice he ordered, "Vickersham, would you mind stepping outside?"

"Yes, sir. But may I emphasize—"

"No, you may not. Outside, please."

Hunter didn't break eye contact with Briggs. A line had clearly been drawn when Briggs had prepared the reprimand—a line that Hunter had no intention of ignoring.

When the door closed behind Vic, Briggs leaned toward Hunter with his fists planted on the desk. Still in the menacing low tone Briggs said, "Now you listen to me, you self-righteous prig! You had no right as *acting* superintendent to pass judgment over those orders. And you *certainly* had no right to take this matter to the commissioner without first discussing it with me." He paused, and a predator's smile tugged at the corners of his mouth. "Listen to me, Stone, because I'm only going to say this once. If you don't do an about-face and start seeing things more clearly, I'll have your rank. Do you understand?"

"Yes, sir," Hunter answered tightly.

"And that goes for your Indian-loving girlfriend, too. If I hear of her making any trouble—" Briggs stopped abruptly and took a step back when Hunter leaped to his feet. His eyes were round with surprise and a trace of fear.

Hunter said through tight lips, "I think the major had better stop himself before he goes too far. The threat of harm to a civilian is a serious offense."

"You're dismissed, Stone!"

Hunter turned and went to the door, then paused and said, "You can be sure, Major Briggs, that I'll be appealing that reprimand." For good measure, Hunter slammed the door solidly behind himself when he left.

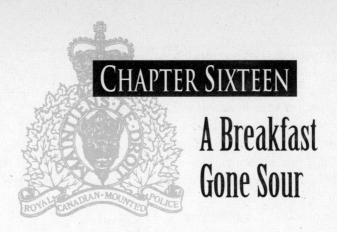

CHAPTER SIXTEEN

A Breakfast Gone Sour

Dirk and the rest of the Mounties had pitched tents outside the schoolhouse in order to be more available if they were needed. Dirk had expected a fight on his hands from Duke Dillard when he suggested this. After all, they would be away from warm stoves and fully prepared meals three times a day. To Dirk's surprise, Duke was delighted.

"Stay here? You betcha." The other men nodded with him.

"You mean you're not going to moan and groan about it? None of you?"

"Are you kidding?" Duke asked with a grin. "The farther we are from that gargoyle Briggs, the happier I am. This'll be like a vacation after a week with him."

The morning after their first night at the school, Dirk rose with a groan from the cot that was too short for him. Duke was still snoring soundly on the other side of the tent, so Dirk threw a dirty rolled-up sock at his head.

"Hey!"

"Rise and shine, valentine."

Duke threw the sock back at him, then sat up and squinted

at the oil lamp Dirk had just lit. With a groan he said, "It's still dark out there! What are you trying to do, become like Briggs?"

"Hardly. You want breakfast, don't you? We don't have a cook to be at your beck and call. *We're* the cooks."

Duke fell back on the cot and covered his head with the pillow. "I'm not hungry. I'd rather sleep."

Pulling on his boots, Dirk said calmly, "Duke, if you're not out of bed and dressed in two minutes, I'll send you back to the major."

Duke was out of bed instantly. "I'm up, I'm up!"

As Dirk stepped outside into the heavy dew, he remembered that today was the day Jenny was supposed to take all to herself. He'd asked Simone about it the previous evening, and after a little persuasion he'd agreed, then commented, "The gallant warrior watching out for the maiden, eh?" Dirk still wasn't sure if the doctor was mocking or merely trying to establish a comradeship.

He woke the other men and told them to start breakfast, then went into the schoolhouse just as the sun broke over the horizon in an orange blaze. Inside the door he was met by Mrs. Branson, who'd agreed to be the night nurse. She was a birdlike woman, fine boned, with a habit of fluttering a hand against her breastbone like a broken wing. At the moment her hand was working overtime.

"Oh, Sergeant, I'm glad you're here. Mr. Slade passed on during the night." She motioned with the hand that wasn't fluttering over to one of the beds, where a very pale man lay with a sheet pulled up to his neck.

"Mrs. Branson, why didn't you cover his face?"

"I didn't want any of the others to know they were near a dead man all night. They've got enough to worry about without that, the poor dears."

"I'll take care of removing him, Mrs. Branson. But the next time this happens—and I pray it won't—please come wake us."

"But you boys need your rest, too," she protested.

Dirk placed a reassuring hand on her arm. "It's our job, Mrs.

Branson. It's what we're here for." He was glad to note that the distracting fluttering of her hand stopped momentarily, not only for her sake but because it was driving him crazy. "Now, what time does the doctor usually get here in the mornings?"

"Oh, he told me he'd be late today, I don't know why."

Dirk stared at her in confusion for a moment, then he had a sinking feeling. *I'll bet I know why.*

––––––––––

Jenny woke to the early morning sun flowing in through the sole window right onto her face. Squinting and turning away from it, she nevertheless smiled and mentally thanked Dirk for making her take a day off. The night before she'd been calm and relaxed, knowing that she wouldn't have to face the horrors of sickness today. She'd enjoyed some of Dickens' *Pickwick Papers* but didn't remember falling asleep. Thinking it must have been about ten o'clock when she'd dozed off, she looked at the clock by her bed and saw that she'd slept nine and a half hours. She couldn't remember the last time she'd done that.

Sitting up and stretching luxuriously, she reflected on what she wanted to do with her day. Maybe go visit Megan and little Jaye. Or take a ride into the countryside toward the foothills and walk through the sighing aspens. "Or both, or neither," she said to herself with a grin.

She brushed her teeth and hummed a tune as she dressed, noting how fine she felt after only one good night's sleep. When she opened her door to go downstairs, she gasped in surprise. "Doctor! What are you doing here?"

Phillippe, sitting in a chair across the hall, rose to his feet and grinned. "Why, waiting for you, of course. Your chariot awaits."

"My what?"

He took a step toward her, his small hands laced in front of his chest, and looked at her appreciatively. "Dear Jenny, you're as fresh as a daisy on a summer day."

"What are you doing here, Doctor? Why aren't you at the school? Is something wrong?"

"Jenny, one question at a time! I've taken the liberty of having Mrs. Howe bake us some nice blueberry muffins and throw some fruit in a basket for our breakfast by the river. I've found a wonderful place beneath some cottonwoods—"

Jenny shook her head in confusion. "You can't be serious! What about the sick people who need you?"

"Mrs. Branson and your Mountie friend are perfectly able to handle things, don't you think?"

Backing into her room, Jenny said, "No, I think one of us should be there—"

Phillippe reached out and took her hand to stop her progress. "Aren't I allowed a small break from work, too? After all, I've been working as hard as you have. Come on, Jenny, I'm only talking about a couple of hours, not the whole day as you have."

Still Jenny hesitated. Somehow it didn't seem right. Yet she had no plans, and it was only for two hours, wasn't it? It was kind of him to make the arrangements. Wouldn't it be rude to turn him down? And Mrs. Branson *was* capable of tending to the patients with Dirk's help. *Dirk. What would he think of this?*

"Take a deep breath, Jenny," Phillippe whispered, drawing close to her. "Can't you smell the muffins Mrs. Howe baked just for us? I can. And they're probably still warm in that basket that's waiting for us downstairs."

Jenny couldn't smell the muffins, but she could smell the mint on his breath. There was something about him so intriguing that she couldn't seem to resist his invitation. "All right, Doctor."

He held up his index finger in front of her face and waggled it from side to side, saying, "No, no, no, the whole thing's off if you don't start calling me Phillippe."

"All right . . . Phillippe."

"There! Now that wasn't so hard, was it?"

"Well, a little," she said with a smile.

He took her arm and steered her toward the stairs. "You'll

get used to it. And I sure like the way it sounds coming from your lips.''

Jenny felt as if she were being swept down a river in a boat with no way to steer. Instead of being frightened, it excited her.

———————

The muffins weren't warm, but they were delicious. Usually if Jenny had breakfast at all, she ate very little. But she had three muffins, some wild strawberries, and two slices of melon. Phillippe watched her with amusement in his eyes, but he, too, ate as much as she, if not more.

They were in a crook of the river in the shade of the cottonwood trees, lounging on a blanket Phillippe had brought. Small, cottonlike blooms from the trees danced in the light wind all around them. Jenny thought it was a very relaxing place and was glad she'd decided to take him up on his offer. They seemed miles and miles from the depressing schoolhouse and the smell of sickness and death.

"What are you thinking?" Phillippe asked. He was lying on his side with his head propped up by one hand, looking at her with lazy, brilliant blue eyes.

"I was thinking that this place is nice, and that this was a good idea."

"I have a confession to make," he said, removing the basket from between them.

"What is it?" Jenny was leaning against a tree, beginning to feel a drowsiness brought on by overeating.

"I couldn't stop thinking about you last night, Jenny," he confessed, scooting himself closer to her. "There I was, I'd given you today off, and . . .''

"And what?"

He stopped when he was right beside her, looking up into her eyes. "And I realized that I didn't want to go the whole day without seeing you."

Jenny waited for him to go on, but he only kept gazing at

her. "Well . . . um . . . thank you, Doctor—I mean, Phillippe. That's very sweet."

"You're blushing."

"I am?"

"Kiss me, Jenny."

"I . . . I barely know you."

"Then I'll kiss you."

He leaned toward her slowly, and Jenny felt herself go rigid with tension. They were far from the fort and all alone. What was she doing out here without a chaperon? She really *didn't* know him very well. What if he attacked her?

When his lips touched hers, it broke her trance, and she moved away quickly. "No, this isn't right."

A flash of anger crossed his face, then was gone. "What do you mean? I just wanted a kiss. I'm not going to hurt you."

Jenny stood and brushed herself off. "I think we should go now."

"But we just got here!"

"Are you going to take me home, or do I start walking?"

"Why are you angry?"

"I'm not angry, I'm . . . I'm . . . all right, I *am* angry, but I don't know why yet." Phillippe stood and reached for her, but she pushed his hands away, again seeing the momentary dark look of his own anger. This time, there seemed to be a bit of danger lurking there. What had she gotten herself into?

Phillippe visibly calmed himself down, then turned and began gathering his things. "You don't have anything to be mad about, Jenny. Nothing at all. But, yes, I'll take you home now."

They didn't speak all the way back to the boardinghouse until the wagon stopped. Casually, as if nothing had happened, Phillippe said, "Enjoy the rest of your day, Jenny."

"Thank you," Jenny said, but as she went to her room, a cloud of uneasiness settled over her.

Dirk and his men were washing linens when Phillippe pulled

up in the wagon. Dirk had been pondering all morning whether he should say something to the doctor about coming in late. He'd decided to let it go until one of the patients, a teenaged girl named Louise, had awakened to violent coughing. He and Mrs. Branson hadn't known what to do for her, but thankfully the coughing had stopped as suddenly as it had started, leaving the girl breathless and spent. The event had angered Dirk, both from the intense feeling of helplessness and the absence of Simone.

Simone dismounted from the wagon and threw a casual wave toward Dirk. "Nice day for washing, isn't it?"

"Can I have a word with you, Doctor?" Dirk walked over to him, noting the sudden wariness in his eyes.

"Is everything in order around here, Sergeant?"

"No. We've had a death during the night, and a young girl almost coughed herself to death this morning. Where have you been, Doctor?"

"That's absolutely none of your business." He turned to take the steps, but Dirk stopped him with a firm hand on his arm.

"I think it is. You're the only doctor this town has, and you think you can sleep in like a baby?"

Phillippe looked down at Dirk's hand with disdain. "Take your hand off me, Sergeant. I'm not one of your constables you can order about."

Dirk let him go but stepped closer to him.

"And for your information, I wasn't sleeping."

"I don't care what you were doing. You have a responsibility to—"

"Are you sure?" Phillippe asked, giving a half smile.

"Am I sure about what?"

"That you're not interested in what I was doing? Why don't you just say it, Sergeant?"

Dirk shook his head. "I have no idea what you're talking about."

"Of course you do. This is all about Jenny, isn't it?"

"I haven't said a word about Jenny." Dirk's heart sank when he realized where the doctor might have been.

Phillippe switched his doctor's bag from one hand to the other, full of confidence again. "The stresses of taking care of the sick are enormous, Sergeant Becker, but I wouldn't expect you to understand that. Jenny and I have been working almost nonstop all week, and when you requested a day off for her, I thought why not take"—he consulted his pocket watch—"an hour and a half for myself? An hour and a half, Sergeant. Surely you won't begrudge me that?"

Dirk had thought it was almost noon, but he saw from the timepiece that it was only nine-thirty. That combined with Simone's reasonable tone made Dirk begin to think that he'd made a mistake to confront him.

"I didn't think so. May I go inside now, Sergeant?"

A muscle twitched in Dirk's jaw, but he nodded. "I'm sure Mrs. Branson is ready for some rest."

"Thank you." Phillippe took two of the steps, then turned and said, "Jenny and I had a very pleasant breakfast together. No need to worry, I'm not trying to steal her away from you. She's just a very sweet girl to be around. I thought you'd like for me to be up front about it. Enjoy your washing." He climbed the rest of the steps and disappeared inside.

Dirk clenched and unclenched his hands. *So that's how it's going to be.* Simone hadn't needed to tell Dirk where he'd been. It was just a way of twisting the knife after making Dirk look foolish for his questioning. "You want to be up front," he whispered, "we'll be up front."

Duke Dillard appeared at his side. "Everything all right, Sarge?"

Dirk looked at him, and whatever Duke saw in his face, it made his eyes widen. "I'd say that things couldn't be much worse, Duke."

CHAPTER SEVENTEEN

Unwelcome News

Constable Frank Jeter angrily kicked a rock against the gloom of the fort's southside wall. It made a satisfying *clack!* and ricocheted off somewhere in the night.

Jeter, of medium height with a stocky build, was fully armed with a holstered Adams revolver and Winchester Model 1876. The repeating rifles had just arrived the previous week, replacing the hopelessly outdated Snider-Enfield single shot carbine. Training with the Winchester had been the only thing Jeter had enjoyed since becoming a Mountie in January.

"Night guard duty," he muttered to himself, looking for something else to kick. "The stupidest job in the force. Guard against what, marauding settlers?" He snorted derisively and moved on toward the southeast guard tower, which was his post. He hated the tower, just as he hated the northeast tower and the northwest tower and so on. They were so cramped that he had to get out and walk every hour or so to keep from going mad.

Why had he ever let his father talk him into joining the Mounties? The pay was terrible, there was absolutely nothing to do in your spare time, and now they had an ogre for a superintendent who was a brutal dictator. How could it get any worse?

Now he was stuck, having signed on for three years. He should have stayed home and learned cabinetmaking from his uncle, who made a fine living and lived in a mansion in Dufferin. But no. He'd been ignorant and signed on for the most boring job in the world. "I just wish something would *happen*!" he told himself as he passed the horse corral. "Nothing ever happens around here."

Jeter stopped to pet the nose of a bay mare as she edged against the fence. "It's three o'clock in the morning and quiet as a tomb, girl. I think you and me are the only ones who aren't asleep within miles." The mare nudged his chest as if in acknowledgment.

Moving on, Jeter did a quick head count of the horses, as he always did when he passed by. It was difficult to do in the darkness, with the only light being thrown from an oil lamp in the guard tower. "Twenty-nine, thirty, thirty-one—" He stopped suddenly. "Thirty-two." The last time he'd passed by there'd been forty-four horses in the corral.

"Naw, that can't be right," he said with agitation. Some of the horses were as black as the night. He'd probably just missed a few. But as he recounted, he reflected that twelve horses were more than "a few."

The closer he got to thirty-two the slower he counted, and his stomach began to churn. "Thirty-one, thirty-two." A light sheen of sweat broke out on Jeter's upper lip, though the night was cool. He stood frozen in place, barely breathing, until the realization of what had happened fully hit him. "Oh no!" He had a vision of Major Briggs' face, stormy and apoplectic, mouth spouting thunderous oaths reserved only for Jeter.

The southeast guard tower directly overlooked the horse corral, and Jeter had heard and seen nothing. Absolutely nothing. Briggs was going to have him for breakfast.

"Or I could leave," he whispered. "Just go away and never come back." The thought was tempting until he reasoned that they might think *he* stole the horses.

With no other choice, Jeter sprinted for the north, toward the other guard, Manning, screaming his name.

———

Blue Bear smiled to himself as he herded the horses across the prairie. It had been ridiculously easy. He'd watched the guards for the previous two nights to see how well they watched over their stock and had noted that one of them liked to leave his tower a little too often and walk around. He also foolishly took the same route for his walks, enabling Blue Bear to sneak in and take the horses when the guard was at the far corner of the fort. If Blue Bear had had some help, he could have made off with the whole group. Instead, he'd taken only twelve— enough to send a message to the Mounties that they weren't invincible and enough to replenish his tribe's dwindling herd.

He would take a roundabout way back to his village, corral the horses a few miles from there, then recruit some help to divide the herd. They would each take their string and roam all around the area to confuse trackers, eventually returning to the village.

Blue Bear's smile turned into a full grin when he visualized his increased standing in the tribe for his heroics. It would have to remain a secret from most of the people—especially the missionary woman—to be sure that no one would turn him in to the Mounties. But Plenty Trees and the other braves would know of it, and Blue Bear would receive praise and rewards.

Taking a deep, satisfied breath, he urged the leader of the horses, a chestnut stallion, forward at a faster pace. He wanted to reach his destination before dawn to escape any prying eyes. And to be all the closer to his rewards.

———

Hunter knew something was wrong when he was shaken awake. He squinted up at Sergeant Stride, who was holding a lamp and wearing an anxious look.

"Sir, the major wants to see you immediately."

Hunter could hear commotion in the room next to him, which was the enlisted men's barracks. "What's happened?" he asked groggily, sitting up and reaching for his trousers.

"Some horses were stolen."

"What? Who would be dumb enough to rob from us?"

Stride only looked at him.

Hunter held up a hand and said, "Never mind, that was a dumb question. We've both seen some of the riffraff floating around on the prairie." He recalled the albino, Matsen, who'd come to reclaim his horses from Plenty Trees' braves. Though he claimed to be a legitimate rancher, Hunter wouldn't have been at all surprised to hear that Matsen had pulled off this trick. Hunter had sensed Matsen was one short step from crossing the line into crime, and there were too many men like him to count on the vast plains.

He dressed quickly, buttoning his tunic as he made his way to Briggs' office. The major would be in a foul mood and was probably looking for a scapegoat to vent his anger on. Hunter didn't envy whoever had been on guard duty.

Two ashen-faced constables emerged from the library just as Hunter reached the door. One of them was named Jeter, he thought, but he couldn't remember the other one's name. "Is the major in his office?" he asked them.

Jeter nodded, swallowing hard. "Oh yes, sir, he's in there, all right. That is, if he's not out forming a firing squad for us."

"You were the guards?"

"Yes, sir."

"What happened?"

Jeter's Adam's apple bobbed up and down his neck like a cork as he swallowed again. Hunter wondered if he wasn't about to throw up.

"Didn't see or hear a thing, sir. I made my three o'clock count, and they were just . . . gone."

Hunter nodded, then passed by them to Briggs' office. After knocking and receiving an unintelligible reply, he opened the door. Briggs was behind his desk, scowling, and when he saw it was Hunter, the lines in his face deepened.

"Have you heard, Stone?"

"Yes, sir."

"What do you propose to do about it?"

"Why, go after them at first light, Major. What else is there to do?"

"Precisely. Take a scout and ten men and bring these scoundrel Indians back to me. As magistrate, I intend to bring the full consequences of the law against them."

Hunter hesitated, then asked carefully, "How do you know they're Indians?"

"Of course they're Indians!" Someone knocked on the door and he roared, "Come in!"

Vic came in, saluted, and said, "Good morning, sir."

"Ah, Vickersham," Briggs greeted with genuine warmth. "Glad you could join us. How's your son doing?"

"Very good, Major, thank you. He seems to be adjusting quite well, actually."

"Splendid news." The scowl returned as he motioned to Hunter. "I was just telling Stone here to organize a tracking party for these thieves. I say they're Indians, and he questions that. What do you say, Vickersham?"

Vic glanced at Hunter, who shook his head very slightly. "I . . . er . . . I wouldn't know, Major."

Briggs let it pass with a final sour glance at Hunter. "You'll be staying here, Vickersham, helping me organize some letters of transfer. Most of the force here will be going to Fort Walsh, down around the Cypress Hills. That's going to be the new headquarters beginning in '78 because of that scoundrel Sitting Bull moving up here. They'll want to keep a close eye on that one."

Hunter and Vic exchanged identical puzzled glances. Vic asked, "Do we already know who's going to be transferred?"

"A few, but not all." Briggs looked at Hunter. "You're one of them, Stone."

"Me? Why me?" His thoughts turned to Reena at once. They had it very good at the moment, since the Blackfoot were so close to the fort. They'd been able to see each other often and spend time with their friends. Hunter had wondered what she would do when the Blackfoot went to the reservation, but he hadn't asked because he'd been afraid of the answer. Now it would be *him* who'd be causing their separation.

"I don't know 'why you,' Stone. They didn't send along an explanation for every man. Is there a problem?"

"Well . . ."

Vic broke in and said, "We've been here for nearly three years now, Major. It's sort of like a home to us—especially for me, since I have my own house, but I'm sure it's the same for Hunter."

"Your name's not on the list, Vickersham, so I think you'll be allowed to stay."

Hunter thought, *Great, I'll lose Reena* and *my best friend.* "Major, can these orders be appealed?"

Briggs gave him a look of intense dislike when he said, "You're very high on appealing orders, aren't you, Stone? Have you always had trouble with authority? I shouldn't think there'd be a place for someone like you in the Mounties."

Hunter felt his face burn, but he managed to hold his tongue. The only consolation he could find in the news was that at least he'd be away from Briggs. But thinking about Reena and Vic staying behind, he knew he'd endure any abuse to be able to stay, too.

"Get your party together, Stone, it's almost dawn."

Hunter saluted and left. Outside in the cool, damp air, he took a deep breath and closed his eyes. *Don't let this happen, Lord. Please don't let this happen.*

———

Reena convinced Plenty Trees and Raindrop that the best course of action in containing the flu was to separate those who'd contracted it from those who hadn't. They didn't understand at first, and Raindrop had flatly refused. The family unit was sacred to the Blackfoot, and splitting up family members was unheard of. But Reena told them that it was a white man's disease, and they would have to trust her on how to deal with it.

They chose four newly built lodges that were near the corn-field to use for the sick. Reena sincerely hoped they wouldn't need any more. Currently there were only about twenty people who were ailing, and the severity of it seemed less serious than what Reena had seen around Fort Macleod. The Indians also had medicines derived from boiled bear root such as *be-cigodji-biguk* that worked wonders at dispelling fever and chills. Reena knew, for she'd been very sick once, and though the concoction tasted horrible, it had gotten her back on her feet quickly. She prayed that it would do the same against this strain of flu.

The people were remarkably cooperative in bringing their loved ones to the lodges. Reena received a few dark looks, but for the most part they trusted her judgment. She supposed that part of the reason might have been their superstitious fear of the white man's diseases, with many painful memories of smallpox deaths. Whatever the reason, Reena was relieved at the ease of the transition.

Reena prayed with everyone who was sick and hoped that it helped in their fear and suffering. One of them was Sun Flower, the little girl who'd been surprised that Reena wouldn't throw sticks at Hunter if he started seeing another lady. That happy day when Reena and the children had laughed and talked seemed a long time ago now, though it had been only a month.

Sun Flower rested on a bed of deer skins. Her dark eyes were slightly glazed, and every so often she coughed deeply. Reena took her hand and prayed for her, and when she looked up, Sun Flower was smiling.

"I like to hear you pray, Reena."

"Thank you. I *like* to pray, don't you?"

Sun Flower pursed her lips. "Sometimes it's hard because I don't know what to say."

"That doesn't matter," Reena said, patting her hand. "God

knows what's in your heart, and that's enough."

"Reena, will you come with us when we go to that place?"

Reena knew what "that place" was, and she felt a wrench in her heart. "I don't know, Sun Flower. I go where God tells me to go, and He hasn't given me an answer on that."

"What do you call it? 'Res . . . res . . .' "

"Reservation." Reena had come to hate the word.

"I'm scared of that place. What if there are no trees, or no stream to swim in? What if there are no birds or antelope?"

Reena didn't want to tell her that all of those things would be there and then it not be so. With a deep sadness inside her from the innocent questions, she said, "They may not be there, but then they might be, too. But try not to worry about that right now. You're a very sick little girl, and we have to get you well."

"Reena?"

"Yes."

"Will you pray that those things will be there? And that we'll be happy?"

Reena felt her eyes begin to burn and willed herself not to cry. The little girl wanted to see strength right now, not weakness. Forcing a smile, she said, "Of course I will. And you can pray for that, too, you know. There's nothing wrong with wanting to be happy, because that's what God wants for us."

Sun Flower squeezed Reena's hand weakly and closed her eyes. "I'm going to sleep now."

Reena sat with her until she was breathing evenly, wondering what it would be like if she were told where and how to live. She couldn't bring herself to imagine it.

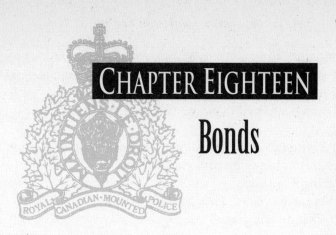

CHAPTER EIGHTEEN

Bonds

Y ou're mighty quiet today, lad," Faron said to Hunter. "Somethin' on your mind?"

"You could say that."

They were having no trouble tracking the stolen horses. Faron had determined by the number of prints that there was only one rider herding them. Hunter had been surprised, but he trusted Faron's judgment. However, the thief had a good four or five hour start on them, so Hunter had driven his men hard. He had a feeling they were gaining on the herd.

"Well?" Faron asked when Hunter didn't say any more. "What is it, boy? Ye look like ye just lost your pet dog."

"No, I think I've lost a bit more than that. Major Briggs says I'm being transferred to Fort Walsh in the Cypress Hills sometime soon."

Faron raised his bushy eyebrows in surprise. "The Cypress Hills? It's pretty country, but I see what ye mean—it's over a hundred miles away."

"Right."

"Could put a serious dent in a relationship."

"Right."

Faron eyed him closely, then said in a low voice, "Unless she were to go with ye."

Hunter returned the look. "Do you think that's a possibility?"

"Anything's possible, Hunter, me boy. But the question is, do you *want* her to go with you?"

"Of course I do!"

"Aye, aye . . . may I ask, in what capacity?"

"What do you mean?"

Faron produced a plug of tobacco from his coat pocket and bit off a chunk of it. "What I mean is," he said around the mouthful, "are ye just goin' to go up to me niece and say, 'Reena, darlin', I'll be goin' south a hundred miles, but you're welcome to come along. You'll have to find yer own place, ya see, but we'll still be within rock-throwin' distance of each other?' " He stopped and grinned, the plug of tobacco tight in his bearded cheek. "Or are ye gonna ask her to marry ye?"

Hunter shifted in the saddle, avoiding his eyes. "I don't know. What do you think she'd say?"

"To which one?"

"To a proposal, of course!"

"My, my, yer awful testy about this, aren't ye?"

"Let's just say I woke up this morning, and things were fine. Now I've got a few huge decisions to make that I don't look forward to, but I can't think about anything else."

Faron smacked his lips with gusto. "Ah, the perils and burdens of youth. I'd give me right eye to have it back."

"What?"

The joviality left Faron's demeanor, and his voice turned gruff. "You've got to snap out of it, lad! It's not like ye to be this way."

"I don't know what you're talking about—"

"Oh yes, ye do. Least ye would if ye was thinkin' straight. Listen to me. Do ye think the good Lord likes to hear His children moanin' about this and groanin' about that? 'Course not! Don't it say in yer Bible not to worry about tomorrow 'cause there's enough on your plate for today?"

"Yes, so to speak."

"And don't it also say somewheres that God's mercies are new every morning?"

"How did you know all this?"

"I can read, can't I! I'm not some heathen barbarian from the North. I like to pick up the Word every now and then. Does that surprise ye?"

Hunter shrugged. "It doesn't surprise me, really—"

"Sure it does! Now, listen to me. Look at ye, a fine-lookin' specimen of a man in the prime o' his youth. Ever since that major got here you've been runnin' like a spooked rabbit. Take yer life by the reins and steer it yourself, fer cryin' out loud, instead of lettin' others do it for ye! Now, do ye love her?"

The question took Hunter by surprise, as did Faron's whole aggressive tirade. "I . . . I . . ."

"Get the mush out o' yer mouth and answer! Do ye love Reena?"

"Yes," Hunter answered firmly, "yes, I do. More than anything in the world."

Faron leaned toward him and spoke slowly, carefully pronouncing each word as if talking to a child. "Then ask her to marry ye."

They'd been riding twenty yards to the front of the rest of the men when a young constable appeared beside them. "Pardon me, sir, but you've lost the tracks. They turned east back there."

Hunter turned to see the rest of the party waiting patiently almost a hundred yards back.

Faron said, "Now see what you've done? You've made me lose *my* concentration! Back we go."

On the way back to the men, Hunter thought about Faron's words. There was sound wisdom in them, there was no doubt about that. Somehow Hunter had allowed himself to become exactly what he wasn't—timid—in the face of whatever circumstances came his way. No more.

Just before they reached the waiting men, Hunter pulled up beside Faron and said simply, "Thanks."

"Don't mention it, lad. Good luck to ye."

To the men Hunter said, "Sorry about that little detour. Faron and I were just having a discussion about rabbits."

They all looked at him as if unsure he still had his sanity.

"Never mind. Speaking of rabbits, we've got our own to catch. With all this zigzagging, he seems to be trying to cover his real destination. I'd say it's time for an all-out run to catch this thief once and for all, wouldn't you?"

The men gave a cheer, and Hunter led them across the rolling prairie with renewed vigor.

———

It only took a few days for Megan and Jaye to work out a comfortable relationship. Megan would fix him oatmeal every morning—he loved it more than anything, she believed—then he would help her with household chores. As they worked together they would talk about all sorts of things. Most of the time it was Jaye asking questions and Megan giving answers. Megan couldn't believe the sheer amount of curiosity and hunger for knowledge in one so small. Vic had mentioned the same thing to her, as he'd been pumped for information during their whole return trip together.

After his chores were done, Jaye would thumb through the children's books that Megan had brought home from the school or play outside. He'd developed a game where he was a Mountie like his father, always riding his "horse," a broken shovel handle, to right a wrong. Megan loved to sit on the porch and watch what his imagination could come up with. Invariably Jaye ended up saving "Sally" from a sure life of misery at the hands of a desperate outlaw.

After lunch Jaye would nap, then in the late afternoon they would both work in the small garden behind the house. On the afternoon that Hunter was chasing a horse thief over the plains and Vic was filling out transfer forms, Megan and Jaye were pulling weeds. The boy was unusually quiet.

"Jaye? What's on your mind? You've hardly said a word."

"I don't know."

Megan pulled off one glove and wiped her brow. "I thought you knew just about everything."

"Naw."

"Is something bothering you?"

He glanced at her as he threw a clump of weeds to the side, then shrugged.

"Come on," Megan urged him, "you can tell me."

"You might tell Daddy."

Vic had been overjoyed the night Jaye had first called him that, and Megan was happy for him. Jaye certainly hadn't called her "Mother" yet, but Megan hoped it would happen in the near future. "I won't tell if you don't want me to."

"Naw."

"Okay," Megan said nonchalantly as she pulled the glove back on. "Suit yourself." She went back to weeding with a secret smile, and sure enough, it didn't take long for Jaye to start talking.

"I'm scared," Jaye said quietly.

"What are you scared of, honey?"

"I don't wanna get that flu and die."

Megan scooted closer to him and put her arm around him. This was something he'd begun to allow only the day before, and Megan liked the feel of him in her arms. "You're not going to get sick, Jaye. That's why your father and I keep you around the house and only around us—to protect you from it. I know you want to get out and explore the town and make friends, but that's something to look forward to later." She reached down and lifted his chin. "Okay? You're not going to get sick."

"What if Daddy does? Or . . . or you?"

"Well, we're just not going to worry about that, all right? Is that all that's bothering you?"

"Um . . . I'm scared of something else, too."

"What?"

He fidgeted around, then rubbed his nose, leaving a dirt smudge at the tip of it. Then he asked, "Is Stella gonna come get me back? 'Cause I don't wanna go back there."

"Of course she's not! Whatever gave you that idea?" Megan took off a glove again, licked the end of her finger, and scrubbed the dirt from his nose, making him giggle.

"That tickles!"

Megan smiled and asked, "Why are you afraid Stella's going to come get you?"

"I don't know. Just am."

Cradling his head against her, Megan said softly, "Well, you can just stop worrying about that right this second, Master Vickersham. No one's going to come and take you away. You're home now." After a moment, surprisingly, he began to cry quietly. Megan waited for whatever was forthcoming.

Jaye became quiet, except for a few sniffles, then stuttered, "Will . . . will you. . . ?"

"Calm down, sweetheart. Take a deep breath and let it out slowly. Now, what do you want to ask me?"

"Will you be my new mother?"

Megan closed her eyes and sent a fervent thanks heavenward. "Look at me, Jaye." He turned to her with red-rimmed eyes— the brown eyes so much like his father's that it still amazed Megan. She quickly wiped his cheeks and placed her hand on the side of his face, looking deep into those eyes. "I've wanted to be your new mother ever since the day I heard you existed."

"Really?"

"Yes, really. I love you, little Jaye." Megan could no longer hold back her own emotions. She took him in her arms and crushed him to her.

Jenny didn't actually ignore Dirk, but neither did she go out of her way to see him. He hadn't seen her arrive that morning, since he and his men had been busy constructing a shed to store more supplies. A church in Fort Benton had sent along a wagonload of blankets, linens, towels, medicine, and all sorts of canned food.

Once Dr. Simone had stuck his head out the window to summon Dirk inside. He saw Jenny just as he stepped through the door. She was washing the face and arms of a woman whose wheezing breath could be heard clearly. Jenny smiled at him tentatively.

"Hi, Jenny."

"Hello. I see you've been working hard."

Dirk looked down at his sweat-sodden undershirt. They'd all stripped off their scarlet jackets to unload the wagon of supplies. "Oh yeah, I forgot. Do you think I should go put on my jacket?"

Chuckling, she said, "No, I don't think that's necessary. We're pretty informal around here."

"Sergeant?" Phillippe called from the back, motioning Dirk forward.

"I'll be right back, Jenny." He went to Simone, who was scowling down at one of the beds holding a very large, over-weight man. The patient's eyes were closed, and for a second Dirk thought he was dead, but then he saw the man's chest rising and falling in hitches.

Phillippe said, "We really need to change this man's linens, but he doesn't have the strength to get out of bed. We're going to have to shift him over to that one." He pointed to the one next to them with clean sheets.

"All right. You take his legs, and I'll take the other end." Dirk moved to the head of the cot while Phillippe got a hold on the huge legs. After slipping his arms under the patient's armpits, Dirk said, "One, two, three, go." He lifted his part, but Phillippe groaned at his burden and had to let go.

"You'd better go get a couple more men for this job," Phillippe told him, wiping his brow. "The man's an ox!"

Without a word, Dirk moved to the side of the man, established a good hold beneath his back and legs, and lifted with a grunt. He was indeed heavy—Dirk estimated at least two-fifty—but he managed to get him to the other bed. When he raised up and bent backward to ease his screaming muscles, he saw Phillippe looking at him speculatively.

"Remind me to choose you for my team if we ever have a tug-of-war game."

Dirk didn't answer and made his way back to Jenny, who said, "That was impressive."

"I wasn't trying to impress anyone. It just needed to be done."

"Dirk, can I talk to you?"

"Sure." He followed Jenny outside onto the steps, where she sat down with a sigh and he joined her. "How was your day off?"

She looked at him quickly, obviously searching for any double meaning. "It was very refreshing."

"Good. I'm glad I twisted your arm."

"Dirk, I have to be honest with you."

He braced himself for possible bad news. Ever since his conversation with Phillippe, he'd tried to prepare himself for the worst. It was negative thinking, but he had no choice. He loved Jenny, and if she was going to break their relationship off, he wanted to be prepared. "All right—be honest with me."

Jenny tucked her hair back behind her ears and said, "I don't know if you've heard, but I had breakfast with Dr. Simone yesterday. It wasn't a planned thing—not by me, anyway—but I . . . I thought it would be nice to . . ." She trailed off and appeared confused. Then, with a new determination she said, "I'm sorry. I told you I'd be honest, and I'm not. The truth is, I was attracted to Dr. Simone and wanted to find out *why* I was attracted to him when I have someone perfectly wonderful like you. Does that make sense?"

Dirk hesitated, then said haltingly, "I don't really—"

"Dr. Simone doesn't hold a candle to you, Dirk," Jenny said quietly.

Pleased beyond belief, Dirk kissed her softly.

"I don't deserve you, Dirk Becker." She hugged him tightly.

"Maybe not, but you're stuck with me now." Dirk couldn't remember the last time he had felt so happy.

Chapter Nineteen

A Matter of the Heart

Blue Bear couldn't have been more surprised if the Mounties had risen up straight out of the earth. One moment he'd been tying the rope to a cottonwood tree to corral the horses, and the next he'd been staring down three rifle barrels. The one in the middle belonged to Hunter Stone, and Blue Bear saw a flash of recognition behind those slate-gray eyes.

"You again," Hunter said grimly. "I would have thought one of Plenty Trees' braves would be smarter than this."

Blue Bear looked at the other two men. One of them was a Mountie with thin, cruel lips. The other was a grizzled old man holding his rifle with only one arm. If Blue Bear could only edge a little closer to him, he could charge him and—

Hunter cocked his rifle, and for an instant Blue Bear thought he was going to shoot him on the spot. Instead, he raised the barrel into the air and fired, then cocked it again and brought its aim back to Blue Bear's chest. "What's your name?"

Blue Bear put on his best defiant gaze and didn't answer. Behind Hunter he saw other riders come into view as they topped a small knoll. His defiance quickly left him as he realized

235

there would be no daring escape.

"Williams," Hunter said to the thin-lipped man, "cut a length of that rope whatever-his-name's holding and tie him up."

"With pleasure, sir," Williams said, stepping up to Blue Bear warily.

To Blue Bear, Hunter said, "I don't want to shoot you. I'd suggest you be real still."

Williams unsheathed Blue Bear's knife, cut the rope, and began tying his hands behind his back. The other Mounties rode up and surrounded the stolen horses behind them.

"Why did you think you'd get away with this?" Hunter asked. "Don't you know this is the worst possible thing you could have done for your people?"

Blue Bear winced slightly when he felt the rope biting into his wrists, but he said nothing.

Faron glanced at Hunter wryly and said in his strange accent, "Not a real talkative fellow, is he? Do ye think he can't speak English?"

"No, I *know* he can. We've met before under like circumstances, I'm afraid." To Blue Bear, he said, "I warned you back when the white men came to get their horses that it wouldn't go well for horse thieves in the Territory. You've made a big mistake. Get him on his horse, Williams."

Blue Bear broke from Williams' grasp and snarled, "You have more horses than you need! We have few, and when we have enough, you take them away as you did before. If you do anything to me, my brothers will come and make you pay—all of you!"

Hunter stepped up to him and said, "You have no idea what you're talking about, and you just may have condemned your people to that reservation. I don't know how understanding Commissioner Macleod, the Blackfoot's good friend, will be now after your foolishness. Get him up there, Williams, I'm tired of looking at him."

"You will pay! You will pay! Especially you, Stone Man!"

Over his shoulder Hunter replied, "No, *you're* the one who's going to pay—maybe with your life." He walked over to Faron, ignoring more threats.

"Now what, lad?"

"Take him back to the fort and try to keep Briggs from shooting him before I get back."

"Where are ye goin'?"

"To tell Plenty Trees."

Faron gave him a knowing look. "And?"

"And see Reena." Hunter shrugged and half smiled. "I've got to know."

———

Plenty Trees was understandably outraged when he learned of Blue Bear's thievery. He paced back and forth outside one of the lodges that held the sick, slamming his fist into his palm over and over. "I warned him! I warned all of them. We were going to trade for horses with our corn crop. Now we will have no corn crop because we'll be at a reservation!" He muttered something in his native tongue, bringing a small gasp from Reena and Raindrop, who were watching Plenty Trees' growing anger with trepidation.

Raindrop said to Reena, "Maybe you and Stone Man should come back when my husband is calmer. Sometimes he . . . says a word he doesn't mean."

Reena nodded, still blushing. "I think we will." She turned to Hunter and held out her hand. "Shall we?"

As they walked down a path to the creek, Reena told him about the "hospital" they'd set up and asked about the one at the schoolhouse.

"I'm ashamed to say that I haven't even been down there yet. Briggs has kept me jumping ever since he got here. Dirk's there, though, with a few other men, helping out."

A squirrel darted across their path, making scolding noises. Reena tried to think of something pleasant to talk about, but nothing came to her at the moment. When they reached the gurgling creek, a secluded spot they'd been to many times, Reena sat down on the embankment with a sigh. "I just don't know what Blue Bear was thinking." Plenty Trees had known who the thief was by Hunter's description. Reena didn't know the man, but she had seen him many times since Matsen had come for his horses, talking with other braves privately. She'd wondered what the secret was, and now she knew that he'd probably been trying to sway them to his radical side.

Hunter squatted down beside her and picked up a smooth pebble to run between his fingers. "He wasn't thinking, obviously."

"What do you think Briggs will do to him?"

Hunter looked at her impassively.

"That's what I was afraid of," Reena said quietly.

They could see small fish lazily floating by in the clear stream. On the other bank more squirrels scampered around, and Reena noticed a pronghorn wandering by in the near distance, nosing for roots or good grass. It was a peaceful place and always had a calming effect on her.

Hunter tossed the pebble into the water and picked up another. Reena watched his gaze move restlessly over the forest, as if guarding against some sort of attack. His thumb and forefinger rolled the pebble around in circles. "Hunter, why are you here?"

"I wanted to tell Plenty Trees the bad news myself. And I wanted to talk to you."

"For a man who wants to talk, you sure don't have much to say."

His mouth turned up in a lopsided smile, but with no humor. "I've got a lot to say. I just don't know how to say it."

Reena heard warning bells go off in her head at his words and demeanor. Something was wrong, and it wasn't just about Blue Bear. Something had happened. All of sudden she wasn't at all sure if she wanted to hear what he had to say.

He tossed the pebble after the previous one and sat down beside her. "Do you remember back in the Cypress Hills, when you took care of me after I almost got killed?"

"Of course."

"What did you think of me?"

"Think of you? What do you mean?" Reena was really beginning to worry with the strange questions and his almost melancholy mood. This wasn't the Hunter she knew.

"I've been thinking about that time on the ride over here. I was almost crazy, it's true, but even then . . ." He trailed off, then flashed a self-conscious grin. "I guess I'm not making much sense here, am I?"

Reena threaded her arm through his and said, "Just talk it out, Hunter. Sometimes that's the best way to get to what you want to say."

He continued gazing at her with an intense scrutiny, then finally said, "All right. I'll do that." He took a deep breath and continued. "Like I said, I was thinking as I rode over here. I love the prairie on a clear day. Sometimes you can be riding along in the broad, incredible openness—you don't really have to be thinking about anything in particular—and you'll come face-to-face with yourself. I'm talking about a flash of awareness that hits you right between the eyes. I know that probably doesn't make sense either, but that's the only way I know how to describe it."

He shifted a bit and took her hand. "I realized it way back then, right after Betsy was killed and I was crazy for revenge. I sensed that you would somehow have a special place in my life. I don't know if you felt that way about me or not." He ended the sentence with the rising tone of a question.

Reena thought about it, then said gently, "I didn't really think you had much of a future, to be honest. I thought you and Red Wolf would probably end up killing each other. You both were filled with so much hate."

He chuckled lightly and said, "I can't blame you there. Anyway, it doesn't really matter." He stood, pulling her up with him, and wrapped his arms around her.

Reena sensed that he'd come to the point he was wanting to make and held her breath.

"Honey, Briggs told me that I'm being transferred to Fort Walsh soon. I want you to come with me."

It was the last thing Reena had expected to hear, and her heart skipped a beat. What did he mean by "come with me"? Her thoughts ricocheted around in her head, finally lighting on the Blackfoot. How could she leave them at a time like this? When was he talking about leaving?

"Reena, I can see I've confused you by springing this on you, but there's no easy way to ask this. My three-year term of service is coming up this year. At that time I can either sign up again on a yearly basis or take the one hundred sixty acres promised me after three years' service and build a ranch again." He stopped and kissed her lightly on the lips. "Either way, I want you to help me make that decision—as my wife. Reena . . . will you marry me?"

Reena felt her knees go weak, and her first instinct was to kiss him and say yes. But something stopped her. This was the moment she'd been contemplating for the past few months, and yet she hadn't come up with an answer. One still eluded her now.

Hunter's face registered mild surprise, then disappointment softened his features.

"Hunter, I . . . I don't know what to say." *Help me, Lord! What do I do?*

"It's okay, Reena—"

"No, it's not okay! I really *don't* know what to say. I want to say yes, but I keep thinking about my calling from the Lord and don't know if it's time to give that up yet. The Blackfoot need me right now more than ever before, and I don't . . ." She stopped, searching for the right words, but couldn't find them. Shrugging, not quite believing she was saying what she was, she blurted, "I just don't know what to say."

He released her and stepped back, looking as confused as she felt. "I, um . . . I'd better get back now."

"Hunter, wait—"

Starting back up the trail, he said over his shoulder, "I'll check on you when I get time."

She caught up with him and clutched his arm. "Wait a minute! You've got to give me time to *think*—"

"Reena, I'll say it again—it's all right. Really it is. Now, I've got to go."

Reena was shocked to see that his eyes were wet. "Hunter, listen to me. Not everyone is like you. They don't have instant answers to everything. Everything's not in black and white! You're all or nothing. You always have been and always will be—"

"What's wrong with that?"

"Nothing! But you expect everyone around you to be the same way, and that's not fair."

He stepped up to her and caressed her face, his eyes shining. "I asked you a question about a matter of the heart. You looked into your heart, and I have my answer. Good-bye, Reena." He turned and started away with a determined stride.

"Hunter, please!" she called, beginning to sob. In frustration she bent down and picked up a rock of her own and threw it as hard as she could into the water.

———

All the way back to Fort Macleod, the same question went round and round in his mind. *How could she say no?*

He knew she loved him and no other and had for years. Why did she act unsure now?

Eventually, the farther he got from the Blackfoot village, the more he began to understand Reena's reluctance to give him an immediate answer. First he had stunned her with the news of his transfer, and then he had asked her to leave her calling as a missionary and come with him. Reena was right. He had expected an instant, joyful answer of "Yes!" He prayed for God's calming influence to help him think clearly.

Out loud he reasoned, "Maybe you really aren't through with Reena's work, Lord. If that's true, I had no right to treat her the way I did. Maybe I handled it wrong all around—I don't know. But I truly felt your pleasure when I decided to propose. Was I wrong about that, too?"

There was no answer but the whistling wind.

By the time he reached the fort at dusk, Hunter had decided that he'd apologize to Reena the next time he saw her. He should have been more understanding and less selfish. He'd tried to tell himself that his behavior was justified because of his disappointment, but this was the woman he loved—she deserved understanding instead of rejection.

His mood quickly changed for the worse when Vic and Del met him just inside the gates. The grim look on Vic's face told tales that Hunter didn't want to hear. "What is it now?" he asked resignedly as he dismounted. "Is Blue Bear still alive, or has Briggs killed him?"

"You may be speaking sarcastically, old boy, but it's not very funny."

"You got that right," Del muttered darkly.

"What are you talking about?" Hunter demanded, handing the reins of his horse to a livery worker who'd come for Buck.

Vic looked around the parade ground in a conspiratorial manner, then answered, "Briggs told me he was going to sentence him to hang."

Hunter was stunned. "But . . . he can't do that! We're not allowed to *hang* anyone. We only have the power to imprison."

"Tell that to Briggs. He seems to make up his own set of rules as he goes."

"No, this has gone far enough," Hunter said, shaking his head. "I'm going to see him and—"

"He ain't here," Del informed him. "Catchin' Blue Bear and the idea of hangin' him put the major in a fine mood. He took the wifey for a buggy ride and picnic."

"Besides," Vic asked, "how are you going to stop him? How can any of us stop him?"

Hunter could only stare at him, sure he was mirroring his friend's helpless look.

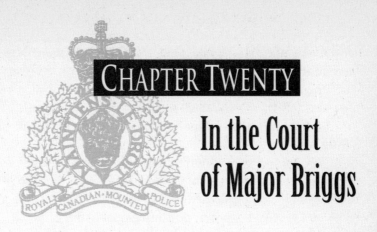

CHAPTER TWENTY

In the Court of Major Briggs

The small courtroom next to the library was jammed with Mounties the next morning. Hunter sat in the front row with Vic, Del, and Faron. All of them fixed their eyes on Blue Bear, who was standing in the small defendant's box. The Indian's black eyes scanned the room full of scarlet jackets and white faces, trying to appear unperturbed. To Hunter, the false bravado seemed pitiful, since it was obvious that the young brave was scared out of his wits. As Del had commented when they'd brought Blue Bear in, "He looks as if a possum just trotted over his grave."

They were waiting for Major Briggs. Hunter believed that he was intentionally making them wait in order to make a grand entrance. Hunter hadn't slept well the night before, and that combined with the stuffy, hot air in the room was making him irritable. He took out a handkerchief and wiped his brow and upper lip.

"Stifling in here, isn't it?" Vic commented.

"Briggs shouldn't have allowed this to be open to everyone. This feels like a saloon-show atmosphere."

"You're not going to keep the major from having his moment in the sun, are you?"

"There are a lot of things I'd like to deny the major, but unfortunately there's the small matter of being outranked."

"I don't know why. It's never stopped you before," Vic said lightly.

"Very funny." Vic was referring to the time Hunter had disobeyed a direct order from Colonel Macleod in order to save Reena from the renegade Red Wolf. That time Hunter had been lucky and received a promotion instead of a discharge. If he crossed Briggs, that would never happen.

"Are you feeling any better about Reena?" Vic whispered.

Hunter thought a moment, then answered, "I don't know if better is the word. More at ease about it, I guess, since I put it in God's hands last night."

"Good man. You know, I think Megan was just as surprised as you were. I thought she was going to faint when I told her."

Hunter raised an eyebrow and showed a humorless smile. "Believe me, she wasn't as surprised as I was."

"Attention in the courtroom!" Sergeant Stride bellowed from the door.

They all stood at attention while Major Briggs strolled down the center aisle in full dress uniform. "My, my," he commented as he passed by Hunter and Vic, "quite an audience we have today." He sounded pleased with himself, as if they'd all come just to see him. As the major passed Blue Bear he gave him a baleful glance, then took his seat behind the desk on the rostrum.

"Let's make this short and smooth," Briggs announced, clasping his hands together. "Sub-Inspector Stone, to the witness box, if you please."

Hunter wished it were someone besides himself being called. He didn't like the appearance that he was being instrumental in Briggs' charades. When he stepped up to the railing across from Blue Bear, he saw a growing tension in the young brave that was palpable. Gone was any attempt at defiance. Blue Briggs gauged

Briggs for the man he was in the brief, malevolent glance he had received from him.

Briggs crossed his arms and leaned back in his chair. "Sub-Inspector Stone, please tell the court what you witnessed yesterday concerning this Indian."

"I took a party of ten men and one scout to track whoever had stolen twelve horses the night before. After about twenty miles, we came upon this man with the horses and arrested him."

"Did he resist arrest?"

"No, he did not."

"Is there any doubt in your mind, Stone, that this man acted alone?"

"No, sir."

"Is there any doubt in your mind that he needs to be punished?"

Hunter looked over at Blue Bear, wishing again that he wasn't the one having to do this. "No doubt, Major."

Briggs looked out over the gathering and asked, "Is there anyone out there who was in Stone's party and wishes to dispute what he's said?"

No one moved.

"Is there anyone out there who wishes to *add* to Stone's testimony?"

Faron stood up. "I'd like to add somethin', sir."

"And who are you?" Briggs scowled.

"Faron O'Donnell. I was the scout on that little excursion."

"And?" Briggs asked testily. It was obvious that the major was displeased because someone had interrupted his script.

Unflappable, Faron said, "Well, ye see, Hunter went on to the Blackfoot camp to tell Chief Plenty Trees about this youngster's stupidity, so he don't know about this. But when we were bringin' Blue Bear back here, he told me that he was sorry for what he did. Seemed real sincere, too, if'n ye ask me."

"Of course he was sorry!" Briggs roared. "But he wasn't sorry he did it. He was sorry he was caught."

"That's not the way me and the lads took him to mean it, sir—"

"Sit down, scout. I'm not interested in your opinion on this man's meaning. I'm only interested in *facts*. Did you or did you not find this man with stolen horses?"

Faron looked at Blue Bear helplessly. "Yes, sir, that we did."

"Thank you." Briggs fixed Blue Bear with a hostile glare. "Do you have anything to say for yourself before I pronounce sentencing?"

Clearly uncomfortable and unsure of how to proceed in a white man's courtroom, Blue Bear's gaze went from Faron to Hunter and back to Briggs. "I said I was sorry for taking the horses. In my tribe, it is not a crime to steal horses, it is—"

Briggs cut him off with a slashing gesture of his hand. "I'm not interested in Blackfoot law. What do you have to say for yourself concerning this incident of thievery?"

Blue Bear's demeanor now revealed true defeat as his shoulders slumped perceptively. "That I am sorry, and I wish I had never thought of it."

"Fine. The sentencing of this court is that you be taken out in the morning and hanged by the neck until dead. And may God have mercy—"

Briggs was cut off by many surprised outcries and both Hunter and Vic shouting, "No!" at the same time.

"You can't do that, Major!" Hunter said forcefully.

Vic jumped to his feet. "This is an outrage, sir, and—"

Briggs picked up his gavel and began relentlessly pounding it until every protest was drowned out. "Now you men listen to me!" he roared, his eyes seeming to threaten to pop from his head. "*I* am the magistrate in charge of this Territory, and *I* am the superintendent in charge of this fort! Anyone not carrying out my orders will be thrown in the brig! Is that clear?"

Hunter stepped around the railing of the witness box to stand directly in front of the desk. Pointing at Blue Bear he said, "That man can't be put to death by this court! Only a jury of his peers can sentence him to—"

"You will stand down, Stone, or I'll have you arrested! Sergeant Stride to the front!"

Stride marched up the aisle quickly, throwing a nervous glance at Hunter and Vic on the way. "Yes, sir?"

Briggs pointed the gavel at Hunter and ordered, "If this man opens his mouth again, take him to the brig. Do you understand?"

Stride hesitated as he stared straight ahead.

A pulsing vein zigzagged across Briggs' broad forehead like a lightning bolt. In a dangerous tone he repeated, "Do you understand, Sergeant?"

"Yes, sir." He glanced at Hunter with a plea for restraint in his eyes.

Vic stepped forward. "Sir, I must protest also. This is not the British military. This is the North-West Mounted Police. Police, sir! We do *not* give execution orders—"

"Sergeant Stride, what I said also goes for Sub-Inspector Vickersham." Briggs stood, and with one last blazing look at Blue Bear, Hunter, and Vic, he made his way toward the door. All eyes in the gallery followed him until he opened the door and faced them. "Don't you men have duties to see to?"

Many of them glanced back at Hunter and Vic, but mostly they shuffled out the door, avoiding the major's eyes. Stride and two men escorted Blue Bear out, leaving only Hunter, Vic, and Major Briggs. The major, his lip curled upward in distaste, growled, "It's a junior officer's duty to give a good example to the men by showing support for his superior, whether he agrees with him or not. Both of you should remember that in the future." Briggs turned on a heel smartly and went out.

Hunter banged his fist on the witness box railing. "I can't believe this is happening!"

"What are we going to do?" Vic considered Hunter's face and said, "Uh-oh. I've seen that look before, and some nasty business usually follows close behind it."

"This hanging isn't going to take place, Vic. I won't allow it."

"What are you going to do?"

Hunter clapped him on the shoulder. "It's probably best that you don't know. Prior knowledge and all that."

Vic looked at the hand on his shoulder suspiciously. "I don't know whether to be grateful or outraged."

"Be grateful. But you'll owe me one."

"Now *that's* a frightening thought."

———

Reena, too, had slept little—if at all—the night before. She'd replayed the scene with Hunter over and over, imagining a different word or phrase here and there, a nuance real or imagined at different points of the conversation. The phrase that kept coming back to her was his talking about "coming face-to-face with yourself." The meaning of that had eluded her, until sometime in the early hours of the morning she understood. God had spoken to him and revealed something profound—and it had been about her. And if God had told Hunter to propose to her, who was she to turn him down?

Fervently she began praying that God would show her what to do.

By morning she felt a new peace, though no clearer understanding of God's will for her. Her eyes were gritty from lack of sleep. Not bothering with breakfast, she quickly washed her face and went to the sick lodges to see how Sun Flower was doing. The little girl's condition had also weighed heavily on Reena.

Raindrop was already there cooking and tending to the needy. When she saw Reena, she went to her and said, "Sun Flower has already been awake and asking for you."

"How is she?" Reena asked, alarmed.

"She is a little better but still very weak. I think she fell asleep again, but she made me promise to wake her when you came."

They went over to the girl, who was indeed asleep. On her chest was a Bible Reena had left for her, open to the book of Malachi. "Oh, Raindrop, do we have to wake her?"

She shrugged her shoulders. "A promise is a promise." Then

she knelt by Sun Flower and shook her arm gently. "Reena is here, little one."

"Reena?" Sun Flower said, opening feverish, bloodshot eyes.

"Yes, I'm here." She took Raindrop's place beside the girl as someone called out for the chief's wife. "Why did you want us to wake you up? You need your rest."

"I woke up last night and couldn't go back to sleep, so I read some of this," she said, gesturing to the Bible.

Reena smiled. "You were reading Malachi?"

"Is that how you say it? I thought it was 'ch' like in cherry. Malachi," she said softly, testing the name on her tongue.

"Why were you reading there? That's a strange book for a little girl to be reading." Reena tried to think of the last time she'd read Malachi but couldn't remember when she'd done so.

"I just prayed and opened it up and there it was. Look." Sun Flower pointed to the first part of a verse in chapter four. It was highlighted by the deep crease probably made by her fingernail.

Reena read, " 'But unto you that fear my name shall the Sun of righteousness arise with healing in his wings.' That's a beautiful verse, Sun Flower. I'd say it's just the thing a sick little girl needed to read last night, isn't it?"

"It's not just for me. It's for you, too."

"What? But I'm not sick." Something stirred inside Reena at that moment—a feeling or notion she couldn't quite grasp.

"You're not sick, but I could tell you felt very bad last night." She placed her hand over her heart. "In here."

Reena almost caught the idea that was trying to form in her mind, but suddenly it was gone, leaving her with the distinct feeling that if she'd grasped it, her life would be altered in a permanent way. She tried concentrating very hard to bring it back again, but to no avail.

"Do you like the verse, Reena?"

Reena smiled down at her. "I like it very much. You're a very perceptive young lady."

"What does that mean?"

"It means you have the ability to sometimes feel what people are feeling when they're hurting. That's very special."

"You're that way, aren't you? I want to be just like you, Reena."

Reena leaned down and kissed her forehead, whispering, "Thank you, Sun Flower. Now I want you to get some sleep, okay?"

"Okay."

Reena went to work helping others, thinking that she'd been teetering on the edge of something important. Maybe later tonight when she was feeling more focused and calm she could bring it back again.

———

Dirk watched Jenny bound down the steps of the school with a light step. From his position outside his tent, she appeared to actually be happy, an emotion that seemed to elude her lately. Somewhere inside her, he reflected as he had so many times, there was a deep sadness that seemed to be waiting to swallow her whole. He prayed every day that it wouldn't.

The late afternoon sun reflected golden highlights in her hair as she came up to him, smiling. "I think the flu's going away."

"Really? That's wonderful! What happened?"

"Remember Mrs. Reilly, the nice woman with that huge mole on her cheek? We'd almost given her up for dead the day before yesterday, and now she's sitting up and gulping down sandwiches. Not only her, but for the first time since they've gotten here, no one's gotten worse today, only better."

"That *is* good news. And I'm sure it all has to do with their wonderful nurse."

Jenny grinned and said, "But of course!"

"How's Dr. Simone been treating you?"

"Like a leper, thank you. I believe he's set his sights on Marcia Lederer just up the road here."

"Not much for rejection, is he?"

"Not at all." She took his hand. "Come on. I'm taking you

to supper. Mrs. Howe is baking one of her famous hams to-night."

"All right. Let me tell Duke where I'm going." He ducked inside the tent where Duke was napping and shook him awake.

"Whaaa? Aw, Sarge, what is it now?"

"I'm going for supper at the boardinghouse. Be back later."

"You know something?"

"What?"

Duke closed his eyes again and said while yawning, "I sure will be glad to get back to my old bunkmate, 'cause I'm tired of waking up to your face all the time. I'd rather get back to my usual self and ignore the bugles when they blast 'em in the middle of the night."

"You'll be glad to know that may be sooner than you think."

"Good."

———

Jenny placed her tiny hand in his when they were in the wagon and rolling down the street. "I'm sorry, Dirk."

"For what? And if you're apologizing for Simone again, I don't want to hear it. Didn't even happen, as far as I'm concerned."

She rested her head against his shoulder and was silent for a while. "Why do you think it happened?"

"Why do *you* think it happened?"

She made a face at him. "I hate it when you do that." Taking a deep breath, her face became contemplative. "I guess maybe it's because . . . he's completely the opposite of you? Maybe I was wondering what someone like that would be like?"

He gave a little shrug and said, "Maybe," nonchalantly, but it was exactly what he'd been thinking.

They rode on in comfortable silence again, until Jenny said, "I can't help it, Dirk, I still feel bad about this. Is there something I could do to make it up to you?"

"Jenny, stop punishing yourself! Now you want to do penance?" He suddenly had an idea. "I'll tell you what. I know something you can do that would please me and end up pleasing you more."

"What is it?"

"You know that Bible I gave you? Read one chapter out of it every night before you go to bed and every morning when you get up."

"Just one chapter?"

"Just one. But I have to warn you—you won't want to stop with one, you'll want to keep going."

"Okay," Jenny said simply. "I've looked through it a few times, but it's pretty hard to understand. Tell me an easy place to start."

Dirk held up a finger. "Not the easy place—the most important place. The life and teachings of Jesus."

"Where's that?"

"Matthew, Mark, Luke, or John."

"All right. Which one?"

"Mmmm, how about John?"

Jenny nodded and slipped her arm through his. "Why don't we start after this big, luscious supper I'm going to stuff you with? You read to me."

Dirk grinned at her, not quite believing how easy it had been. In the past whenever he had tried to talk to her about God, an invisible barrier would rise between them. He'd never understood how she was able to summon that wall, but he was elated that it hadn't appeared right now. "Tonight I'll read you the story about the birth of Jesus. The best one's in Luke."

Jenny leaned her head on him again. "All right. I like baby stories."

Dirk laughed softly, intensely happy. "I think it's safe to say you've never heard one like this."

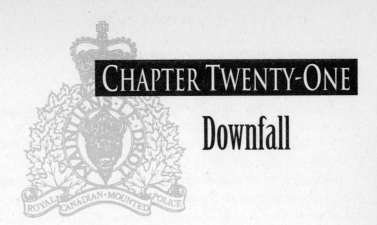

CHAPTER TWENTY-ONE

Downfall

At one-thirty in the morning, Hunter strolled into the jail as if it were the most natural thing in the world. The jailor this night was Jerry Strotham, though everyone called him "Edgy" because of his naturally nervous disposition. For some reason Edgy could never sleep more than two or three hours a night, leaving him to be the obvious choice for jailor if there were any prisoners. When Hunter opened the door, Edgy jumped out of his chair to his feet, dropping the book he'd been reading and fumbling for his sidearm.

"At ease, Edgy," Hunter told him, then smiled at what he'd just said.

"Sir, you almost scared me plumb out of my britches! I suggest you knock at this hour of the night."

Hunter glanced over at Blue Bear in one of the three cells. He was sitting with his back against the wall, legs drawn up, and arms crossed. "How's our prisoner?"

Edgy, rail-thin and scarecrowlike, pointed a skinny finger at the Indian. "You see how he's sitting? I ain't seen him move from that position. It's like he's frozen there." He moved closer to Hunter and whispered, "Gives me the spooks. Seems like he never blinks, just like a snake, and he keeps staring at me."

"He's locked up, Edgy. He can't hurt you."

"Do you know," Edgy said, "that some of them Indians believe they can change into animals? Did you know that?"

"I've heard that some of the more powerful medicine men believe that."

Edgy glanced over at Blue Bear warily, then asked, "Well, what if he's one of *them*? What if he turns into a snake and gets out of those bars?"

Hunter noticed the book on the floor that Edgy had dropped on his entrance and picked it up. "Edgy, do you really think that you of all people should be reading *Tales of the Grotesque and Arabesque* by Edgar Allan Poe in the middle of the night?"

His brow wrinkled in puzzlement. "What's wrong with that?"

"Never mind. Give me the key, Edgy."

After fumbling in his trouser pocket, Edgy produced the key and handed it over. Hunter went to the cell, opened it, and closed it behind him without relocking. Blue Bear watched his every move without moving. Hunter sat on the bunk opposite him with his back to Edgy for privacy. He was sure Edgy would be listening for all he was worth to find out why an officer was here in the middle of the night.

Blue Bear's eyes were solid black onyx, revealing none of his thoughts, and Hunter could find no fear in them now as he'd seen in the courtroom. Somehow, he'd made his peace with the idea of a neck-breaking swing from a rope only hours from now.

Hunter said admiringly, "You seem calm."

"Why should I be afraid? You have already taken my freedom. After that, taking my life is a blessing."

Hunter leaned forward and placed his elbows on his knees. "What you did was wrong, Blue Bear. I know that your laws are different from ours, but by treaty you've agreed to follow our chief's laws."

"*I* didn't agree. Plenty Trees agreed."

"Plenty Trees is your elected leader. It's your duty to follow his wishes."

Blue Bear gazed at him sullenly. "Why did you come here, Stone Man? To make fun of me? To show that you are a better man than me by catching me? I thought you were a friend of the Blackfoot."

Hunter would have liked to talk to him more because he knew he'd never see him again. But he also knew time was a consideration now. "I've come here to let you go."

Blue Bear's eyes widened. With a cautious glance at Edgy, he swung his legs over the side of the bed until their faces were only a foot apart. "Let me go?" he whispered. "Then they will put *you* in here!"

"Turn left when you go outside and stay in the shadows. Your horse is around the corner. I've already talked to the guards outside, and they'll let you go, but don't get careless. If you get caught again, it's out of my hands."

Blue Bear kept his eyes locked on Hunter. "Why do you do this?"

"I have my own reasons," Hunter said as he stood. "Let's go."

Edgy's eyes rounded as he saw Blue Bear follow Hunter out of the cell. "Uh, sir? You forgot to lock the door behind you."

"Close your eyes, Edgy."

"Huh?"

"You heard me—close them." When Edgy did, Hunter turned to the brave. "Go now."

Blue Bear hesitated, then held out his hand. "I will not forget this."

"Just stay out of trouble from now on, all right? And if I were you, I wouldn't go back to Plenty Trees, or *he* might hang you. But wherever you go, ride hard tonight." Hunter watched him leave, then pulled up a chair opposite Edgy. "Okay, Edgy, you can open them."

Edgy opened them and looked around the room in disbelief. "You let him go? Briggs will kill me!"

Hunter grinned at him. Now that the deed was done, he felt better than he'd expected. "Reach behind you and get that checkerboard. I might be rusty for a few games, but eventually I'll give you a challenge."

Jerry "Edgy" Strotham looked at Hunter as if he'd lost his mind. Just another thing to worry about on this strange night.

———

When Reena awoke, two owls were trading calls in the sleepy darkness, but that wasn't what had roused her.

But unto you that fear my name shall the Sun of righteousness arise with healing in his wings.

Reena sat up and brushed back the hair from her eyes with her fingers. In the gloomy light thrown from the dying fire across the tepee, she saw the Bible by her bed opened to that very verse that had formed in her mind at waking.

Yawning, she reached over and lit the oil lamp on the table beside the Bible. "What is it, Lord?" she asked sleepily. "It's a wonderful promise, but what does it have to do with me?"

Then her eyes fell on the second half of the verse: " '. . . and ye shall go forth, and grow up as calves of the stall.' " Reena caught her breath, and all of a sudden she was wide awake. "Oh, Lord . . . oh, Lord," she repeated. Sitting straight up, she exclaimed with joy, "It's your promise! It's . . . it's . . . ." She wrung her hands together, desperately trying to form what was being given to her.

All at once she stopped fidgeting and became very still, experiencing a peace she'd never known. Closing her eyes, she said with fervent gratefulness, "Thank you, Father. Thank you, Jesus. Thank you, Holy Spirit."

Reena lay back on the bed and let the peace roll over her, filling her with joy. Tears streamed down her cheeks and onto her pillow. The noises of the night couldn't disturb the perfect calmness of spirit that she was experiencing now.

Eventually, with a smile on her face, Reena extinguished the lamp and succumbed to a dreamless, tranquil sleep.

————————

Hunter gave Blue Bear a four-hour start before knocking on the door of Major Briggs' quarters. He thought grimly that this would be the second night this week that Briggs would be awakened to bad news. "Oh, well," he sighed, with fist raised to the door, "maybe it'll give him character."

After giving four big blows to the door, he waited calmly. No longer did he fear the major's wrath or punishment. He'd thought about this moment all day and night, at the beginning with trepidation and eventually with indifference. It was in God's hands now.

Heavy footfalls stopped on the other side of the door, then it opened to reveal Briggs, hair in disarray and pulling on a silk robe. "Stone? What's the meaning of this?" He stepped outside and closed the door, eyes darting around the parade ground as if searching for an attack.

"It's the prisoner, Major. He's escaped."

"*Escaped?* What are you talking about?"

"I mean he's gone." Hunter was glad for the gloom of the quickly approaching dawn, or Briggs would have seen the amusement in his face. Why had he been afraid of this man? It was the first time Hunter had seen Briggs in any appearance except a stern military manner and sharply tailored uniform. At the moment, with hair standing straight up, a shadow of a heavy beard, in nightshirt and robe, he seemed a far sight from dangerous.

Briggs stuttered around, searching for words. "That's . . . he can't . . . how could he escape? He was the only prisoner in there! I'll get to the bottom of this. Follow me, Stone." He set off in the direction of the jail, but Hunter's words stopped him.

"That won't be necessary, sir."

"Why not?"

"Because I know how he got away."

Briggs came back to him with his head cocked to the side like a bird. "How?"

"I *let* him get away, with the aid of no one. Just me."

After a moment of thunderous silence, Briggs began to tremble. There was enough light to see his eyes and lips narrow into slits and his jaw begin clenching spasmodically. "You . . . you traitor!" he bellowed, coming around with a sweeping right fist at Hunter's face. Hunter dodged easily, grabbed his arm, and spun him away.

"Careful, Major. Striking another officer is a serious offense."

Briggs came back instantly and pointed a finger in Hunter's face. Spittle flew from his tight lips as he growled, "I'll have you *beaten* from this fort! Guard! You up there! Get down here, now!"

From behind and above Hunter he heard, "Sir, there are riders coming! From the direction of town."

Briggs looked confused. "Riders?" he whispered. Then he called up, "What do you mean riders? Are they Indians?"

"Can't tell, sir."

Briggs said to Hunter, "Hand over your side arm, Stone."

Hunter unholstered the Adams and gave it to him just as Sergeant Stride and a dozen other men tumbled out of their barracks in various dress. When he turned back to Briggs, his own pistol was aimed at his chest.

"Major, is that you?" Stride called as he ran toward them.

Briggs cocked the hammer of the Adams and slowly brought its aim to Hunter's face. His arm was trembling, and Hunter could see white teeth grinding together. Hunter realized that he might have underestimated Briggs' hatred of him and took a full step back.

From the shadows of the quartermaster's office next to Briggs' residence emerged a figure holding a pistol. "Lower that weapon, Major."

Briggs did so immediately, spinning around in surprise. "Vickersham?"

"Maybe you should hand that pistol over to me," Vic said.

Hunter felt a surge of relief. He had begun to wonder what was taking Vic so long to make his presence known.

Briggs sounded offended when he said, "I'm perfectly capable of handling a firearm, Vickersham."

Stride and the other men arrived, and in the gray light, Hunter could see them staring in confusion.

Vic said, "Sergeant Stride, the guard says we have visitors coming. Take some men and go see about it."

"Not so fast, Vickersham," Briggs countered and pointed to two men. "You and you . . . place Sub-Inspector Stone under arrest at once."

The constables exchanged nervous, disbelieving glances.

"You heard me!"

Tentatively, the two men came to stand by Hunter but didn't hold their weapons on him.

Briggs turned back to Stride. "You have your orders, Sergeant. Go see about our visitors."

"Yes, sir." Stride obviously didn't care for Hunter being arrested, but his iron discipline took over, and he led the men away.

Turning back to Vic, Briggs looked surprised and asked, "Vickersham, why are you holding that gun on me? Put it away!"

Vic hesitated, then asked, "Are you all right, Major?"

"Of course I'm all right! I was just placing Stone here under arrest." His malevolent glare came back around to Hunter. "Oh, you're going to pay for your acts, Stone! Mark my words." He put his hands behind his back and began pacing back and forth as he said confidently, "Vickersham, we have a little mission on which to embark this day."

Vic and Hunter exchanged uneasy glances.

"I want twenty men left here to garrison the fort," Briggs said. "The rest I want in full battle dress. Issue thirty rounds of ammunition per man and prepare those cannons for transport."

Hunter couldn't believe what he was hearing. "What for?" he blurted.

"Are you still here, Stone? You men, take him to the jail at once."

"No, I want to know what you're up to, Major!" Hunter said defiantly.

"It's none of your affair! You're a prisoner and no longer on active duty with this force!"

Vic stepped forward and said, "Then kindly tell *me*, the one you're issuing these orders to, what it is you're planning, Major?"

"We have orders that were received weeks ago to gather those Blackfoot Indians and fence them on a reservation. Hunter buried them in other papers so I didn't find them. That order will be carried out beginning today. If they resist us . . ." Briggs paused and a smile touched his lips. "Then they'll have a little war on their hands that they won't soon forget."

"This is outrageous!" Hunter exploded, taking a step toward Briggs. Vic placed a restraining hand on Hunter's arm, and when Hunter turned to him, he was shocked to find him smiling. "Vic?"

"Look over there."

Hunter turned and saw what he was grinning about. "Oh, thank God," Hunter breathed.

Making his way across the parade ground in long strides was Commissioner James Farquharson Macleod and his personal escort. The commissioner, a tall, handsome man with auburn-streaked hair and full beard, could make himself an imposing presence with little effort. Now, as Hunter watched him strut purposefully toward them, was one of those times.

Hunter was satisfied to see that Briggs was duly horrified. "What's the matter, Major? You look like you've seen a ghost."

Macleod nodded to Hunter and Vic as he stopped in front of them. "Stone, Vickersham . . . what's all this commotion, Superintendent Briggs?"

Looking down at his bedclothes self-consciously, Briggs gave a weak laugh and said, "Good morning, Commissioner. This is quite a surprise."

"I can see that by your high color. Maybe that explains why you didn't answer my question."

Briggs, still holding the pistol, switched it to his other hand and halfheartedly attempted to hide it in the folds of his robe. "We've had a major breach of conduct on Sub-Inspector Stone's part during the night. I was just placing him under arrest."

Macleod's eyebrows arched. "Oh? Perhaps you'd like to get properly dressed and tell me about it in your office." He didn't wait for an answer but instead turned to one of his officers and said, "See about some breakfast, Anderson. I'm starved. Stone, Vickersham, come with me."

Briggs watched Macleod walk by him with no acknowledgment whatsoever, then asked, "Um, where are you going, sir?"

"Why, to your office to await you. I think I can find my way, since it *was* originally mine. Is there a problem, Briggs?"

Briggs waved his hands helplessly, inadvertently swinging the pistol past Macleod's body.

"Good heavens, Briggs, put that gun away before you shoot someone!"

Briggs looked down at his robe and realized he had no pockets.

With a heavy sigh, Macleod said, "Stone, take the pistol, please. I believe it *is* yours, isn't it?"

"Yes, sir." Hunter couldn't resist a smile as he tugged the Adams from Briggs' grasp.

"You were saying, Briggs?" Macleod prompted.

"Saying? Oh yes, um . . . I have a number of personal papers in my office that are of a private nature, and—"

Macleod stepped toward him, towering over the smaller Briggs. "Private papers? Too private for the commissioner of this force to see? Interesting."

"Well, it's not like that, sir, it's—"

"Get dressed, Briggs," Macleod ordered, then turned on a heel and led Hunter and Vic away.

———

"This is the only thing I've found so far, sir," Vic was saying as he shuffled through a stack of papers on the desk.

Macleod studied the paper Vic had just given him with creased forehead. "Mmm. So what you're saying, Vickersham, is that this is the list of names Briggs wrote out for you, and this"—he reached for the paper in Vic's hand—"is the official list that he received."

"That's right, Commissioner. And as you can see, Hunter's name isn't on the official list of men to be transferred to Fort Walsh. He added it. He's brutal to the men, sir. He was fully prepared to hang a man when he had no authority, and he was actually issuing orders to me to prepare for a war. On the whole—"

"Yes, Vickersham, I can see the picture developing here." Macleod placed both papers on the desk, sighed, and rubbed his eyes. "I was afraid of this. I don't know what moron recommended Briggs for this post, but I intend to find out."

There was a tentative knock on the door, then Briggs entered in full-dress uniform. Hunter was satisfied to note that his demeanor was much more humble and subdued than at any time since he'd known the man.

"Superintendent Briggs," Macleod began without preamble, then paused. "Or should I address you as 'Major'? Oh, never mind—I think all of us here know what your proper title is, so let's proceed. I received a disturbing letter from Stone and Miss Reena O'Donnell, two people whose instincts I trust without question. They expressed doubts about your ability to run this post in a smooth manner. I arrived just in time to witness myself that you can't."

"I can explain, sir—"

"Can you now? Can you explain your habit of falsifying documents to suit your will? Can you explain the sadistic treatment of your men? Men whom, I might add, I trained and were excellent policemen when I left them? And now, *Major*, their morale is at an all-time low and they must be *re*-trained. Can you explain all of that?"

Briggs' mouth opened and closed twice before he answered, "I . . . I must say, sir, with all due respect, that I honestly ran this post to the best of my ability and judgment—"

"Judgment!" Macleod roared, coming up out of his chair. "Judgment? Briggs, if you have an ounce of sound judgment in your body, it's well hidden! Don't speak to me, sir, of your ability, either. You *have* no ability to effectively perform a duty of this nature. I also must add that I'm appalled at your lack of moral principles in dealing with the men under your command."

Briggs was sweating now, and Hunter noticed his hands trembling. Hunter didn't pity him, but he wondered how a man could develop such a cold and cruel personality that Briggs possessed. What terrible events had molded him?

Macleod continued in a calmer tone. "Under the circumstances, Briggs, I have no choice but to relieve you of your command, effective immediately. I want you off this post in twenty-four hours. Is that clear?"

Briggs' throat contracted with a clicking noise when he swallowed. With a sheepish glance at Hunter he said, "I'd like to appeal the commissioner's decision, if I may."

"Appeal all you want," Macleod said casually as he sat back down, "but just do it somewhere other than Fort Macleod. That's all."

Briggs looked as if he wanted to say something else but decided against it. Without looking at either Hunter or Vic, he turned and left.

Hunter breathed an inner sigh of relief. No more waking up and dreading whatever abuse Briggs had thought up during the night. No more trying to justify senseless orders to the men when he'd had to issue them. No more Briggs.

Macleod looked around the desk top cluttered with papers. "I'd say we have a lot to do, gentlemen, to get this fort back into shape. But not before a good breakfast, eh?"

Hunter stepped back and opened the door for him. Just before Macleod went through it, he stopped and gave Hunter a gauging look.

"You were acting superintendent before Briggs arrived, weren't you, Stone?"

Oh no. "Yes, sir, I was."

"You don't sound as if you enjoyed it."

"In all honesty—no, Commissioner."

Macleod rubbed his chin thoughtfully, then asked with a sparkle in his eye, "Would the job be more enticing if, after Irvine returns in two weeks, you'd hold the rank of full inspector?"

Over Macleod's shoulder Hunter saw Vic's look of surprise, then vigorous nodding of the head. The rank of inspector was only one step below superintendent and a significant pay raise. "Would the commissioner be offering me a bribe, sir?"

Macleod looked dutifully offended. "A bribe? Absolutely not!" His bearded face split into a grin. "What do you say, Hunter?"

"Could I take the day to decide, sir? I need to . . . consult with someone."

"Would that someone have dark hair and sky-blue eyes?"

"Yes, sir, they would."

"Then, by all means—consult! Come along, boys, our feast awaits." They were following him through the library when he asked over his shoulder, "By the way, Stone, why haven't you asked that fine gal to marry you yet?"

Hunter and Vic exchanged grins, then Hunter answered, "I'm working on that, sir."

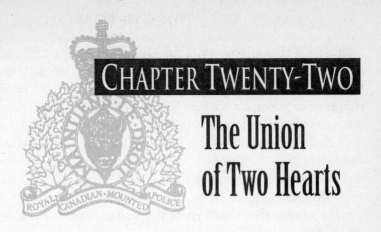

CHAPTER TWENTY-TWO

The Union of Two Hearts

As Reena rode along the natural trail that had been beaten down between the Blackfoot tribe and the fort, she was having trouble defeating a nagging thought: what if she were too late? What if he'd already been transferred? She calmed the fear with the certainty that he wouldn't leave without telling her good-bye. Would he? Had she hurt him that badly?

She urged the horse into a run. She rushed through a scattering of trees, through the smell of wildflowers, fresh sap, and musky undergrowth. After bursting from the forest, the pony nimbly crossed a gorge and a swelling of the ground that grew into a ridge.

"Just a few more miles," she told the horse breathlessly, "then you can rest."

The ridge eventually gave way to open prairie on the right, with a ten-foot wall of shale on their left. The shale ran for a few hundred yards until it ended abruptly, then the trail took a sharp left around the corner of the rock.

Suddenly, there was a flash of color at the edge of her vision. She felt a solid bump and had to hang on to the saddle horn with all her strength to keep from falling. The horse screamed in protest as it went down on its hindquarters, and Reena found herself on one side of the horse, grimly determined not to hit the ground. When the pony gained its feet, it stood there, panting, tail swishing in protest.

"Hello?" Reena heard from the other side of where she was barely hanging on. Carefully she eased her feet to the ground and stood there on shaky legs.

"Are you all right over there?"

The voice snapped her back to the present from almost fainting. "Hunter?"

He came around the front of her mount, making soothing noises to the frightened animal. Reena gave a cry and ran into his arms. "Oh, I can't believe it! What are you doing out here?"

"Coming to see you, of course." His face was full of concern as he held her back to look at her. "That was some collision. Are you all right?"

"Yes," she assured him, still out of breath, holding on to his arms and still trying to acknowledge the fact that he was really there.

"You were in a mighty big hurry. Is something wrong?"

"Yes! I mean, no, nothing's—"

"Come over here and sit down in the shade." Hunter led her to a shelflike outcropping from the shale wall, where he helped her sit down and kneeled in front of her, still looking for bruises or cuts.

Reena put her face in her hands for a moment to calm herself, then raised her eyes to his. "It's you . . . it's really you! I've got—oh, Hunter, can you forgive me?"

"Wait a minute," he said soothingly with a little amusement. "Slow down. You could have broken your pretty neck, so why don't you take a few deep breaths while I get you some water, okay?"

Reena only nodded, not trusting herself to speak until she was totally in control. She still couldn't believe that of all the people to run into on the trail, it would be him. Was it coincidence, or did it go deeper than that?

Hunter handed her his canteen, saying, "Take little sips of it, not big gulps."

Reena did as he said, noticing that he was watching her the whole time with a little smile playing at his lips. "Are you laughing at me?"

"Of course not."

"Then what are you smiling about?"

"I've got some news that—"

"Wait!" Reena said quickly, capping the canteen and setting it aside. "Me first, okay? I've been dying to talk to you ever since I got up this morning."

He inclined his head. "Go ahead."

Reena half turned to face him and took his hands in hers. "I've been so upset about our . . . about what happened the other day, and couldn't help blaming myself for—wait, don't say anything—blaming myself for not giving you a better reason or explanation." She told him about Sun Flower finding the verse in Malachi, and how it had seemed important but she hadn't been able to make any sense of it. Then she quoted the first part for him.

"So last night I woke up with the verse going around in my head, and I lit the lamp and read it again—the *whole* verse, not just the part that Sun Flower had shown me. And then . . . I don't really know how to describe what happened then except to use your own words—I came face-to-face with myself. But not only myself, with you, and us."

Hunter said, "Now it's you who's not making sense."

"The second part of the verse is, '. . . and ye shall go forth, and grow up as calves of the stall.' Don't you see? The first part of the verse was meant for you, and the second for me."

"The healing part is for me? How?"

"Hunter, underneath our whole relationship has been the death of your wife, Betsy. Wait, let me finish! You know that it took you years to stop blaming yourself for it, and then whenever she came up in conversation, you still had a hurt look in your eyes like you still missed her. I know, I've seen it time and time again."

"Reena, I forgave Red Wolf for killing her when I became a Christian."

"I know that, and that's wonderful, but it's not what I'm talking about. I'm talking about *healing*, darling—*your* healing. It all became so clear to me that you've been healed from the wound in your heart that was caused by her death. First of all, there's no way you would ask me to marry you if you still carried the burden of her inside you. That's just not like you. And secondly—"she paused and took his face in her hands, stroking his cleft chin with her thumb—"when you look at me, I don't see pain for her anymore. I only see love for me."

He watched her for a long time before saying, "You're right. You only see that because it's the only thing there."

Reena kissed him softly, feeling more love for him than ever before or that she could ever imagine. The feeling was so deep and intense that she never wanted it to go away. Finally she drew back reluctantly. "I have to tell you that Betsy was always in the back of my mind, right up until you asked me to marry you. I didn't want to have to compete with her as your wife. I didn't want to be compared to someone I've never even known."

"I never would have—"

"I know that now, don't you see? Now, but not before. All I had when I dared to think about us getting married was worry for the future. That's my part of Malachi chapter four. It's only six verses, but it's all about the future where *God* is in control, not Reena O'Donnell. It's about the hope that springs from that promise, the hope that I've been searching for concerning us. You've seen what happens when calves are released from the stall in the mornings. They run, they play and frolic with pure joy. And that's how we should be, because the future is in God's hands, and everything will be made right for those who believe."

Reena stopped and took a deep breath. "Because of that, I know that He'll take care of Plenty Trees and his people. I'm not any sort of a guarantee that their future will be bright if I stay with them. Only God is. I've helped plant the seed, and I believe that was the mission God sent me to do. I feel it's finished now, and I'm comfortable with moving on."

A smile was growing on Hunter's lips as she spoke, a smile filled with the hope that she felt so strongly. "Does this mean what I think it means?"

"Please ask me again, Hunter. Please?" Reena could feel her eyes begin to brim with tears, and though she'd promised herself that she wouldn't cry, she didn't care. There was too much love shining in his face—just for her.

"Reena, I love you," Hunter said in a husky whisper. "I promise to love you and no other until the day I die. Will you marry me?"

With lower lip trembling, Reena's voice broke when she answered, "Yes. I'd be honored to be your wife."

They embraced in the shadow of the colorful shale wall, and time lost its meaning. Reena clung to him, running her fingers through his hair and letting her tears fall freely. Never in her life had she felt as fully interlocked into God's plan than at that moment, and the steady peace that she'd found in the middle of the night returned to her in the rush of a warm glow. She sensed that Hunter felt it, too, because he held her tighter to him and began a slow, soothing rocking motion that she found dreamlike.

Reena didn't know how long they stayed like that, bound together by loving arms and tranquil hearts. When they finally released each other by silent, mutual consent, the shadows seemed to have creeped a bit farther away, as if they'd been there for quite a while.

Hunter kissed her lightly. "We'd better be getting back. Will you come with me?"

"Of course I will. My sister would kill me if she found out about our news from Vic." Reena remembered something Hunter had said earlier. "You said you had good news, too?"

"Yes, but now I don't want to tell you because you might change your mind about marrying me."

"Never in a million years. If they've decided to transfer you somewhere other than Fort Walsh, I'd go anywhere with you."

Hunter chuckled and said, "Just the opposite. It turns out that I wasn't supposed to be transferred at all. It was Briggs up to his usual mischief. I'm staying at Fort Macleod, and, my lady, you might like to know that you'll be marrying a full inspector."

It took a moment for what he'd said to sink in, and when it did she laughed and said, "Hunter, that's wonderful!"

He took her hand and brought her to her feet with him.

"Hunter?"

"Yes?"

Reena moved against him and rested her head on his chest. "Say it for me once more. Say you'll always love me and no one else."

"Look up there, Reena. Look at that sky as deep as royal blue, and beyond it—God's heaven. He's watching us right now, and I can feel His approval, can't you?"

"Oh yes."

Hunter kissed her upturned mouth. "Then He's watching me when I promise you that I'll never love anyone else my whole life."

"Thank you, my darling." Reena placed her head against his chest again, feeling the strong, confident beat of his heart.

"God is watching," Hunter whispered.

Date Due

B&H

JUN 02 1999		
JUL 11 1999		
OCT 13 1999		
FEB 02 2000		
MAR 19 2000		
APR 6 '03		
JUL 3 7 2011		
DEC 1 4 2014		